For
Bella

Paul N. Thompson

Thirteen Per Cent

P N Thompson

In Loving Memory

Paul Britton

(29-03-1958) - (01-09-2008)

Gordon (Spike) Hughes

(27-12-1958) - (14-04-2016)

Never forgotten

Sharon

Thank you

Part One

Ella

Your last few world history lessons

To become a world history teacher such as myself, one must first learn to tell these particular lessons by word of mouth which is what I will begin to do today. My aim is to ensure that my voice will have more impact than any written word. This is in fact my first time telling it although I was obviously never there, the story that I am about to tell you begins way back during the year of two thousand and twenty eight.

You students are now thirteen years of age, after these final lessons you will leave here to join the world, many of you will become farmers, some will travel the width and breadth of the country when you become message carriers, one of you might become a representative of the people once known as a politician, although they were very different back then and you never know, one of you here may one day reach the heights to become a teacher of history, in my humble opinion the most important work in the world today.

We are reasonably ignorant with regard to the planet prior to when she almost ended our existence, what we do know is that the biggest problem of all regarding the year of two thousand and twenty eight was global climate change. The entire world was considerably warming although for the most part, it was ignored by the masses and when I use the word masses, allow me to offer you an example. There were back then believe it or not, close to seven and a half billion people walking upon this earth, not the fifteen million or so that we know of today, can you imagine that?

Many reports were published around a decade prior to that year, one of which informed the politicians that the entire world was already one degree warmer than during the preindustrial levels and that a line was now drawn in the sand. This was told to them not long after devastating hurricanes at what was then known as the United States of America. At that same meeting, they were warned that if the global temperature climbed another one and a half degrees, the risks of drought, flooding, extreme heat and those hurricanes would considerably increase, as would climate related poverty.

For those of you seated in front of me wondering how climate related poverty occurs it's really simple to explain. Fewer crops thanks to a slowly but steadily boiling planet, obviously means less food for a world of seven and a half billion people but fear not, our ancestors would never make it to that point.

With those hurricanes at the Americas, this country along with most others experienced the first example of that extreme heat a decade earlier during the year of two thousand and eighteen when the most important meeting between politicians and scientists took place, when all temperature records were broken, when London was still our thriving capital city with more than seven million people living there.

Seven million people all living at London, I know that's difficult to imagine considering how London looks today, but it's the accurate truth of the matter, it was once I assure you, a thriving and bustling multi-cultural city.

The oceans around the world were already suffering elevated acidity and lower levels of oxygen, the politicians were warned during two thousand and eighteen, that fisheries would lose more than three million tonnes of produce per year if global temperatures climbed another one degree. Fewer fish also equates to less food, another case of how global climate related poverty can be successfully achieved, but again none of that mattered.

The politicians attending that meeting with scientists at Katowitz, Poland arrived there in fuel laden jets to airports where they climbed into fuel laden cars to travel to a stark meeting where they listened to the findings of noted scientists. The politicians later returned to their own countries where they briefly and quietly preached what they were told before they got on with their everyday lives in politics. Nobody really did enough to stop what would happen around ten years from that day although they could have, there was back then probably still time.

The oil rich countries around the globe in fact quietly condemned the reports and called them fiction, scare mongering as did a few other now unknown world leaders, but the entire planet was on course for a cataclysmic three degree temperature shift, not the mere two degrees that was ultimately feared.

You children, very soon to become young adults inherited this world from your ancestors, some of whom you will learn the truth of during these lessons, I am in fact myself a direct descendant of one of them.

Remember that this tale is always the last thing that any pupil will ever learn at any school, the most important lesson of all is that we never make the mistakes that they made leading up to the August of two thousand and twenty eight and for a brief while beyond.

Listen and learn this particular lesson well, I will tell you the story before you finally begin to make your own decisions and choices. Remember that yours one day might make a world of difference.

Sunday December 31ˢᵗ 2028

Cambridge, United Kingdom

A pale blue single engine aircraft sped north-east along the recently cleared lone runway at Cambridge International Airport, just forty five miles north from the flight's destination that was to be the capital city of London. The two pilots inside wanted to view some of the eastern coastline along the way because of a dreaded theory.

When the plane lifted from the tarmac, Steve and Hannah Madison headed east as they climbed to an altitude of eight hundred feet. Hannah pulled on a dark blue headset with an attached microphone so that she could communicate with Steve despite the noisy, recently repaired engine.

Thirty two year old Steve sat on the left side pilot seat, his thirty year old wife sat to his right although she was also a fully qualified commercial pilot. As the aircraft climbed, they both stared at the bright blue cloudless sky that today looked like none of it ever happened.

He was a well-built man of five feet nine inches with short dark brown hair, he eventually stared down at the ground as the plane levelled off, he then glanced across at Hannah but she already stared at him. At first, neither said a word about what they could see from a bird's eye view for the very first time as they flew above vacant flat green fields.

"Looking at the sky, you wouldn't know any of it ever happened." Hannah eventually commented through the microphone. Steve nodded because she was right, everything today seemed so calm and serene from the air, but that serenity was to be very short lived as they would soon discover. Those vacant fields below were unlike almost every other area across the entire country.

Hannah was an attractive woman of five feet six with long wavy blonde hair that was today pulled into a ponytail from high at the back of her head and she possessed pale blue eyes that stared back down at the ground. Her heart began to pound a little harder and faster from the moment that they all suddenly started to appear down there.

"This already looks worse than we thought." She said with an anxious tremble in her tone, despite that she tried to remain calm and objective. Steve again nodded although his just as anxious heart also pounded, from what he could now see he believed that she was right, this was much worse than they initially believed. They soon stared down at what used to be the town of Newmarket that once boasted a thriving population of more than nineteen thousand souls.

"Holy crap look at that." Steve uttered, as he shook his head with disbelief. He said it mostly to himself but Hannah obviously heard it, she also heard the tremble in his tone although she didn't reply because she stared down at the same incredible sight.

The town of Newmarket was the first that she would record as a completely lifeless area after the plane circled overhead twice just to be sure, but nothing at all down there moved, nobody emerged from the rubble and absolute devastation.

"They're all dead." Steve quietly assured her. Hannah nodded as she stared down at the same lifeless bodies along with all manner of dead animals, partially standing and completely obliterated buildings and so many crushed or overturned vehicles of all shapes, colours and sizes. They could both clearly see that Newmarket was, as a town no more and that every one of those nineteen thousand plus people that once lived there were dead.

Every last one of them dead, although it would later transpire that many of the corpses down on the ground did not in fact begin their journey at Newmarket.

It took just a few minutes to continue east and fly directly above Bury St Edmunds, an area twice the size of Newmarket with a population of forty two thousand plus, but again they stared down at what looked to be every one of them just like back at Newmarket, scattered motionless, twisted and contorted around more pulverised partial buildings, more smashed or overturned vehicles and many of those corpses were only now beginning to properly decay.

"I've flown over here hundreds of times, I don't recognize any part of it." Hannah blurted through the microphone. She knew that Bury St Edmunds was about to become the second lifeless area on her list although not even this sight could prepare her for what lay ahead, but this second town was also without doubt no longer home to anybody.

The plane climbed to an altitude of one thousand feet as it headed out toward the eastern coastline and in less than ten minutes, they would fly over not where Southwold would be, but where it once stood. As they would discover it was also gone, but not like the mere lifeless situation back at Newmarket and Bury St Edmunds, Southwold was literally gone, no longer visible even from the air.

The situation was the same at Walberswick to the south and at Reydon to the north of Southwold, in fact the new coastline started way past the submerged main road some two miles to the west of where the beach used to be. This sight caused Steve and Hannah to once again stare at each other with utter disbelief.

They both knew that no good would come of today's flight, but the sight below was much more devastating than either could have possibly imagined before they flew out today for the very first time. They expected to see at least some survivors and they were not yet counting the cost, but after just thirty minutes in the air, the current death toll stood at more than sixty thousand men, women and children. An anxious doubt slowly crept into the back of both their minds although neither said it. They began to wonder if it was even conceivable that they were the only people to have made it out alive because they were yet to see another living person down on the ground.

Steve banked the plane right and headed south above the eastern coastline as the plane again began to descend, they flew over where Dunwich also used to be, but a little farther south they saw that the beach at Sizewell was still partially visible. At that moment, it dawned on Hannah that they now stared down at the permanent new shape of the British eastern coastline.

She considered that after centuries of looking how it did until just five months ago, it now appeared nothing like it would on any current, previous or even ancient map because so many eastern coastal towns and areas were submerged deep beneath the North Sea. A little farther south at Thorpeness, they stared down at the sandy beach with brand new dismay.

They initially believed it to be a motionless beached Whale, but as they neared, it appeared to be somehow broken in half. Steve banked the aircraft left and headed out over the North Sea as they descended to just three hundred feet so that they could turn back and take a closer look at the long, narrow black broken object.

"Is that what I think it is?" Hannah anxiously asked. Her heart continued to pound as they slowly flew past it again at the much lower altitude. When she turned again to stare at Steve she saw that he nodded.

"It's not just a submarine either, it's nuclear and it could be carrying warheads." He finally replied and shook his head with more dismay. Hannah immediately returned her stare out of the window and back down at it with renewed horror.

"How the hell did it get there and why is it broken in half like that?" She asked, although she didn't believe that he had a readily available answer and she was right, he only displayed a look of startled confusion as he also stared down at it, again he shook his head with thoughts of the possible implications of such a monstrous sight.

"It looks like it was picked up from the sea and thrown against the cliff or something, but that couldn't have happened because a Tsunami didn't do this." He assured her. Hannah returned her stare to him and for a few moments, they simply stared at each other.

"A Tsunami big enough to pick up a submarine from the ocean and throw it like this would've taken out Cambridge from here and we were underground, we wouldn't have survived." He added.

Hannah continued to stare at him as her heart pounded so heavily against her chest, the same terrifying thought continued to lurk at the back of her mind since they flew over Newmarket. They had already seen so much horrific devastation and so many scattered, motionless corpses and they now stared down at the epitome of death and destruction, a beached and very heavily damaged nuclear submarine.

They couldn't possibly know that the Dolphin class submarine was in fact German and not British, or that five months ago she was on secret manoeuvres beneath the North Sea just eighteen miles from the north-east British coastline.

They were also unaware that she was violently wrenched up from the ocean by *the Viking* during the very early hours of August twelfth and sometime later, even more violently hurtled south-west to impact the cliff's edge at Thorpeness breaking her almost into two halves, but that was precisely what happened and obviously not a single crew member could have survived the incredible, multiple impacts.

They also couldn't know that there were thankfully no nuclear warheads on-board, those manoeuvres were a mere training exercise. Germany was in no way hostile toward the United Kingdom and besides, they fared no better five months ago, if anything they fared worse although Steve and Hannah still didn't yet know that. All they knew for certain was that this catastrophic event happened to the United Kingdom, but in truth it happened to the entire world and at so many countries the situation was much, much worse.

London

It was around fifty minutes later, Steve gently banked the plane right and they headed west above the now considerably wider mouth of the River Thames that they would follow all the way into the heart of the capital. A city that was once a leading worldwide political, commercial and financial giant and home to more than seven million people, they both knew that they would now see at least some survivors on the ground.

As they followed the vast old river toward the city, the first thing that they saw From Hannah's window on the right side was that Foulness Island directly below was no longer visible, it now lay deep beneath the murky brown river as did Southend-On-Sea and Canvey Island.

From Steve's view on the left, the Isle of Grain, Allhallows and Cliffe were also completely submerged and because there was never any kind of warning prior to the event, they knew that nobody could have made it out alive from any of those areas. This was easily confirmed because thousands of the still rotting dead now floated on the water there, directly above where people once lived.

"This is incredible it can't be, it's much worse than I ever imagined." Steve uttered in a state of stunned shock. They would soon discover that every inch of land at Tilbury, Gravesend, Northfleet, Swanscombe and Greenhithe was also completely submerged, thousands more corpses floated above there and the horrific sights were not about to improve.

Directly ahead was where the enormous white cable stayed Queen Elizabeth II Bridge that connected the counties of Kent to the south and Essex to the north should have been. There was nothing but a void it was gone, completely missing and only a few concrete and twisted steel sections remained to show that it was ever once there at all. That vast bridge was built to withstand a strike from a ship weighing anything up to sixty five thousand tonnes.

"Where the hell is the bridge?" Hannah blurted with a startled gasp. She stared directly at where the huge iconic four hundred and twenty six feet long and one hundred and seventy feet tall structure should have been, but at an altitude of just three hundred feet they almost flew straight through where it once proudly stood.

They would soon discover so many more horrific sights, but the situation beneath them at Dartford was in fact much worse than they could possibly comprehend. The biggest catastrophe there lay beneath the overflowed, considerably wider and deeper murky brown River Thames, but the heavier tides had long since pushed most of them into what remained of the city centre.

The plane climbed to an altitude of five hundred feet, still directly above the river where ahead they saw with more horror the remains of only partial men, women, children and animals that floated lifeless upon it. They both temporarily lost the ability to speak because this incredible new sight couldn't be a possibility.

Steve and Hannah continued to stare in stunned silence when they saw that the Isle of Dogs ahead on the right was completely submerged, thousands more corpses floated there and the huge building known as Canary Wharf was just like the vast bridge behind them gone. Most of the seven hundred and seventy feet tall structure was no longer there, it was ripped apart and whatever remained of the base lay beneath the muddy brown water. All of Rotherhithe to the south of the river there was also completely submerged.

Hannah again gasped when they both saw that ahead Tower Bridge, London Bridge, Millennium Bridge, Blackfriars Bridge and Waterloo Bridge were also just like the Queen Elizabeth II Bridge back at Dartford, completely obliterated and they were all once also huge constructions, but now only remnants remained.

She stared down from her window to see that all of Westminster was also submerged beneath at least sixty feet of dark brown river water. This sight included the House of Commons and more than the top half of the iconic clock tower Big Ben, just like every other tall building around it was missing.

As Steve continued to stare with astonishment, he tried to remain focussed on the purpose of the flight. He eventually banked the plane right before they flew through voids where clusters of tall buildings once stood so that he could again circle the city, but Hannah didn't deal with the situation quite so well.

Just like back and Newmarket and Bury St Edmunds, Steve hoped that the sound of the plane's engine would entice people out from wherever they hid down there, if anybody was in fact still alive amongst the floating corpses and pulverised rubble. His wife now wiped tears from her eyes as they continued to search for any sign of life, London of course previously boasted that population of more than seven million.

Most of the city centre was however now submerged and the rest of it lay in obliterated ruins, although they still optimistically believed that surely some of those people had to have survived, they couldn't all have died. Again, just like at Newmarket and Bury St Edmunds and all the way down the eastern coastline from Southwold, they saw nothing, no movement, no living no breathing anything or anybody at all.

"There were millions of people down there, they can't all be dead!" Hannah blurted through the microphone. Steve heard that same tremble in her voice and he glanced back at her with a lump in his own throat, but he said nothing because yes they could all be dead in fact yes, it looked like they all were.

They circled the city once more at an altitude of seven hundred feet, if anybody had made it they would have without doubt by now heard the plane's engine. There had been nothing in the air for five months, but they still saw nobody alive down there, still no movement whatsoever only so, so many dead for as far as the eye could see.

"Let's fly over Birmingham before we head back to Cambridge for the night." Steve suggested, as he banked the aircraft to the right for a final time. They headed north-west to fly over the next once heavily populated city, as Hannah continued to quietly sob.

One Hundred and Forty Five Days Earlier

Tuesday August 8th

Huntsville Alabama, The United States of America

On yet another stifling hot morning, American Airlines flight A-17 departed from the Ronald Reagan Washington International Airport, bound south for Jackson Wiley Evers International at Jackson Mississippi, carrying two hundred and twenty nine passengers and laden with around seventy thousand litres of fuel. After a little more than two hours into the flight, the aircraft would still hold some thirty eight thousand litres when, for no known or apparent reason everything electrical on-board suddenly shut down including the computerised engines, navigation and communication systems, according to much later very vague reports.

After an earlier transmission from the plane's cockpit to ATC (Air Traffic Control) at eight twenty one that reported nothing out of the ordinary, there were no more from the huge aircraft that weighed more than three hundred tonnes. With no warning whatsoever, it suddenly and silently plummeted toward the ground from eighteen thousand feet, already travelling at more than three hundred and fifty miles per hour before it began to free-fall and spin out of control.

Across the Atlantic Ocean around two hours after this event occurred, the United Kingdom learned of what became a tragic incident during the national six o'clock evening television news broadcast, that an American Airlines flight for no known or apparent reason, crashed into what was thankfully an almost unpopulated William B. Bankhead forest some sixty seven miles south-west of Huntsville, Alabama.

Of course, none of the two hundred and twenty nine passengers or the crew of five could have possibly survived when the huge jet impacted the ground and broke into thousands of separate pieces, after the initial explosion that killed another fourteen on the ground.

The heat generated from that explosion was so intense that no human remains would ever be discovered, everything and everybody for five miles around the impact site was completely vapourised after it collided tail first at more than six hundred miles per hour.

The flight still held around thirty thousand litres of highly combustible fuel after no computerised emergency jettison occurred and the staggering global heatwave at the time only served to intensify the horrific situation that had just taken place. The investigation into how and why flight A-17 so suddenly fell from the sky began with immediate effect.

Many initially believed that a new form of terrorist attack was responsible for it to down so abruptly and with no warning whatsoever, particularly so close to the anniversary of the horrific September Eleventh twin towers attack of two thousand and one.

This time, no group claimed responsibility for the catastrophe because none were responsible for it. Today it is widely accepted that what happened to flight A-17 did so because the entire planet was somehow charged in preparation for what would soon begin or a giant, possibly several giant solar flares were responsible for the occurrence and there is some unproven evidence to support this particular theory, although of course nobody is a scientist.

Gansu, China

A little more than two hours after the tragic American incident, a much smaller aircraft, a single engine private flight just as suddenly lost communication with ATC over Gansu, China some seven thousand five hundred miles from Huntsville Alabama. This second flight, again for no known reason collided into a fifty five storey apartment block where the pilot, a lone passenger and one hundred and fifty three men, women and children inside the apartments were incinerated in a ball of flames, in this very similar tragedy involving a much smaller and very different type of aircraft.

The body count for aircraft impact incidents on this day alone so far stood at four hundred and three souls in two completely different although both stifling hot climates, but the day was not yet over and there would be more that would not be revealed until much later, long after the last clock stopped and that time approached.

Glasgow, Scotland

As the United Kingdom watched devastating live footage of the American Airlines flight during an extended television news broadcast, a lone Sea King helicopter impacted the ground from an altitude of six hundred feet at Queen Elizabeth Forest Park, thirty six miles north-east from the city of Glasgow, Scotland. This third aircraft impact of the day was again so sudden and without warning and immediately killed the pilot and co-pilot, the navigator and twelve soldiers, but this incident would never be reported by the government or by the military.

No report was ever made public as was often the case regarding military operations, but this time not because the fifteen Royal Marines were on any kind of top secret assignment, they were in fact taking part in a mere joint training exercise with Germany. The helicopter headed south-east for the North Sea in search of a disarmed German Dolphin class nuclear submarine that would intermittently surface.

It is today common knowledge that all types of satellite and ground communications started to disrupt and fail, all digital systems would also later die on this day never to return and from that moment all flights private, commercial and military were suspended although the general public was never made aware of why.

What the world once knew as the Internet died on this day and was also never to return, as Mother Earth finally reached her boiling tolerance levels, but the reason that the incident involving the British helicopter was never revealed was because it was simply too late, time was up. The last clock ticked down toward a near total extinction level event. No twist of fate would occur, no superhero would arrive to save the day like they watched back then in their movies and for those that would not make it and so many would not make it, their time on earth would soon be over.

The first real warning signs came as I explained before, a decade earlier during the incredibly hot summer of two thousand and eighteen and those signs did finally cause concerns regarding global climate change because during that year. Taiwan endured a new record high of 40.3C at Tianxiang and on July fifth at the Sahara Desert, the temperature reached 51.3C but it would be nothing in comparison to two thousand and twenty eight. From the April of that year, the world endured the hottest national and global termperatures recorded in living history and day by day those stifling temperatures steadily increased.

On Monday August seventh, the town of Slough, Berkshire witnessed and suffered Britain's hottest ever day when the temperature soared to staggering 41.2C equivalent to 117 Fahrenheit and in comparison, the previous known record was as far as we know, set on August tenth during the year of two thousand and three when it reached just over thirty eight, recorded at the town of Gravesend, Kent south-east England.

On this day, August eighth two thousand and twenty eight, the entire country would be hotter than yesterday, a brand new record breaking temperature would reach an incredible forty two degrees at just after three in the afternoon, at what was then the small slate town of Blaenau Ffestiniog, northern Wales.

Much later discovered records show that at around the same time on August eighth, a dark blue Range Rover car pulled onto the hard shoulder of the westbound M4 motorway just a few miles from the town of Newbury, Berkshire. It was where twenty nine year old Clay Drummond climbed out from the driver seat to make a call to emergency services as he stared at thick white plumes of steam that billowed up from his engine. His recorded call was made to one of the already overstretched and outsourced emergency roadside assistance services, as his vehicle overheated under the intense and still rising temperature.

'Your call and location have been logged, please wait inside your vehicle for roadside assistance.' Was the automated response to his call.

Shortly after that call, those digital communication systems completely failed on a global scale, which meant that he could do nothing but wait. A few moments later, there was a loud explosion when the chunky front right tyre of his car violently exploded and a there was another when the rear left did the same, then the rear right followed by the front left.

Those large, chunky and wider than average tyres actually melted and exploded on the scorching white concrete road. Clay Drummond chose not to wait inside his vehicle and was found standing nowhere near it on the same hard shoulder of the motorway when more than thirteen hours later, that roadside assistance finally arrived as all completely overwhelmed emergency services continued to break down.

Every clean water reservoir across the entire country was by this time severely depleted and at some areas completely empty after four months of incredible heat, but also because it hadn't rained a single drop for more than six months since early January, long before the intense heatwave began.

Three weeks prior to this day, the national government was forced to implement measures banning the unnecessary use of water under a national crisis situation and it shortly after became a criminal offence to take a bath after six in the morning or before six in the evening, until water companies finally disconnected all private supplies during those times in a bid to save as much water as possible.

All Accident and Emergency facilities were overwhelmed on a twenty four hour daily basis, with heat related illnesses, injuries and deaths. One hundred and twenty seven heat related deaths occurred yesterday at the United Kingdom alone and a similar number on this day and the day after.

It was also on August eighth that fishermen operating in the English Channel just five miles from the coastal town of Folkestone, Kent spotted and reported several Sharks. The reason that they were immediately reported was that they were not the type of Blue Shark occasionally seen in those waters prior to this day, but they were with hindsight notice of what approached.

Every ocean around the entire globe was by now far, far warmer than ever before and those ocean temperatures would soon cause the biggest heat related catastrophe of all. The Great White Sharks that were spotted just five miles from the coast of Folkestone provided the evidence.

The ocean temperatures surrounding the British Isles were by now no different to those at any tropical island, it was exactly how and why *she* would soon come into existence. The situation was the same everywhere, every ocean temperature had risen to the point that it could no longer be stopped just a decade after those warnings came from scientists. It was already too late for those promises of drastic change.

She was verified by twenty nine year old Alan Driscoll at the MET Office (Meteorological Office) at thirty two minutes past four that afternoon, positioned around one hundred and twenty miles south-east of Baltimore, southern Ireland. He sought special approval to designate her unlisted name. It was also Driscoll that monitored her out on the Celtic Sea for much of that afternoon as she very slowly headed west toward Canada, until she suddenly vanished from his computer screen.

She was officially designated 'Hurricane Ella' after his three month old daughter, but like so many to follow she would become no ordinary Hurricane, if that's what she ever was at all. To put things into perspective, more than a decade earlier, Hurricane Mathew formed near Haiti over the Caribbean Sea and Mathew started life as a category five hurricane with windspeeds of more than one hundred and sixty miles per hour and would claim more than one thousand lives.

Around a year after Mathew, Hurricane Harvey tore a bloody path through Houston, Texas and this one was just as, if not more devastating. More would follow over the next decade, but Mathew and Harvey were like tiny baby brothers in comparison to what Ella and so many that shortly followed her would become.

Much of her early life can be validated as fact, the country was informed of her existence, a category three at that time during the same six o'clock evening news broadcast, when the nation watched the tragic fate of the American Airlines flight although Ella was a minor, secondary story moving at six miles per hour and away from the United Kingdom, heading west toward the North Atlantic Ocean. The nation was assured that she would dissipate long before she reached the east coast of Canada at her current size, speed and estimated lifespan.

At some time after seven that evening, she changed course and headed south or possibly south-west according to two separate visual reports and on a path with what was believed to be north-west Spain. By this time, she would have been upgraded to a category four with windspeeds of more than one hundred and fifty miles per hour, not yet as vast as hurricanes Mathew or Harvey, but Ella was still only just getting started.

Conspiracy theorists would have you believe that she was kept undisclosed by the MET Office by order of the government because there was nothing that anybody could do to protect or save the population and they wanted to avert panic, riots and looting, that there was some kind of pre-planned New World Order for the aftermath.

Another and more plausible theory involves strange, never previously encountered atmospheric conditions that included those giant solar flares, that the entire planet was somehow charged in preparation and the MET Office could simply no longer see her, or see that she had turned and now headed south toward Spain.

This second theory would mean that they also couldn't know that she would later turn again and once more after that and of course it is widely accepted that the worldwide satellite disruptions began on this day although nobody can know anything as fact, but maybe this second theory is closer to the truth when one thinks back to the American Airlines flight and the smaller aircraft over Gansu followed by the Sea King helicopter over Scotland, that all failed in the same way courtesy of those satellite disruptions.

The technology that they were completely dependent upon was suddenly gone, never to return.

Thursday August 10th

The Dancing Planes at Scilly

With a combined population of just two thousand five hundred and seventy three, Scilly was a group of small islands situated just thirty miles south-west from Land's End, the most south-westerly point of mainland Britain. Much later recovered records reveal that at just after seven on this evening, a very peculiar incident occurred involving three small stationary and now grounded aircraft on the airstrip at St Mary's, the largest of the handful of inhabited islands.

According to a handwritten incident report, the aircraft that were mostly used to transport passengers to and from the mainland, were seen to gently lift from the tarmac where they appeared to hover or *'float around three feet from the ground for about a minute each time'* as the report described, before they just as gently bounced back down onto the incredibly hot tarmac.

It would have been a very peculiar sight and would continue for the next three hours, but all three engines were switched off long before this event started to occur. It was reported to the mainland, but because high winds and light rain were also recorded for the very first time in more than two hundred days no further action was taken, but it did seem that the incredible stifling hot drought was about to finally break.

Ella was still nowhere near the size that she would become, but she was now positioned around one hundred miles north-west from the small French island Ushant where it was also raining and around the same distance south-west from the Isles of Scilly. With worldwide satellite systems down, nobody could see her. Nobody knew that she was there and it is very doubtful that Alan Driscoll or anybody at the MET Office knew. Ella earlier turned again and headed in an easterly direction, but she would at some point later adjust one last time and the population of the United Kingdom would still have no idea of what headed straight for them.

Her outer winds were responsible for *The Dancing Planes at Scilly* and when she did later turn for what is believed to be the final time before she reached dry land, she would head north-east on a direct path toward the Cornish coastal town of Porthleven, who of course had no idea that she was coming.

What was coming would be no ordinary Hurricane and at that time, The Scilly Isles and Ushant would be grateful for the sudden, unexpected start of even light rain after such an incredible long arid drought that seemed to be finally ending and those clean water reservoirs could at last begin to refill and end the dire water shortage.

Ella would maintain the same six miles per hour travelling speed, but she was still growing in colossal size and ferocity at a seemingly impossible rate. She would have without doubt by this time been upgraded to a category five with windspeeds of much more than one hundred and sixty miles per hour, if they at the MET office ever knew that she was there. Her eye alone would span at least seven or eight miles across and she brought rain more than one hundred miles away in all directions, but she would continue to grow and already much, much more than a category five would head straight for the south-west shores of the United Kingdom.

Friday August 11th

Porthleven, Cornwall, South West England

The picturesque coastal town of Porthleven, on the south-west tip of England with a recorded population of three thousand five hundred and ninety three, was where Ella's vast eye arrived onto dry land at almost eleven o'clock during the darkness of night.

She brought with her incredible earth shaking thunder, almost continuous lightning, impossible torrential rain and by that time, her eye would span more than twelve miles, in her entirety she was somewhere around one hundred and eighty to two hundred miles when she slowly engulfed the entire small harbour town, where almost all of the buildings in front and at both sides of Mounts bay were shredded as if made from paper.

The residents at Porthleven were the first to fully understand that the most powerful and destructive winds of a hurricane are those just outside of the eye and the first of those impacted every inch of the surrounding areas exceeding not the one hundred and sixty miles per hour of a category five, but an incredible three hundred and ninety. She was obviously something that nobody on earth had ever witnessed and no remaining record books reveal anything remotely similar, probably because theoretically, Ella couldn't possibly exist.

Before her colossal eye reached the small harbour, her incredible turning winds wrenched the water from the small deep port out to the Celtic Sea and when she very slowly travelled directly above the wet muddy bed, there was no movement at all only an almost serene calm as she very slowly continued north-west.

At that silent paused moment in time, it would be as if she wasn't there at all but that warm still, almost tingling sensation was merely her vast eye slowly passing just one hundred metres overhead, without carnage or devastation inside, only that dead still calm. That six minutes was when whoever initially survived at Porthleven, slowly emerged from whatever was left of their homes, they emerged dazed, confused and terrified whilst standing directly inside her vast eye.

A short while later, a second just as incredible impact from behind her arrived and just as violently wrenched that ocean water back into the harbour with an absolute vengeance, completely submerging at least half of the small town beneath eight feet of Celtic seawater. Earlier that evening, she was merely the storm that finally brought the much needed rain and of course, no information emerged from the Meteorological Office as a warning because they were blinded at that time, they still wouldn't know that she was there, although by this time they would know that it thankfully raining across the entire country.

As she slowly passed directly over the entire town, ripping apart everything in her path on all three sides and then after the comparative calm inside her eye, those incredible destructive now already four hundred miles per hour winds behind would bring a just as devastating second impact to anything that somehow earlier remained in front.

Porthcurno to the south-west of Porthleven became completely submerged as far inland as the villages of Treen and Trethewy, the Penberth River assisted there when it violently burst its banks and just north of Porthcurno, the coastal village of Mousehole was just as quickly beneath twelve feet of Celtic seawater, as were Newlyn and Penzance with a combined population of more than twenty five thousand who all immediately drowned. So many at that time would be in their beds, anxiously waiting for her to pass over.

The area was used to incredibly violent storms, they occurred approximately every one hundred years although nothing before could stand in comparison to this one. Hopefully those people would have known nothing or at least very little about the very sudden emergence and absolutely devastating multiple impacts of Ella.

The entire coastal area around Mount's bay was completely submerged for at least eight miles inland as her vast and still growing eye passed over every inch of Porthleven with a brief, very false sense of serene calm directly beneath it.

Between twenty and thirty small fishing boats were earlier ripped from their moorings and sucked up into the swirling black night sky along with vehicles, uprooted trees and partial buildings of all shapes and sizes, as was any other object that was or was not bolted down. What remained of a dark blue Jaguar car that was registered to a Mr. A. Treglown and would have been parked at Porthleven that night, was much later discovered crushed on its side through a small hanger around four miles to the north-east at Culdrose airfield.

The identified, twisted and contorted remains of twenty nine year old Police Officer Colin Ambrose, who was definitely on-duty at Porthleven that night was also discovered. His broken, decayed corpse was much later found just south of Redruth almost twelve miles to the north. That was where he finally landed or at least what was left of him, although Colin Ambrose would have been thankfully dead or at least completely unconscious long before he impacted the ground at more than four hundred miles per hour.

As Ella continued north, more vehicles, trees, large farming equipment and live animals continued to be wrenched up from the ground and more buildings joined them, almost whole or in pieces and many with the terrified screaming occupants still inside. The entire region was ripped apart and completely submerged, now beneath at least twenty feet of Celtic Sea and it all happened in less than twenty five minutes at Ella's mere walking speed, which was the worst thing possible.

She was so powerful, yet travelled so slowly that she missed absolutely nothing and nobody at all. It is extremely doubtful that anybody around that part of the country could have survived or escaped the onslaught. Nobody knew that she was headed their way and of course the wrenched incoming seawater from three directions was an additional, major factor.

Only three hours earlier when the rain began to pour, she was simply the much needed storm that brought the rain to break the incredible drought, but nobody on mainland Britain could have known at the time that the Scilly Isles, just forty six miles south-west of Porthleven were an hour ago, completely submerged and the two thousand five hundred and seventy three men women and children that lived there drowned, if they didn't join the terror in the skies.

There have been no discovered records of visitors at that time and the Isles of Scilly are all today still deep under water, the only thing for certain about the area is that those dancing planes, they danced no more.

The town of Porthleven along with everywhere around it was also completely submerged and void of any life. It's widely believed that nobody at all survived anywhere around the region when it happened, they simply couldn't have, nobody was ever given the opportunity to flee.

The rest of the United Kingdom still had no idea of what had just happened to Porthleven, or that Ella continued to head north-west. Nobody knew that she was still only just getting started or that she would not come alone. She slowly continued toward Truro who at just twenty miles away, were already enduring the most devastating storm that history would ever recall.

Truro

It was previously believed that a hurricane would begin to dissipate from the moment that it reached dry land, that is now known not to be fact because Ella most certainly didn't, but she was no ordinary weather system. Instead she continued to grow in both size and speed not the mention terrifying awesome destructive power and travelled along the still warmed white concrete road that seemed to feed and fuel her.

She now headed on a direct path for the city of Truro and more than twenty four thousand people, who were by now aware that this was much more than a mere storm but were also still quietly grateful for the almost impossible, torrential downpour. They were without doubt unaware of what really headed their way and they were right, but also wrong to stay inside their homes. With hindsight they should have tried to flee because Ella had already left absolutely nothing and nobody in her wake.

Truro just like Porthleven, was by no means prepared for Ella and she would be bigger, more powerful and still growing when she arrived there. It was at just after midnight when Carrick Roads, Truro River, Tresillian River and Channel's Creek all burst their banks and completely flooded the city centre, as high rise apartment blocks were ripped apart and sucked up in pieces by Ella's now four hundred and fifty miles per hour winds.

Again, large objects such as vehicles, partial and almost entire buildings and terrified livestock that did try to flee for their lives now filled the black turning debris-filled skies. There was then a just as sudden, paused dead still calm across the entire city and no movement whatsoever. It was that same calm, peaceful warm tranquility that Porthleven experienced around an hour ago.

What remained of the terrified residents of Truro, around three thousand survivors from the previous twenty four thousand plus also began to emerge dazed and confused onto the flooded streets in need of help, but it was as if she waited for them to do that and in defence of those desperate people, when a storm has passed over, a storm has usually passed over.

Some eight to ten minutes later, those incredible destructive winds suddenly impacted again when she slowly passed over, as screaming people cluttered the turning skies around her vast eye. If any of them knew much of the horror will never be known because of course none could have possibly survived and just like Police Officer Colin Ambrose from Porthleven, they would have been hurled and scattered, eventually impacting the ground at much more than four hundred miles per hour, many miles from where they were violently wrenched up from it.

Take some solace that nobody up there should have known anything of it, they should have been completely unconscious long before they impacted the ground. It is estimated that an individual man, woman, child or animal would be hurtled around her vast and still growing eye at much more four hundred miles per hour, for some twenty eight minutes.

To demonstrate the sheer awesome power of Ella, two stationary trains that did not join the carnage in the skies were completely derailed at Truro station, one of which would be crushed on its side more than three hundred feet away at the far end of Avondale Road where it was much later discovered, partially embedded into what remained of three terraced houses.

The areas around St Austell, Lostwithiel and Liskeard to the north of Truro were soon completely wiped from the face of the earth along with everybody that lived there, as Ella again adjusted course and now headed north-east, tearing up the next warmed main road on a direct path with the much more heavily populated city of Exeter.

By this time, the death toll surrounding St Austell was somewhere around twenty three thousand plus, at Plymouth there were around two hundred and seventy two thousand, at Torquay, more than sixty eight thousand and they're all gone, every single one of them without doubt died on this day, although Ella was still to reach her full potential.

The city of Bristol lost around a quarter of a million, Taunton, Somerset one hundred and thirteen thousand and the Welsh city of Swansea fell with more than a quarter of a million. These are merely the areas noted and not the only places that were completely obliterated by Ella. Nobody living anywhere near any of them could have possibly made it out, nobody was prepared because nobody knew that she was coming and every last one of them also without doubt, perished on this day.

The Question

Ella continued to grow, but Exeter should have been more fortunate than Truro, they would have by now known that something vast and terrible headed straight for them, but take a moment to ponder on a question, it was the one question that would find absolutely everybody, nobody on earth could avoid answering it. Where you sit right now, I want you to try to imagine, put yourself in the more fortunate position than those at Porthleven, Truro or anywhere around them which was of course everywhere.

Try to imagine that you know that you now have around seven minutes to protect yourself, to simply survive her absolute rage, to live past that day and please feel free to raise your hand if and when you can answer the only question that at that time truly mattered. Let's do that from where you sit, I'm asking you personally and if this story later becomes a ledger, the question will appear, readers can ask themselves wherever they sit to read it.

Where on earth would you hide?

It would take her vast eye just seven minutes to reach Exeter from Truro, not because she now was travelling faster, but because she was still growing at an incredible rate and remember that she would rip apart everything in her path along the way. You would have less than seven minutes to survive if you lived anywhere near Exeter at that time, so think of somewhere right now, think of somewhere that could possibly protect you from a vast super-hurricane like the world has never seen.

From this very moment it would be time to ask yourself the question, she is heading straight for you with pure vengeance and to seek you out with wind speeds of more than four hundred and eighty miles per hour so think very carefully, but think very quickly because you now have six minutes to live.

Where would you hide right now?

It would seem that nobody at Exeter found the answer to the question although it's not known for certain, but nobody that lived anywhere else ever met or heard of anybody that survived there during that terrible night. It's probably because it is believed that over Exeter, Ella's eye spanned some fourteen or fifteen miles. There were more than half a million people that lived in and around that area alone. In her entirety, Ella now covered all of the United Kingdom along with much of the west coasts of France, Belgium and Holland and she continued to grow.

The River Exe at Exeter was the first to be pushed right out to sea leaving her wet muddy bed completely void of water, but it would later return with more pure vengeance and although the Exe may have been the first famous waterway to do this she certainly wouldn't be the last, another very famous old lady would later do the same with even more devastating consequences.

You now have five minutes to live, by the way.

The River Severn to the north didn't do it, but both vast bridges that led into southern Wales were completely ripped apart to join the terror in the skies. The Welsh capital city of Cardiff was also destroyed beyond recognition and there alone another half a million plus were lost. No survivor ever met a single person from there either, but maybe not courtesy of only Ella. Where did you think of to hide from her in the time that it took for her to reach Exeter from the northern outskirts of Truro?

If you don't have the answer which you probably don't, it's already too late you have around two minutes to live and it's very doubtful that yours came from there either, more than half a million people died in and around Exeter alone, but like I earlier said, maybe not courtesy of only Ella.

LMS

As Ella raged over all of Exeter, a second city destroying colossus very suddenly formed over the Irish Sea with the Isle of Man to her north, Dublin, Ireland to her west and Anglesey to her south, but nobody knew anything of this second giant nightmare until much, much later.

Everything at that time would have been about the incredible singular storm that was alone ripping the south of the country to pieces, although from above it would look very different. There were now two giant weather systems over the United Kingdom alone.

This one would later become known to survivors as *LMS* because she was primarily responsible for the total annihilation of Liverpool, Manchester and Sheffield and the combined deaths of more than six and a half million people at those three cities alone.

All three were systematically reduced to nothing but rubble filled destruction because unlike Ella, LMS very suddenly formed in a matter of hours, not over days and within an hour and a half of her emergence, the Isle of Man was completely submerged beneath eighty feet of water and drowned a population of more than a million people, as was most of Dublin to the west and Anglesey to the south soon followed suit.

Again, nobody could have possibly made it out alive, there was nowhere to run to and nowhere to hide as she started to head east at a much faster pace. This one very soon passed directly over the city of Liverpool with the same terrifying consequences as at Porthleven, Truro, Exeter and everywhere around and between them.

LMS was however about to destroy so much more, she was very quickly at least equal to Ella in all departments and whatever she really was, would later become even more devastating after Blackpool, Leeds and Nottingham to name just a few fell beneath her, absolutely devastated and completely lifeless from her awesome destructive power and impossible five hundred miles per hour winds.

Within a matter of hours, the United Kingdom would become completely covered by these two giant turning weather systems and nothing of the country would have been visible from above, but something incredible, even under the unimaginable circumstances would occur.

Five or six hours later, LMS headed out to the North Sea toward the already flooded and battered Dutch coastline, but Holland was suffering catastrophes of the same terrifying magnitude courtesy of her own turning nightmares, as was by this time everywhere else on earth.

According to more very vague later reports, over the North Sea, LMS merged with a third super-hurricane that was also much later named and would become known as '*The Viking*' because this new huge system apparently formed just outside of Scandinavia and was also headed for the shores of the United Kingdom where it met LMS with more devastating consequences.

The Viking was in fact another reason that survivors are certain that the Meteorological Office could not see Ella just before she turned toward Spain. According to more much later accounts, at around seven o'clock on the evening of August tenth, the Viking formed over the North Sea around forty miles south-west of Borhaug, southern Norway. Nobody at the United Kingdom ever knew of its existence and no records were discovered at what remained of the Met office headquarters, that were ironically situated at Exeter.

This would mean that they probably knew nothing of The Viking because of those satellite disruptions and the Scandinavian born colossus, unlike LMS but just like Ella very slowly grew as it headed south-west toward the coast of the United Kingdom.

LMS and The Viking would merge, twisting, turning and pulling each other around and around to form *super-twins* that combined became almost five times the size of Ella at the south of the country. LMS would then return her attention to mainland Britain, but this time she would bring the Viking with her.

Birmingham, Coventry and Leicester were just a few of the first to join the list of lifeless fallen cities as a result along with many, many more heavily populated areas. Those regions would obviously include all of Scotland, all of Wales and all of Ireland, as arm in arm they later headed out and across the North Atlantic Ocean, where they apparently much later dissipated not far from the east coast of Canada, just as Ella should have.

By this time, the death toll for the United Kingdom would stand at around forty million men women and children, more than half of the population. Church, Mosque, Synagogue and Temple, they destroyed them all without prejudice or distinction, but the day was still very young and Mother Nature was by no means finished with humanity.

Basingstoke

When Ella reached the town of Basingstoke at just before six that morning, her eye spanned more than eighteen miles and her outskirts merged deep within LMS and the Viking as far as five hundred miles to the north. Those most powerful winds directly outside of her eye now tore effortlessly through everything in her path at more than seven hundred and eighty miles per hour. As far as anybody knows, history had never witnessed anything like her although with hindsight, she and the others were always inevitable.

By this time, the muddy bed of the River Thames was just like the River Exe completely void of water, forced north for four miles from Twickenham to Brentford and was still being pushed, but now east and toward the capital. It would later cause one of the most terrifying catastrophic disasters of all.

At Westminster, the Prime Minister and several cabinet members of Parliament along with other available politicians were apparently taken to a secret underground bunker complex, where they would wait out the wrath of Ella so that the country could later maintain a working, emergency cross-party government. They would never re-emerge and it's believed that they're still down there wherever there is, probably somewhere beneath the House of Commons beside the rapidly emptying River Thames.

Some members of the royal family earlier fled London and Ella by way of separate helicopters, but those flights were an impossible act of desperation and none would make it to wherever they were destined. They couldn't possibly travel south and instead would head straight into LMS to avoid Ella, but by then, the second giant nightmare covered everywhere to the north of the country, although of course nobody could have known of her at that time.

Ella did not pass directly over the capital although they were by no means safe from her. At a much later date, one of the huge faces of the iconic clock tower Big Ben at Westminster would be discovered some one hundred miles away just north of Peterborough. Now you'll understand that it's more than doubtful that any of the bodies scattered around it came from there either, they would have also impacted the ground from elsewhere many, many miles away.

Gatwick International Airport was destroyed beyond recognition as was Heathrow both just to the north-east of Basingstoke, but at Heathrow something incredible, even under the circumstances occurred.

Most of a huge aircraft with a two hundred a fifty feet hinged wingspan would be hurtled tail-first into what remained of a high rise block of residential flats around eight miles away at the town of Slough. We ancestors of those that survived know that it's still there today, to serve as a reminder of just what Mother Nature can do when her wrath is incurred.

The Tragedy at Dartford

At the far south of the country, the estuary known as Southampton Water was also forced out to sea along with the deep water Solent between the coastlines of Southampton and the Isle of Wight. Just like the River Exe, they were soon both completely void of water and some eighty miles north of Southampton, more than one hundred miles of the River Thames was by this time forced east, toward the North Sea.

Ella's incredible force was so powerful that she also pushed millions upon millions of gallons of seawater out from Southampton into the English Channel, the sea bed from the awaiting Isle of Wight for at least twenty miles was nothing but wet sand and sunken shipwrecks toward the French coastline. As a result, the French coastal towns of Cherbourg, Cabourg and Le Harve were completely submerged as were the British Isles of Jersey and Guernsey. Of course everybody at all of those places immediately drowned if they didn't join the raging carnage in their own skies.

A short while later, Ella's eye passed directly over all of Croydon, Micham, Tooting and Addington at the southern outskirts of London, as the River Thames was forced even further east and finally out to the North Sea. That was when the vast Queen Elizabeth II Bridge at Dartford was completely and effortlessly ripped apart and hurtled in all directions. When the river was finally pushed into the ocean, the Dutch cities of Rotterdam and Roosendaal were also submerged as a result.

Back at the now empty Thames riverbed, the bridges that faced north to south including London Bridge and Tower Bridge were completely ripped apart although Chelsea Bridge, Vauxhall Bridge, Lambeth Bridge and Westminster Bridge that all coincidentally faced east to west somehow withstood.

Officials at Dartford earlier organised protection from the incoming eye of whatever Ella truly was, inside the two now fully exposed road tunnels that passed four thousand six hundred and ninety feet beneath where the River Thames should have been.

The riverbed itself was now completely void of water and visibly showed both grey tunnels beside where the vast cable stayed Dartford Bridge earlier stood, but when Ella's now twenty mile wide eye passed directly over, that same water was suddenly and very, very violently pulled back in to refill the empty riverbed.

Because the Thames Estuary leading into London from the east back then bottlenecked toward the river from the North Sea, the Kent coastal towns of Margate, Broadstairs, Ramsgate, Herne Bay and Whitstable to the south, became like so many others completely submerged, as did Foulness Island, the Isle of Sheppey and Canvey Island at the northern side of where the river should have been.

Ella wrenched back so much water that she earlier forced out, but when it returned because of that bottlenecked Estuary, all of those coastal towns and the surrounding areas were completely submerged in a matter of eleven or twelve minutes. Nobody at any of them stood a chance as the pressurized water was pulled back in to more than refill the two hundred and fifteen miles of empty Thames riverbed.

Those Dartford officials unwittingly led local residents to take shelter inside the two earlier considered safe, but now fully exposed tunnels. It's understood that the same idea was used at the northern end at Thurrock, Essex. Now take another moment, but this time to consider the sheer ferocity of what happened next.

Both Dartford crossing tunnels were impacted with such incredible force, the force of much more than the four thousand five hundred *million* gallons of returning pressurised water that earlier filled the entire riverbed. It returned with an absolute vengeance thanks to the bottlenecked estuary and under that incredible pressure, neither tunnel could possibly withstand.

Four thousand two hundred and twenty seven men, women and children plus the nineteen local officials that took refuge at the southern end immediately drowned, if they weren't ripped apart by the sudden impacts when both shelters were completely obliterated by the sheer mass and weight of incoming water, whatever remained of them at both ends completely filled. If the stories are true that residents from Essex took shelter at the northern end, the exact same fate would have been bestowed upon them.

Within half an hour of the tragedy at Dartford, the inner city of London including Westminster was also completely submerged as that mass of water rushed back in to refill the riverbed, it's more than likely why those politicians were never seen again.

The Isle of Wight

A short while after the tragedy at Dartford, the English Channel at the far south of the country also returned to Southampton with as much if not more vengeance and completely submerged the Isle of Wight in around seven minutes. It also more than refilled the deep water Solent along with Southampton water and every inch of the southern English coastline.

The population of the Isle of Wight at that time, stood at around one hundred and fifty thousand and obviously, everybody there drowned or had already joined the devastation in the skies when this next event took place. You can now appreciate why I earlier referred to the Isle of Wight as awaiting. Portland was also gone and just like the Isle of Wight, would remain submerged as did the Scilly Isles, both the Isle of Man and Anglesey in the Irish Sea. In fact every one of the two hundred and sixty seven small inhabited islands that surrounded the United Kingdom suffered that fate, obviously nobody on any of them could have possibly made it out.

What was left of the United Kingdom was nothing but dust-filled rubble and the start of wild burning fires, the death toll would stand at an incredible sixty nine to seventy million people. Fifteen years earlier, that would have been the entire population and what was once known as Great Britain would have become like so many other islands completely uninhabited, a lifeless plot of land in less than twenty four hours, but thankfully some on the mainland did somehow survive.

Ella continued east across the North Sea, on a direct path with the Dutch city of Rotterdam that was already battered and mostly submerged by her. It's believed that she finally dissipated somewhere near Hanover, northern Germany on the evening of Sunday August thirteenth. Holland and Germany however, along with every other country on earth had by that time and many were still experiencing their own catastrophes of the same terrifying magnitude.

It is today widely accepted that there were around five hundred and fifty Ella sized weather systems around the entire globe at that same time, too many of them colossus merged super-twins like LMS and the Viking.

Sixty seven were later estimated and widely acknowledged over the Americas alone, sixty one over Russia and at least sixty five over China, but the worldwide problems were far from over even after they all much later dissipated. Around the world, those that somehow survived were left with no power of any kind, no running water and no means of communication when entire civilisations turned dark.

It is extremely doubtful that anybody realised the true extent of what happened to the entire planet over the past twenty four hours and was still happening over many countries, most isolated survivors for many months after believed that it happened only to them.

As she slowly subsided, Ella's three hundred and fifty miles per hour plus tailwinds with those from LMS and the Viking, continued to batter the entire United Kingdom long after they left and crossed the North Sea into mainland Europe and the North Atlantic Ocean toward the east coast of Canada, but Mother Nature's purge of humanity was not yet over.

Wednesday August 16th

The First Survivors

Too many of the two million or more that somehow survived at the United Kingdom, would emerge from whatever shelter earlier saved them when they needed medical supplies, food, water and help or to search for loved ones. They really should have stayed where they were.

It was as if Karma and Mother Nature knew each other well and had seen enough. It seemed that they had finally seen enough of humanity and patiently waited for those that survived to re-emerge so that they could continue with the purge of the roach that was mankind.

At around fifteen minutes past five on this evening, when so many survivors roamed the decimated and still burning streets far enough from their havens with nowhere to run to, giant sized hailstones formed and at the United Kingdom, they returned the still blustering skies to night before they hurtled down at around six hundred miles per hour.

For most, this was down to incredible timing and pure bad luck, but it would not have felt that way at the time. It would have felt like Hell on Earth when billions upon billions of giant compacted balls of ice hurtled straight down and impacted whatever and whoever stood or ran in their paths across the entire planet. Those huge rocks continued to relentlessly rain down well into the next day and by that time, so many terrified and confused people had re-emerged only to face this new horror. This is known as fact because they were later found or at least parts of them were.

Try to imagine four kilogramme lumps of frozen rock hurtling down toward the earth at six, or maybe even seven hundred miles per hour to understand that those terrified and confused, roaming people never really stood a chance and should have stayed wherever they were.

Some in blind panic took refuge beside or beneath already pulverised and overturned vehicles that were earlier slammed down to the ground by the hurricanes, or that never left because they were protected by partial buildings. Others took new refuge inside what remained of buildings that were for whatever reasons vacated by their previous occupants, some even tried to hide beneath corpses that already lay scattered upon the ground.

Be it from naivety or sheer terrified blind panic, no car and no remains of a tiled or flat roof let alone another human body, would protect anybody from a four kilogramme lump of frozen compacted ice that rained down to earth and smashed through whatever and whoever stood or lay in its path and there were of course billions of those hailstones.

It is said that there was apparently one giant boulder for every six feet of land and they didn't discriminate between city street, rural countryside, council housing estate or stately home. Those solid compacted rocks created another two million corpses, most of them headless providing the clear evidence of what happened to them. They were the easily identified souls who tried to run for their lives when they should have stayed wherever they somehow earlier survived.

The country was no longer similar to a stifling hot tropical island, it was now pulverised and void of life just like everywhere else on earth. All that remained was a very thick white floating dust that almost blocked out the sun.

Burning rubble with lifeless contorted corpses that were scattered absolutely everywhere for as far as the eye could see from anywhere one stood. The only people to survive that incredible day long hailstorm were the remaining three or four thousand that stayed inside the havens that earlier saved them from the colossal super-storms.

Three or four thousand survivors from more than seventy two million. The United Kingdom came that close to becoming an uninhabited island.

When the World Turned Dark

On August eighth, more than four hundred million people across the United States of America watched their television screens with utter horror, when news broke of the devastating air disaster that was American Airlines flight A-17 out of Washington.

Like everywhere else on Earth, most immediately assumed with outrage that it was caused by some new kind of terrorist attack and there were several outbreaks of revenge violence. That all changed two days later when they endured their own incredible vast storms that impacted every inch of land.

It changed because the terrible air disaster was promptly forgotten by those that survived the catastrophic events, such is human nature. Today, here and now is always the only real day in existence, the only one that truly matters, yesterday is gone, tomorrow is yet to come and memories from both will fade in a very short space of time.

It is believed that the sixty seven validated, Ella sized super-hurricanes arrived over the United States alone, not the mere three that completely destroyed this country. Theirs left an estimated live body count of a little more than just three million from some four hundred million.

Approximately three hundred and ninety six million men, women and children perished before their own giant hailstorms just as suddenly and silently hurtled down from the skies, this time concealed by the darkness of night. They claimed another one and a half million or more, the additional headless corpses joined those already lying there and were also left strewn across the vast American landscape and were again the easily identified.

Some areas of the United States were prepared for violent hurricanes and other extreme weather systems, but many of those people also later re-emerged after theirs and so many didn't make it back to their underground havens when the giant hailstones suddenly rained down although out of pure fear, a few earlier remained where they were and again survived.

Bustling New York, where nine million people once lived was abruptly void of any life when at the same time Manhattan Island, Rhode Island and Long Island were all submerged beneath the Atlantic Ocean as was most of the east coast including New Jersey, Delaware, Philadelphia and South Carolina. Those areas are still void of life although they did much later very slowly begin to resurface at some areas of higher ground.

Florida no longer exists as a land mass and still rests beneath the Ocean, as does most of what became the small island of Mexico to the south while Cuba, The Bahamas, The Cayman Islands, Haiti, The Dominican Republic, Puerto Rico and Jamaica are no longer there at all.

With the exception of the tiny lifeless remaining patch of Mexico that now stretches around one hundred miles by one hundred miles, they're all gone as are their ancient cultures just like every island around that region. Costa Rica along with Panama also submerged as a joint region, turning South America into a completely separated, almost lifeless continent.

The American capital back then known as Washington DC, lost more than ten million including the President and all staff when, just like at the House of Commons at London, they hid deep beneath what remained of the White House and would never re-emerge. They did the same at the Pentagon and the Ronald Reagan National Airport from where the American Airlines flight departed on August eighth, when it all so suddenly began with no warning whatsoever.

Shortly after they all hid, the vast Potomac River took care of whatever remained when some nine hundred thousand *million* gallons of North Atlantic Ocean was pushed inland to more than violently burst her banks.

Just like at the House of Commons beside the River Thames, the American Politicians hid deep beneath the Whitehouse to save themselves from the storms to later maintain a working government, but unfortunately no matter how deep they waited, the vastly overfilled Potomac followed and she found and drowned every last one of them.

The purge of life continued.

Survivors only later understood that the place to wait out those horrific giant super-storms was obviously underground, but hiding underground beside a vast waterway such as the River Thames, the Potomac or any ocean proved to be nothing short of involuntary suicide. Hindsight is such a wonderful notion but rarely a reality when, with help from Mother Nature a pinch of blind panic is thrown in for good measure.

The souls that lived through those horrific days would be forgiven for thinking of nations in order of the superpower status that existed back then, but of course there was no distinction. The most powerful countries on Earth were just like every other region and their religions, utterly destroyed.

Before the catastrophic worldwide events took place, China boasted the largest population with almost one and a half billion people and there is still no accurate record of how many survived there but it would not be many. It is believed that around sixty five vast super hurricanes, again all at least equal to Ella passed over those lands. As a result, Beijing was lost as was Taiwan and most of the Great Wall that withstood every previous test of time, but not this time.

India boasted a population of much more than a billion when she, just like every other nation was reduced to nothing but pulverised rubble and lifeless corpses that were scattered everywhere. Brazil with two hundred and twenty five million plus, they all died and at Russia one hundred and fifty two million met with the same fate.

What remains of Mexico is of course completely void of life, but that population once stood at almost one hundred and twenty eight million.

Germany lost eighty two million with Stuttgart, Frankfurt and Hamburg just a few of the many German cities that were completely wiped from the face of the earth. It is said that four of those colossal turning eyes with seven hundred miles per hour plus winds impacted Berlin alone, one after another after another just to be absolutely sure, although whether or not it was the same storm that returned over and over will never be known because nobody at all survived at Berlin.

Iran, where there were once eighty six million men women and children is now a barren desolate landscape and no records have been discovered regarding her neighbour Iraq, but there it's also believed to be completely lifeless.

France was also lost with the deaths of almost seventy million on the day that the Eiffel Tower fell at Paris, along with other estimated death tolls such as Canada thirty seven million, Italy sixty three million, where both Rome and Vatican City were effortlessly wiped from the face of the planet, the island of Sicily that once stood to the south-west of Italy was completely submerged.

Argentina lost forty six million, Spain around forty million and Saudi Arabia more than thirty million. The proud old seafaring Scandinavian nation of Norway with a population of just five million was completely submerged beneath the North Sea along with Denmark to her south, still with no known or even estimated Danish body count.

That was when the entire world from the view of the International Space Station turned dark other than the raging fires and at that time, nobody that survived on Earth knew anything for certain about anywhere other than where they lived and where they lived was lifeless, absolutely pulverised and so much of it ablaze after Hell paid a visit to Earth.

The Astronauts on-board the International Space Station would have stared down at the planet that was at one point completely covered with vast white, swirling super-giant storm systems. Those just as unfortunate souls up there may have been safe from them, but they had their own problems to consider or to come to terms with.

They would have known as they watched the entire planet being ripped apart, that when this catastrophic world-wide event was finally over, they would never return home, home was gone. Florida was no more as was most of Russia along with the technology to communicate and use the same technology to return.

They would have watched it and all means of ever coming back being destroyed, they would observe entire continents change their natural shape and when the storms finally dissipated, they would also see that most island countries were no longer visible because they were gone, that meant that everybody on them had to have died.

Those seven astronauts still circle the globe today but they are of course also long time dead, just like the seven billion or more lifeless souls who all lay motionless down on planet earth.

Thursday August 17th

Living, breathing people

Thirty year old Amelia West slowly opened her blurred pale green eyes, for a few moments they stared up and into the darkness before she suddenly sat bolt upright with a terrified gasp on the reclined front passenger seat of her dust covered car. It suddenly dawned on her that what she had lived through was no terrible dream, it really did happen.

She was of athletic build and stood at around five feet seven inches, she had wavy shoulder length brunette hair and was dressed in the same, although now filthy clothing that she wore when she fled the apartment during the early hours of Friday morning. On her way out, she grabbed Mark's old grey trench coat, but he wasn't with her.

As her senses slowly returned, she again began to tremble as she anxiously stared out through the dust covered window around the very dimly lit underground car park. She thought only of the whereabouts of her partner of four years Mark Bristow because this really did happen, it was no mere terrible dream.

She sat wrapped in a thick grey blanket that she kept in her car for emergencies, along with minimal non-perishable food that was eaten two days ago with a small bottle of tap water. She sat terrified, two thick concrete floors beneath the apartment block since the raging carnage worsened at around five o'clock on Friday morning.

In a state of sheer terrified panic, Amelia fled and hurried down the internal, communal staircase and into the private underground car park after the windows of her fourth floor apartment were pressed so hard that all of them smashed inward. On her way down, she didn't dare to venture outside where unbeknown to her, she would have been sucked up into the debris filled, wildly turning skies just like every one of her neighbours.

She still knew none of this, a short while after she sat inside her car dazed, confused and absolutely terrified, she genuinely believed that the next world war had broken out with no warning whatsoever, that the country was under attack and in one sense she was right, the entire country was under attack. Today however, she sat reasonably calm, in fact somewhat subdued as a result of borderline malnutrition and fatigue, but completely alone inside the dimly lit, dust filled underground car park.

The apartment block above consisted of sixteen privately owned flats and she was still unaware of the true extent, but not one of her neighbours made it, she hadn't seen or spoken to another person in five or six days since early on Thursday evening and that was Mark before he went out to meet with friends. She obviously couldn't know that the now completely pulverised city of Oxford, just like everywhere else around that region was one of so many that incurred the full wraths of Ella, LMS and the Viking combined and that the entire country now lay in unrecognisable burning ruins.

During the early hours of Friday morning, she sat huddled and listened with horrified disbelief to the muffled but still incredible noise above, the terror outside that seemed at the time would never end. She didn't dare to venture out there for fear that bombs were falling and the target would be London just seventy miles to the south-east and that absolutely terrifying, deafening noise that she heard nothing like before had to be the fallout.

She worked much of it out two days ago, when she listened in the darkness to the muffled sound of heavy objects that hurtled down from the skies all day and night and seemed to smash upon impact. She didn't know what those giant compacted boulders were, but she didn't believe that they were any kind of military missile although she couldn't be certain. At times, the impacts came so frequently that that they almost sounded similar to muffled machine gun fire. There was now nothing but deafening silence, with the exception of a very faint low droning sound that came from somewhere above her.

What she did know for certain, was that before today it definitely wasn't safe to even check outside and besides, both ramped entrances that led into and out of the car park were now blocked with rocks and rubble. She also knew that emergency lighting somehow still flickered after it switched over to the diesel run generator that she could hear somewhere above her slowly spluttering and dying out and as soon as it did that, it would leave her and the rest of the underground car park in pitch black darkness.

The otherwise silent environment was filled with floating white dust, she had already lost track of whether it was day or night outside and she was aware that she continuously slipped in and out of consciousness. What today still played heaviest on Amelia's mind was the safety and whereabouts of Mark although she knew that he was resourceful.

She believed that he would have made his way to his sister Ruth's house at the western outskirts of the city if he couldn't get home, so that was where Amelia needed to be.

She had no way of knowing that Elms road where his sister lived around five miles away with her family, was like everywhere else reduced to nothing but smoking rubble and lifeless dust covered carnage, but she did know that she couldn't stay inside her car forever, forever wasn't going to be much longer if she didn't soon eat and drink something.

The internal entrance door that she used to get to her car on Friday morning that led to the communal staircase at the ground floor, for some reason now wouldn't budge after she earlier attempted to take her first anxious look outside.

After conflicting deliberation, she finally opened the car door and again slowly climbed out onto trembling, unsteady weakened legs before this time, she staggered toward the rubble filled drive-in ramps as the white dust began to enter her lungs. With the grey blanket still draped over her shoulders, Amelia began to pull away the smaller rocks that she tossed behind her into the darkened wilderness and heard them echo as they bounced and rolled across the dust covered black tarmac.

Eight or nine minutes later, she still saw no daylight and no breeze brushed her face, she considered that she could be entombed and might die from dehydration inside what was earlier her haven, but she still possessed her stubborn inner strength and refused to panic although her own mind continued to taunt her.

As she pulled away rocks, she wondered if anybody even knew that she was down there and she considered that people, emergency services might be outside busily working to get her out although she couldn't hear a single voice or sounds of any movement out there at all. Hope, albeit terrified hope was her new motivator.

As she continued to pull the smaller lumps from the pile using her left hand while her right covered her nose and mouth to prevent those dust particles from filling her lungs, Amelia couldn't possibly know what was about to happen halfway around world at around that moment in time and if she did, it would have removed all notions of hope.

At the southern hemisphere, the first of five Mega-Tsunami was about to impact the east coast of Japan with an initial three thousand foot wave that was so vast, it would also impact Australia four thousand miles to the south. Within three days and after four more giant waves, both great island countries would become completely submerged beneath the Pacific Ocean with no means of escape, which obviously meant that nobody at all could have possibly survived.

A mere four hundred feet of Mount Fuji can be seen today, the rest of Japan still lies beneath more than two thousand feet of water, as do so many of the one hundred and twenty six million people that lived there at the time. Many of those bones still float rotten above her, the world lost more than thirty one million when Australia also completely disappeared as a land mass.

New Zealand and the Philippines are also gone as a result of the same impacts as are the Indonesian islands, the Malaysian islands and Papua New Guinea. The same fate was bestowed upon Vietnam at the cost of some ninety eight million lives along with her neighbour Cambodia with another one hundred and fourteen million, who all very suddenly disappeared under water although most of them had been dead for days, long before this terrible event occurred.

There are still no estimated body counts for New Zealand, the Philippines, Papua New Guinea or the Indonesian and Malaysian islands but they're all gone. Anybody that still lived at that time anywhere around that region is gone. Nobody could have possibly made it out and the entire area is still under water to this day.

The City of Oxford

It was at around that same time when twenty eight year old Alison Dixon sat inside her small windowless office at the brand new, still unopened and almost completely undamaged Ellington underground shopping centre at Kennington, just south of Oxford. She sat a little more than six miles from Kidlington where Amelia West was trapped inside the underground car park.

Alison sat motionless and incredibly anxious, still in a state of stunned shock with her head buried inside her folded arms on top of her desk, with nothing but thoughts of the very worst case scenario spinning around inside her tormented mind.

She had straight, shoulder length auburn bobbed hair and was dressed in the same pale yellow blouse and faded blue denim jeans that she wore during the very early hours of Friday morning when she and Reg first arrived at the underground complex. Their survival came about only because the power was suddenly knocked out at both of their homes just like everywhere else when the local grid was destroyed by the storm, although Ella still approached Exeter at the time and her full devasting effects had not yet reached Oxford.

Alison was the recently appointed general manager at the shopping centre that was ironically due to open for the first time today, but at just after two o'clock on Friday morning when she arrived, Reg was already at the centre because the power would undoubtedly be knocked out too, but down on the lower basement floor were two brand new, state of the art diesel run generators that could easily power the entire four floors with enough stored fuel to run them both continuously for two whole weeks.

They had not left to return home to their families until now, Reg did so a little more than an hour ago. He would first make his way to his own house around three miles away at Elms Road to find his sixty two year old wife Marcie, then go on with her to find Alison's husband Sid and their three small children. He would then bring everybody back to the Ellington centre to wait for some kind of news and help, underground was without doubt the safest place to be.

All four floors inside the underground complex were completely undamaged, even after Reg watched those terrifying giant hailstones from the protection of an enclosed delivery ramp. Yesterday, they discussed using the entire centre, particularly the upper floor staff canteen to help those in desperate need with hot food and drinks regardless of what the company insurance certificate might have to say, they were both long past caring about strict company policies. Other and more personal, humane matters were on both of their minds.

The entire lower fourth floor was a vast maintenance workshop and ramped delivery area, but the second and third levels comprised of thirty varied, completely filled and ready to open shops, fifteen on both floors including two giant supermarket. The upper floor some fifteen feet beneath solid concrete and steel, was structured into small offices and storage rooms and a fully equipped, ready to use staff canteen that could seat forty people at any one time.

Alison as yet had no real comprehension regarding the true extent of the situation outside, but Reg would learn with a very heavy heart from the rubble and devastation that there was nobody left out there to help. On his way to Marcie, he would climb over and step around so many contorted, so many headless corpses that were slumped and scattered in every direction that he stared, but he saw nobody at all alive.

Twenty eight year old Jason Moran sat on the dusty black floor inside a pitch dark underground car park beneath the superstore where he worked as a night shift manager at Headington, at the southern outskirts of Oxford city centre. He sat around four miles to the north-east of where Alison Dixon sat behind her desk and silently prayed to a God that she didn't believe existed.

Jason was a man of stocky build and five feet nine inches tall with cropped dark brown hair, he stared into the void that was the completely silent underground car park although he wasn't alone down there, but it was so dark that he could see none of the four men that also sat somewhere in front of him. He suddenly glanced up toward the thick reinforced concrete roof above and listened before he returned his stare to the vast pitch black silence in front.

"Who wants to go up top and take another look to see if help's here yet?" He called out. His echoed question was followed by a lengthy silent pause. Seated on the same floor around twenty feet in front of him was the night shift assistant manager thirty year old Alan Robbins, who was of average build and he also had short dark brown hair, he was dressed in identical and just as filthy clothing. Alan lifted his head and stared in the general direction of Jason's voice before he shook his head with a sigh.

"You're the only one that hasn't been up there, why don't you go?" He asked in response. Forty four year old delivery truck driver Paul Richards who sat somewhere between them, stared back down at the ground and he also shook his head.

"Why don't you just shut up for five minutes?" He asked Jason in particular.

Paul Richards was no more than an average looking man of six feet one with short greying brown hair. He was also dressed in the orange company uniform but he was the odd man out, he should never have made it to the store to make his delivery. He somehow did arrive at Oxford in his eighteen-wheeled truck complete with a full cargo, as Ella obliterated Exeter and everywhere surrounding and shortly after LMS formed in the middle of the Irish Sea and turned her full attention toward Liverpool. If he had arrived around forty minutes later, he and his truck would have without doubt joined the terror up in the angered heavens.

Seated to the left of him was twenty year old fork lift truck driver Philip Smith, who was again no more than an average looking man of around five feet eight with short blonde hair, he discretely smirked as he also stared down at the ground. On the right side of Richards sat nineteen year old trainee warehouse manager Jake Jarrett, a slightly rotund young man of six feet one with straight shoulder length reddish brown hair, he glanced up and toward the general direction of wherever Jason sat in the darkness.

"I'll go up again." He called out with a sigh. When Jake slowly climbed to his feet, so did his best friend Phil Smith and together they cautiously made their way toward the concrete staircase that lead up to what remained of the store, which they both already knew was nothing but smouldering grey rubble and was earlier burning in places directly above them.

"Well done lads." Jason called out. Both younger men shook their heads before Jake suddenly stopped walking and turned to face wherever Jason sat in the darkness.

"If you actually went up there just once to look for yourself, you'd already know like we all do that there's nothing but dead people!" He reminded his boss. There was another silent pause before Jake continued.

"And remember this because I'm going to, it was you that made those girls go home when it was all happening." He just as angrily reminded Jason.

Jake couldn't see that Paul Richards, Alan Robbins and Philip Smith all nodded in silent agreement because for reasons known only to himself, on Friday morning Jason sent home only the remaining female members of staff shortly after Richards arrived with his cargo. By that time, Ella had just pulverised Exeter to the south, LMS had done the same to Liverpool at the north-west and the Viking slowly neared the coast at the opposite side of the country.

"First, you told them that they couldn't go home until the truck was emptied and the stock was put away and as soon as it was, you told them that actually now you've got to go home, you can't stay here it's against our health and safety policy!" Jake continued. Again he couldn't see it, but everybody inside the pitch black void nodded as Jason shook his own head in a state of absolute denial.

"That's not what happened." He quietly uttered in response.

The five night shift workers that they all knew that he albeit unwittingly sent to their deaths during the early hours of Friday morning, were discretely recorded by Alan Robbins for future reference. Eighteen year old trainee supervisor Amy Vinton, thirty three year old canteen worker Anita Stone, fifty three year old canteen worker Gwen Vella, twenty year old shelf filler Charlotte Strickland who was of particular importance to one of the men and eighteen year old shelf filler Emma Todd.

Three hundred metres from the destroyed superstore where Jason Moran and the four other men sat beneath the ground, Amy Vinton sat on the passenger seat inside Gwen Vella's dust covered car that was fortunately parked on the lowest floor inside the remains of a darkened, public underground multi-storey car park, Gwen lay reclined on the driver seat beside her.

Amy had long straight auburn hair that was pulled into a ponytail from high at the back of her head. She turned to watch Gwen snooze from sheer exhaustion for a few moments, she then glanced to her left and stared at Anita Stone's dust covered car that was thankfully parked beside in their usual parking spaces, the other three women just as thankfully sat inside it.

"I still can't believe that stupid prick tried to make us go home in the middle of that." Amy quietly uttered. She referred to Jason Moran, but she and the other women were still unaware of what really happened outside. Gwen slowly opened her eyes before she sat upright and again switched on the engine to warm them both.

Still in a state of shock, she suddenly recalled the longest three hundred metre walk of her entire life, from the superstore across to the public underground car park. None of the women could possibly comprehend at the time that just thirty miles away cars, trees, buildings and people were actually wrenched from the ground to be later violently hurtled elsewhere, as they all struggled, holding hands to walk toward the public car park in more than hurricane strong winds, they somehow made it.

"He's a self-important sexist arsehole, you already knew that." She uttered in response. Amy nodded with full acknowledgement and agreement.

"Yeah, well I promise my boyfriend's going to kick the crap out of him when he finds out what he did to us and he can shove his job up his arse!" She angrily replied.

Gwen had curly blonde shoulder length hair and wore blue framed rectangular glasses and like Amy, she still had no idea of just how fortunate they all were to be alive because everybody else was dead, that included Amy's boyfriend. The five women happened to be in the right place at the right time, although if they left the store around twenty minutes later, they certainly would have joined that violent turning terror in the skies. Ella's incredible awesome power simply didn't seek them out in time.

Emma Todd sat on the back seat inside Anita Stone's car and stared through the dust covered windows into the darkness. When she turned her head and stared to her right, she could just see the vague silhouette of Amy seated inside Gwen's car before she again closed her eyes and began to drift off from a result of dehydration. In front of her,

Charlotte Strickland stared down at a photograph of her parents in her hands, as gut wrenching scenarios filled her thoughts. Reclined on the driver seat beside Charlotte with her eyes closed was Anita Stone, who also lay back with her folded arms in front of her.

"I really need something to eat and drink." She quietly croaked. Emma slowly opened her eyes and nodded, but she didn't answer because even that was too much effort. When Anita heard Gwen's car engine start, she opened her own eyes and slowly sat upright to do the same with a sigh as Charlotte watched her.

"We're not going to be able to drive out of here the exit's blocked, if we're leaving and not waiting for help to come we're going to have to climb out." She pointed out in a quiet, croaked voice of her own.

With tear-filled eyes, Ellington underground shopping centre manager Alison Dixon slowly lifted her head from her folded arms, she stared toward her opened office doorway when she heard Reg return through a steel entrance door. Her heart began to race when she listened to his unmistakable heavy footsteps as he climbed down thirty four stone steps and onto a shiny narrow grey tiled corridor that led to her office, but she could hear nobody with him.

Sixty four year old Reginald Simmons was due to retire on his birthday a little more than a week from today. He was the temporary maintenance engineer at the brand new centre mainly because he lived nearby, but also because his knowledge of all types of engineering was very highly respected within the company ranks.

'He's on his own.' Alison convinced herself and her heart began to pound harder and faster with absolute dread. Reg was a rotund man with balding white hair, he always had a smile and even though Alison had only known him for the past three months, she genuinely regretted that he wouldn't be around for much longer because they worked well together, but that was of course before the catastrophic events, everything had now changed.

Like every other day, he wore a dark blue boiler suit over his everyday clothes and on his feet, his old scuffed steel toe capped work boots that suddenly stopped when he stood out of Alison's view just beside her office doorway. Reg then took in a long, long deep breath and very quietly exhaled it to try to compose himself as Alison stared out and trembled with absolute dread. She was now certain that nobody was with him.

His entire body was numb, but he eventually managed to force one foot in front of the other and slowly appeared in the doorway where he very briefly glanced down at her, before he entered and sat on a small black leather chair in front of her desk. He then glanced down at the floor as she continued to stare at him and it was Alison who finally broke the intense silence, she now knew without doubt that he was alone.

"Didn't you find Marcie?" She asked with a very anxious tremble in her tone. Reg still stared down at the floor. He eventually nodded and there was another pause of just as anxious silence whilst Alison's heart continued to pound with dread.

"I'll have to go back and bury her at some point soon." He quietly replied. Alison could clearly see that he was in a state of severe shock as tears continued to fill her own eyes. Her hand covered her mouth when Reg slowly lifted his head and stared back at her, she saw for the first time that his eyes were also filled.

"There's nothing left Ali it's all gone, I had to climb over what was left of my house just to find her, there are bodies everywhere." He uttered.

"There's no police out there, no ambulances or fire brigade nothing, everything's gone, the two hospitals aren't even there anymore." He added. They continued to stare at each other and Reg saw that those tears now began to stream down Alison's reddened cheeks. He knew what she so desperately wanted to ask him, he also knew what he had to tell her and it was about to be the hardest thing that he ever had to do, but Alison instinctively knew and her entire body began to tremble.

"I did go to your house." He finally confirmed. Alison's hand still covered her mouth and tears continued to stream down her face. She continued to stare back at him, she slowly shook her head and silently pleaded with him not to say it because she already knew that he had no good news to tell, but maybe, just maybe her husband and children were safe elsewhere because Sid was incredibly smart. Reg took in another long deep breath that again shuddered when he exhaled it as he stared back at her. Alison could see the tear-filled sorrow in his eyes as she anxiously waited for him to say something, anything.

"Did you actually find them though?" She asked in a trembling, almost whispered tone as they continued to stare at each other before Reg slowly nodded.

"I'm so sorry." He quietly croaked.

The five presumed deceased women from the public underground car park, slowly crossed a wide bridge that passed over the now vastly overflowed River Thames at the south of Oxford. With horrified widened eyes, they stared in all directions, as they stepped around vehicles, rubble and lifeless corpses, they cautiously walked on what remained of the Eastern Bypass Road.

They headed toward the Southern Bypass Road that they would cross to Anita Stone's house at the bottom of Kennington Road because she lived nearest. Everywhere around them was that heavy floating dust. The two teenagers, Amy Vinton and Emma Todd tentatively walked arm in arm at the back of the line along the lifeless rubble filled street, where battered vehicles lay, many of them upside down or on their sides, many crushed with people that actually tried to flee inside them, but none of those people could possibly be alive.

"This can't be happening." Emma quietly blurted as tears streamed down every one of their faces. What none of them had seen so far was life of any kind other than their own. In that eerie, deafening silence they saw no dogs, no cats and no birds in whatever trees that somehow remained, but more importantly there were still no living people.

What they couldn't possibly know, was that there were by this time, a little short of seventy two million corpses that lay scattered across what remained of the United Kingdom. Those corpses already gave off an absolutely foul stench because so many of them now, after five days began to rot in filthy water, this meant that they would decay four times faster.

It was around an hour and a half later, Reg Simmons stepped outside onto the heavily damaged car park roof of the Ellington centre. He stood beside a shiny but battered grey solid steel door. He first stared in front of him at the narrow but overflowed River Thames that led into Oxford from the south. His eyes soon squinted toward the south-east through the thick haze of dust toward the now, very vague grey silhouette of London around seventy miles away in the distance, when he realised something incredible and he slowly shook his head.

'That's impossible!' He thought to himself. His thoughts were about to return to Marcie, but again he refused to envisage her violent death. Just then, movement caught his eye and distracted his thoughts and he stared to his left and again squinted, now in the direction of Oxford city centre.

In the distance, he saw Gwen Vella with her arm around Anita Stone, Charlotte Strickland walked behind them and Amy Vinton with Emma Todd behind her as they headed back on what used to be Kennington Road where Anita Stone used to live, just across the river and a large field from where Reg stood. At that moment he gasped when he suddenly realised for the first time, that there were at least two to three hundred corpses scattered in the field right in front of him that he hadn't even noticed before.

Anita Stone now knew that her entire family and home were no more, this was confirmed because she and her workmates found every last one of them amongst the rubble that was once her semi-detached house. Although Reg knew none of the women, they were the first in fact the only people other than Alison Dixon that he had seen alive since early on Friday morning when he left Marcie at home, but he now knew that there were others. He immediately began to shout at the top of his voice and frantically wave his arms until Gwen Vella heard and then saw him across the corpse ridden field through the haze of thick dust.

To the north at Kidlington, Amelia West felt an icy breeze that gently brushed her cheek as she continued to drag smaller rocks from the blocked ramp inside the dark underground car park beneath her apartment. Because she was so dehydrated, she eventually lay down exhausted on top of the vast pile of rubble, some of which she vaguely recognised but still hadn't worked it out.

She knew that she was almost through to the other side as that cold breeze continued to gently stroke and it felt like she was suddenly breathing icy cold air into her lungs for the very first time in her life. She began to drift off to sleep although she knew that she had to get out and her eyes again suddenly opened.

'Amelia, get up!' She angrily told herself. She stared at a small rock directly in front of her face, she slowly climbed back up onto her knees before she reached forward and pulled it away. That gentle breeze suddenly became a slightly stronger one but she definitely felt the difference. She now squinted at bright blinding broad daylight outside. She slumped back down onto the pile and took in a huge gulp of dust-filled cold air from outside and once again opened her eyes.

'I'm not dying down here, get up!' That same stubborn inner strength insisted. She slowly pulled herself back up

onto her knees and reached forward. She dragged away another rock and the small hole became a slightly larger one, so using both hands she struggled to pull away a much larger boulder that was considerably heavier and had to be rolled down to the bottom of the pile. She soon stared at the hole which was now probably just large enough for her to squeeze through if she removed Mark's thick grey coat, but first she needed just one more break.

From dehydration and sheer exhaustion, she placed her head down onto the back of her hands and closed her eyes for just for a second or two, she knew that she could make it out after this last very short rest.

Alison Dixon sat at one of the long white rectangular tables inside the staff canteen with an arm around the distraught Anita Stone. The two women had something in common which was that they both knew for a fact that they had lost their entire families. Seated around the same table were Gwen Vella, Charlotte Strickland, Amy Vinton and Emma Todd.

"So, this man, this Jason actually sent you all home when it was happening on Friday morning?" She asked with disbelief. She still sat in a state of shock from her own trauma although none of the women knew. She watched them all nod to confirm that she correctly understood their story.

"He had us all help unload a delivery truck and when we finished, he told us that we'd be safer at home but he was going down to the underground car park with the other men so that they could secure the store when the storm was finished." Gwen replied, to a nod from Amy.

"He also told us that because he was sending us home on health and safety grounds, we were no longer covered on the company insurance policy so we had to leave no matter what, he pretty much threw us out." Amy added. Alison raised her eyebrows with more disbelief.

"I hope he's dead, I really hope he's dead." Amy coldly uttered. To Alison's surprise, everybody around the table with the exception of Charlotte Strickland again nodded, this time in agreement with her statement.

A little more than an hour later, Amelia West woke with another terrified gasp and when she opened her eyes, she stared through that small gap to the outside world. For the very first time she saw just a glimpse of the carnage and that there were no salvage teams working to get her out. In fact all she saw was destroyed partial buildings, overturned smashed cars with strewn bodies everywhere and they lay completely still. She stared at it all through that thick haze of dust and the sight caused another gasp.

"What the hell happened?" She quietly croaked. She gradually climbed back up onto her knees and pulled away a few more lumps of broken rubble and without removing Mark's coat, she somehow managed to wriggle her entire body through the small hole and eventually climbed up onto unsteady legs. She was finally outside, she then reached back inside and pulled out the grey blanket behind her.

She now stood and stared through the dust at more totally destroyed buildings, more smashed and overturned cars and many, many more broken lifeless bodies, before she slowly turned to her right and saw more of the same absolutely pulverised carnage. She then slowly turned to her right again to stare at her apartment block and now with absolutely stunned horror.

"My flat's gone!" She blurted with utter disbelief. She stared at nothing but a dust filled void where the four storey apartment block once stood but it was completely missing, none of it was there at all. Her heart pounded against her chest as she continued to stare and at the same time, she considered that at least some of her neighbours had to be inside when it was somehow ripped apart. She hadn't yet worked out that what used to be the building, was in fact much of the rubble that completely blocked the ramped entrance inside the car park that she earlier, vaguely recognised.

"Were we bombed?" She again questioned with that same croaked voice. In a state of shock, she eventually turned to her right one more time and faced south where she stared at yet more destruction. She knew where she needed to be which was at Mark's sister's house, but on the way there she needed to find something to eat and more importantly to drink or she wasn't going to make it. Amelia began to stagger toward Oxford city centre which was a very, very long three and a half miles away in her current physical condition.

Jason Moran made his way south along the devastated Abingdon Road. In a staggered line behind him walked Alan Robbins, Paul Richards, Philip Smith and Jake Jarrett.

"We'll go to my house first, I'll have my wife make you all something to eat and then we'll figure out what to do next." He called out. There was a pause before anybody answered.

Paul Richards studied Jason from behind where he shook his head because in his opinion, the night shift manager was oblivious to what was clearly evident all around them. It was as if Jason didn't care or even see the devastation or the thousands of strewn bodies. Richards suspected that maybe he was in a state of severe shock.

"Where do you live and why is everything always about you before anybody else, what makes you think your house is even still there anyway?" He eventually called out. Jason suddenly stopped walking, turned to face him and he actually smiled.

"It's not far, Abingdon is about eight miles down this road." He replied. Richards immediately nodded.

"I've got to find a way of getting to Maidstone in Kent." He explained. Jason only stared at him for a few moments.

"My family live there it's where I come from, you dickhead!" Paul angrily reminded him.

Reg Simmons stood on the car park roof, he once again stared through that thick haze with disbelief toward the vague grey silhouette of London around seventy miles to the south-east. He turned his attention to the strewn lifeless bodies on the field in front of him when Alison Dixon stepped outside and he turned to see her.

"Are you alright, Reg?" She asked. He somehow forced a smile even though just like her of course he wasn't alright, he placed an arm around Alison and held her.

"Are those girls downstairs alright?" He asked. Alison began to nod her head, but she then changed her mind and instead rigorously shook it.

"Apart from the obvious no, they're all very upset and in shock, of course Anita's in a real state but I'll keep an eye on them all." She replied. Reg returned his stare toward London as he continued to hold Alison in his left arm, but she also had concerns about his state of mind and she studied him for a few moments.

"What are you looking at?" She asked. Using his free right hand, Reg pointed toward London.

"I can't help it, I keep staring at Canary Wharf." He replied. Alison also stared toward London but she had no idea of what Reg actually stared at because before today, she had never taken much interest in the distant outlined sight of the capital from Oxford.

"I don't understand, point it out again I can't see it." She eventually said. There was a momentary pause before Reg shook his head.

"I can't, that's why I keep staring." He replied.

"I used to come up here with a cup of tea every morning and stare at just the top of it with engineer's wonder, I once read that it was seven hundred and seventy one feet tall and that's obviously why you could just about see the top of it from here." He added. Alison continued to stare toward London, but still with confusion.

"I still can't see what you're looking at, where is it?" She asked. Again Reg slowly shook his head, he then shrugged his shoulders.

"It's not there anymore it's gone, Canary Wharf is gone but it was right there." He finally replied. He pointed in the general direction of London. Alison's startled train of thought was suddenly disturbed when she heard a quiet, almost muffled sound that was in fact voices from behind. She spun around to see five silhouettes in the distance out on the main road that led south to Abingdon.

"Reg, there are more people." She uttered. He also turned to see them, so together they began to shout and wave their arms to get the attention of the five silhouettes around a quarter of a mile away. It was Jake Jarrett who spotted them from the back of the line, he nudged Phil Smith in front and pointed before Jason, Paul and Alan also stopped and stared at the two frantically waving people.

"We can't help them, just keep walking." Jason uttered. He continued to head south but nobody else did, when he turned again he saw that the four men now walked toward the two silhouettes in front of the overflowed riverbank.

"My house is this way!" He called out. Paul Richards stopped and turned to stare at Jason for a few moments.

"They're not waving at us to say hello, you idiot." He pointed out the obvious.

At that moment, everybody felt what began as a deep rumble beneath their feet, the ground started to shake and it gradually became more and more heavily defined. They all instinctively froze to the spot as Jake Jarrett and Phil Smith held onto each other to steady their feet, the ground continued to tremble and now even more violently. Reg and Alison also held each other and down inside the staff canteen, the five women stared at each other with absolute horror while they all tightly held the table as everything around them shook.

"It's an earthquake!" Reg yelled. For the first time to date he was wrong, what they all felt was no earthquake.

It was originally believed that on Thursday August seventeenth during the year of two thousand and twenty eight, the United Kingdom felt an earthquake that lasted for around thirteen minutes and another, not quite as violent would occur some five hours later. What they experienced was in fact no earthquake, it was a backlash from the east coasts of Canada and the United States of America.

Four hundred and fifty miles west of Oxford, the first of two Mega-Tsunami impacted the entire west coast of Ireland, submerging every piece of dry land as far as the outskirts of Athlone at the centre of the small island country. The initial impact was felt not only at Oxford, but also at what remained of Dover at the far south-east and at Aberdeen, Scotland at the far north-east. By the next day, Ireland was less than half her original size. That first giant one thousand foot wave also impacted as far north as Fort William, Scotland and submerged that entire area.

It was much later discovered that after this event, there would be no more than fifty four Irish survivors in total after the colossal storms, the giant hailstones and not one, but two Mega-Tsunami onto an island country that previously boasted a population of more than five million. This next terrible happening occurred after the entire east coasts of Canada and the United States of America were hit by waves of similar magnitude some sixteen hours before.

The catastrophic event at Ireland was the backlash as a result.

The first wave headed toward them, growing for much of the day before, as however many Irish that remained at that time, roamed their own battered streets when they searched for loved ones and other survivors after they somehow made it through the storms and the hailstones. They would have no idea that the vast life ending wave headed toward them until it suddenly impacted and of course they never stood a chance.

A week prior to that day, most of the world was dependent upon technology to see something like it coming and the resources to avert this next catastrophe such as mass evacuations after early warning systems. That same technology was gone. Mother Nature and Mother Earth along with their vengeful sister Karma, once again caught everybody off guard.

A short while after the ground stopped shaking, thirty four year old David Wells tentatively opened a small cellar hatch at Abingdon Road, where he reluctantly climbed up into the thick white haze for the very first time and covered his nose and mouth with his hand. He stared around at smouldering rubble because he technically now stood outside, his trendy wine bar didn't withstand in any way. In front of him there was no wall at all, no ceiling above and no flat where he used to live.

"It seems to be ok, come up." He called out, as he continued to stare around at the dust filled destruction that he could see in front of him.

"This is impossible." He very quietly told himself. Twenty five year old barmaid Victoria Annis climbed up from the cellar and stood beside him, she stared with the same horrified disbelief.

"Dave, how could this have happened?" She asked in a whispered tone. He shook his head in response as they both continued to stare at the utter destruction.

"I don't know, but that was an earthquake so we're definitely not safe underground anymore." He finally replied. He glanced beside him at Victoria who had long wavy brunette hair and brown eyes that then stared back down at the cellar hatch.

"Come up, its ok." She said with a false smile of reassurance. Nineteen year old barmaid Wendy Jones was next to nervously climb up onto ground level. She also very anxiously stared around at what used to be the inside of the building, David slowly shook his head.

'Where are the people?' He asked himself. From where they stood, they could see none, only grey smoking rubble through the haze of dust. His sixteen year old stepson Martin Sharpe was the last to climb up to what used to be the wine bar which was once their home. Today there was no flat above and only three partial walls remained at ground level, he immediately stared at David.

"Do you think she's safe?" He specifically asked after his mother, David's partner. She travelled on last Wednesday morning to visit the teenager's ailing grandmother at Shropshire. David turned to stare back at him. He obviously had no truthful answer to give but he would never lie to Martin, instead he chose to avoid answering that particular question.

"Let's get Wendy home to Abingdon and Vikki to hers, then we'll sit down somewhere and find somebody official to talk to and figure everything out." He replied with a false half-smile.

They eventually all made their way toward Wendy's parent's home, which in fact used to be just two hundred metres from where Jason Moran's house also once stood, but they would thankfully never get that far to discover the devastating truth. They would also be seen by Reg Simmons who stood outside the Ellington underground shopping centre with Jake Jarrett. The four from the wine bar would join the other survivors and begin to learn more of what happened to them all by talking and exchanging information.

Amelia West discovered the ruins of a cake shop in a cobbled backstreet at Oxford city centre. She found scraps and crumbs of dust covered food that was strewn across the filthy tiled floor. She hungrily picked up and ate as much as she could find using her bare hands, that was when she also found something that she hadn't seen in weeks thanks to the incredible drought that preceded and finally created the storms.

She found five small, unopened bottles of drinking water that at that time probably saved her life. She immediately drank them all one after another.

An hour or so later, she stood in front of what remained of Mark's sister's unrecognisable house at Elms Road just a few miles south-west of Oxford city centre and she now knew that if he came here, Mark was no longer alive.

Amelia was by this time out of energy and still running on empty, she knew that the task of scrambling through more rubble would be physically, not to mention emotionally impossible. She stared at what remained of the house which was now nothing more than a pile of smouldering rubble and still burning timber just like every other on the street. She slowly turned and headed back toward the main road, now with the knowledge that Mark was just like everybody that she had seen, he was dead.

In her confused and highly emotional state, the notion that she might be the only person left alive began to creep into the back of her mind. She still hadn't seen another living soul only thousands upon thousands of the dead. With tear-filled eyes, she soon reached the end of Elms Road when the ground started to rumble beneath her feet. She instinctively grabbed a pale grey signpost that somehow withstood and she climbed down onto her knees.

'The world's still trying to kill me!' She angrily told herself. With her tear-filled eyes clenched shut, she held onto the post with both hands and waited for an earthquake that would of course never come. She couldn't possibly know that while she knelt and waited, more Irish were dying courtesy of a vast one thousand foot wave.

It was around an hour and a half later, Amy Vinton, Emma Todd and Phil Smith stood in front of the battered grey steel door on the car park roof when Reg Simmons appeared and smiled at them all, he then watched Phil smoke a cigarette.

"You know those things will be the death of you?" He asked, initially with a serious facial expression. Phil stared back at him for a few moments before he grasped the irony that was purposely built into the question when Reg displayed a wry grin. Phil then displayed one of his own.

"I know, but at least they warned me about these on the packet." He finally replied with a chuckle and Reg also laughed. At that moment, the air suddenly became warmer and incredibly calm, too calm in fact. All four of them felt it and they all instinctively stared up at the now darkening grey sky. There was a very eerie, intense almost tingling silent and closing atmosphere that again everybody felt.

"What's happening?" Emma nervously asked. Reg slowly shook his head as he continued to stare up at the still darkening sky.

Well this is something new.' He thought to himself, as he continued to stare up. He then glanced at the three youngsters in turn.

"I think we need to get back inside." He calmly suggested. He returned his stare back up toward the sky for a few more moments, fearing that more giant hailstones might be about to hurtle down onto them. He turned and opened the grey steel door and stepped back inside before it swung closed behind him. Phil eventually nodded before he flicked the remains of his cigarette and followed Reg, as Amy reached beside her and took Emma's hand in hers, they both continued to stare up at the sky.

"I think he's right." Emma quietly said. Both hearts pounded with a combination of fear and dreaded anticipation. Amy nodded before they also turned, but when they did, Emma glanced out toward the main road where she squinted through the haze of dust and saw what she thought was a single, very slowly moving silhouette.

"What's that?" She asked as she pointed toward it. Amy shook her head and for a few moments both girls stared at the vague upright silhouette in the distance.

"I think it's another person!" She finally replied. They both began to shout and scream while they jumped and waved their arms. The silhouette that appeared to slowly head south toward Abingdon, eventually heard their vague distant cries and stopped moving. Whoever it was appeared to stare back at them, but just then, Amy then felt something icy cold gently touch the back of her left hand and she glanced down at whatever it was, she then instinctively stared back up at the sky.

"What the hell was that?" She asked. Whatever just touched her hand was far, far too cold to be rain. As the silhouette began to stagger toward them, Emma also glanced back up and they both saw what appeared to be very large heavy snowflakes that slowly drifted down toward the ground. Amy turned to her right and eventually full circle and saw that the grey, very warm still air all around was now thick with huge, gently falling white snowflakes.

'It's snowing in August!' She told herself, as Amelia West finally stopped in front of them where she bent over, exhausted and out of breath.

"We need to find somewhere to hide from this, what are you idiots doing?" She asked the girls, who were the first living people that she had seen in days. Emma displayed an almost wry smile.

"Yeah, we know." She replied. She then pulled open the grey steel door that led down into the underground shopping centre. Amelia stared with disbelief, first at Amy and then back at Emma.

"Do you want a cup of tea?" Emma asked, as Amelia continued to catch her breath, she still stared with widened eyes back at her.

"What?" She asked with another breathless gasp.

Unfortunately, no more would arrive at the Ellington centre, but the city of Oxford was now already one of the most heavily populated areas of the entire United Kingdom with a live body count of seventeen. On the previous Friday afternoon, there were more than one hundred and fifty five thousand people walking around that particular area.

Abraham's First Three Wishes

Some two hundred miles north at the city of York, forty two year old vehicle mechanic Abraham Bridger sat on his recently acquired powerful Harley Davidson motorcycle with the engine switched off. He stared at the very heavily damaged Cathedral of St Peter through the same thick white haze of dust.

Abraham had been a loner for his entire life, he was an absolutely huge man of six feet seven inches with long greying light brown hair that was always pulled back into a ponytail, he also sported a long thick bushy greying beard. He removed his also recently acquired dark designer sunglasses as his pale blue eyes stared at what remained of the iconic Cathedral building known as York Minster.

He wore no crash helmet which was back then the law of the land, but he was an incredibly intelligent and calculating man, he already knew that there was now no law to stop him from doing whatever he chose and that the entire country, or at least for now the entire destroyed city of York belonged to him.

Of course, York Minster was very heavily damaged just like every other building across the entire country, but the mechanic in Abraham believed that everything was reparable including the Cathedral building. For now he was the new King with no loyal and obedient subjects to speak of, but he knew that there would be other survivors that would rebuild it for him and he knew how he intended to pay for their services.

Abraham already had a very long term plan, this was his often fantasised perfect scenario. He also already knew exactly how to begin his reign. He continued to stare at the obliterated building for a few more moments before he returned his sunglasses and restarted his motorcycle. He slowly pulled away, weaving around battered vehicles, rubble and contorted corpses that were once living breathing people, but he paid those lifeless bodies no attention because they were of no use to him. He slowly weaved his way back to Tang Hall Lane where he used to work and live, which was a little more than three miles to the east of York city centre.

Beneath the ground behind the huge Cathedral, inside a separate building back then known as Treasurer's House, thirty one year old night shift cleaner Rebecca Hamilton sat in the darkness with three work colleagues. They had all been inside the dusty basement since just before LMS tore all of York to shreds and to be certain, later returned with the Viking to make absolutely sure.

"Did you hear that?" She asked in a croaked voice, as everybody else glanced up toward the door. They were all dressed in a filthy white polo shirts beneath dark blue vinyl company issued tabards. Twenty four year old Kate Musgrove, twenty six year old Louise Everett and twenty nine year old Richard Wise sat in the darkness around her, it was Kate who eventually replied.

"I did, what was that?" She asked. Louise Everett climbed to her feet and walked across the basement toward the door that led to twenty five dust covered stone steps.

"I think it was an engine of some sort, let's get up there and find out." She insisted. The sound of Abraham's motorcycle was muffled, which meant that it could have been anything. The three women along with the always very quiet and mild mannered Richard Wise who was a slight man of five feet seven inches, climbed the narrow stone staircase and finally left the basement for the very first time. They were all of course all in desperate need of food, water and news but were previously too afraid to leave the safety of the basement, but it now sounded like the long awaited help was finally arriving.

Around fifteen minutes later, Abraham switched off his motorcycle engine and dismounted. He walked to a grey steel roller shutter door and stepped into a spacious vehicle repair shop that had a very low flat roof and because of that, it was the only building for miles that somehow still had any kind of roof, most other building no longer had upper floors at all.

"I found what's left of another eight supermarkets in and around York." He announced. His former boss, only ever real friend and owner of the workshop, thirty nine year old Clive Henderson who was another well-built man and had a shiny bald head, turned from stacking boxes that came from the destroyed shopping facilities that they had already completely emptied. Helping Henderson was twenty seven year old Andy Clarke, an obese man with short dark brown hair, they both turned to face Bridger.

"We're going to need more storage soon then, Abe." Clive replied. Abraham nodded with acknowledgement.

"Just take over what's left of one of the buildings across the street and start using those, it's not like anybody's going to charge us rent or steal it." He replied, as Clive and Andy continued to stare at him.

"How do we know the authorities aren't going to show up some time soon?" Clarke asked. He watched Abraham walk across the workshop and he quietly chuckled.

"If there were any authorities left we would have heard from them by now, we would've seen or heard from somebody, it's been five days they're definitely all dead or I hope they are, I've got plans." He replied.

The four night shift cleaners stood outside Treasurer's House and stared for the first time in a state of stunned horror at the total devastation that was once York city centre. Kate Musgrove suddenly burst into tears at the sight of completely destroyed buildings, overturned and smashed vehicles and in particular at the sight of so many twisted and contorted dead men, women and children that lay scattered everywhere. Rebecca held her while she, Richard and Louise continued to stare with disbelief at the unrecognisable, dust filled havoc that was once their home city.

"This is insanity." Louise quietly uttered.

"I think it might be a good idea to just stay here and wait for help." Richard suggested. Rebecca stared at him and shook her head with a sigh.

"Don't be stupid, we've got to find something to eat and drink." She reminded him.

"Nobody here has eaten anything in days, we'll starve to death if we just stay here." She added, while she held the sobbing Kate. Again she shook her head as Louise watched them both before she spoke up.

"Let's go and find something to eat and drink and then come back here with it, we can work out what we're going to do after." She suggested.

"We'll think more clearly with food and drink inside us, but Richard's right at least we know here is safe, I don't know about the rest of you, but I don't want to be too far from that basement right now." She added.

It was around two hours later, the four cleaners walked east along the Hull Road and just like those down at Oxford, they stepped around pulverised vehicles and more contorted lifeless corpses, but they all suddenly stopped walking. This time they all heard without doubt a very similar, low droning sound that they first heard inside the basement beneath Treasurer's House.

"It's not the same as before, but it sounded like it came from that direction." Richard said. He pointed south toward the University of York. The three women nodded with agreement as they stared in the direction of what remained of the obliterated university buildings, but there was obviously nothing motorised amongst the smouldering rubble.

"It sounded like a car engine or something this time." Rebecca told them all, again everybody agreed. They continued east and still heard the same intermittent sound until they finally reached a large circular bridge where a main road beneath it ran from north to south. That same low droning din soon became continuous, more defined and without doubt louder. On the large overhead roundabout they stared south as the deep rumble again became a little louder.

"It's a truck or trucks and they're coming this way." Richard assured them all. Kate turned to him.

"It must be help coming." She replied in a trembling tone of desperate hope. In the distance to the south, three large white vans suddenly appeared from around a right hand bend through the haze of floating dust. They weaved around and drove over corpses as they headed toward them.

The four cleaners stood on the bridge and frantically waved before the headlights of the lead van flashed three times to acknowledge them. It then pulled onto the slip road where it weaved around and bumped over more bodies as it travelled up a hill and the two vans behind followed.

"Maybe they know exactly what happened." Louise suggested, as they all watched the vans head their way.

"At least we know we're not the only people left alive." Rebecca replied. The vans eventually pulled up on the bridge beside them, where they met for the first time Abraham Bridger who immediately offered them food, water, safety and security. By way of pure luck, that very moment was when the first giant wave hit the west coasts of Ireland and Fort William, Scotland which was just three hundred and twenty miles to the north-east. Like everybody else that survived the storms, they all believed the catastrophe at Ireland to be an earthquake and that same fear immediately urged the four cleaners to leave with

Bridger and the men inside the two now completely filled vans behind his.

An hour or so later, everybody sat in eerie silence inside Clive Henderson's spacious workshop where they ate straight from tin cans. Rebecca Hamilton glanced around at the stacked piles of large boxes that were filled with food and several tall piles of packed drinking water. She should have taken some comfort in the sight but at the back of her mind and everybody else's, something about these three men now felt very, very wrong. The giant called Abraham who seemed to give instructions whenever he spoke, sat alone while he ate and occasionally raised his head to stare at them, as did Clive Henderson and Andy Clarke.

Abraham eventually glanced across at Clive and then briefly at Andy before he stared at the only other man, the mild mannered and quietly spoken night shift cleaner, Richard Wise.

"Help me bring the vans inside." He instructed. Richard glanced at Rebecca, then at Louise and Kate before he returned his stare toward Bridger and nodded. He placed his tin can down and climbed to his feet before he followed Bridger out of the workshop. The battered grey roller shutter side door slowly swung closed behind them. Rebecca, Kate and Louise glanced at each other after they all then watched Andy Clarke also step outside.

"There's something not right here." Louise whispered. The other two women nervously nodded. Clive Henderson for some reason remained with them.

Richard stood outside directly behind the huge frame of Abraham, he turned to see that Andy Clarke also stepped outside just as the giant opened the passenger door of the white van that he earlier drove. Richard was distracted by the sudden emergence of Clarke which made sense to him, there were three vans and now three drivers.

As he considered this, Abraham discretely reached beneath the closed glove compartment inside his van, he had hidden beneath it a twelve inch long, jagged edged knife that was secured with black duct tape. When Richard again turned to face him, Abraham also turned with the huge blade discretely concealed in his right hand.

He stared down at the much smaller man for a few brief moments and with no warning whatsoever, he suddenly plunged the sharp knife very hard and deep into the side of Richard's stomach. He discovered that it actually felt like cutting through an orange, he then deliberately twisted it just for good measure just like he had seen in the movies. For a few moments, Richard stared up into Abraham's cold blue eyes that stared back down without emotion.

"It's not personal little man, you're just too small and weak to survive in this new world and you're eating my valuable food." Abraham quietly uttered.

"It's *my* new world." He added with a sneer. He placed his left hand onto Richard's shoulder and jerked the knife upward to lift the much smaller and lighter man from the floor using only the knife. As the blade eventually forced its way through and into the bottom of Richard's heart, blood began to trickle from the left corner of his mouth and both nostrils although he was in fact already dead.

Andy Clarke suddenly bent over and began to vomit when he heard the ribcage crack as Abraham continued to stare down at Richard, whose eyes stared back up at him but they were by now lifeless and unmoving. He eventually slumped down onto the floor as the long jagged blade was slowly withdrawn and his lifeless body fell beside where Clarke continued to throw up.

"You're a pussy, you need to toughen up and you need to do it now." Abraham sneered at his former work colleague.

Around twenty minutes after they left the workshop, Bridger stepped back inside with the very pale looking Andy Clarke behind him. The shutter door again slowly swung closed. He glanced at his only real friend Clive Henderson to silently indicate that the deed was done.

"We need to fire up all the heaters, it just started to snow out there." He uttered. Rebecca Hamilton saw that the giant's face was now covered with what looked like tiny blood splatters. She briefly glanced at Louise and then Kate before her stare returned to him.

"Where's Richard?" She asked. All three women anxiously watched Bridger pick up a sawn down, three feet long scaffold pole that was filled with hardened concrete and always intended for would be burglars, he then began to walk toward them.

"He's gone, all of you get in the pit." He instructed. Again, they briefly glanced at each other before they all stared back up at him as he ominously walked toward them with the heavy solid pole in his right hand.

"What do you mean, he's gone?" Louise asked. Abraham slowly shook his head with a sigh.

"If I have to tell you again I'm going to break your legs, all of you." He just as calmly assured them. Kate started to hysterically scream. Rebecca and Louise urgently helped her toward the same narrow repair pit that previously protected Bridger, Madison and Clarke from the storms.

With sheer panic, they quickly climbed down inside it and continued to stare up at Abraham with absolute terror as he and Madison pulled a five inch thick, solid steel plate over to cover it, to at least muffle the sound of Kate's irritating screams and sent the pit into complete darkness. Bridger turned his attention to Andy Clarke.

"Park a car with the wheels on top of it." He instructed. He returned to his seat to continue eating, but he stopped and turned to face them both.

"Those three down there are mine, you find your own." He told them.

At Oxford, as snow continued to heavily fall outside, Amelia West sat at a table inside the staff canteen with Reg Simmons and Alison Dixon. She quietly told the horrific story of where her apartment used to stand, when the superstore night shift manager Jason Moran joined them.

"I was just thinking, a few of us should get to my house it's just down the road." He immediately interrupted, before Reg glanced across at him and shook his head.

"That's not a good idea my friend." He replied. He went on to very quietly whisper to Jason that he doubted that anybody seated inside the canteen had any surviving family members or homes to back go to, after what he personally discovered at his own house that morning.

"And besides, we don't know how long this snow is going to last for, it could go on for days or even weeks, if you get trapped out there you'll all die." He continued. He then went on to suggest that it might be better if and when it was safer to leave the underground haven, that some visit the homes of others including his, to make what he was certain would be absolutely devastating discoveries for those concerned. Alison Dixon nodded with agreement.

"But you can't ask or order anybody to go out in those conditions, especially just for your own needs." She suddenly interjected. Amelia stared down into her coffee cup and told them of what she found when she visited what remained of Mark's sister's house also at Elms Road, before she glanced up at Jason.

"It might be better if somebody else visits your house when it's safer to go out there." She suggested, but Jason had a wife and two small children, he immediately informed them all and this time Alison nodded.

"We've all lost our families, it's not just you." She abruptly reminded him. He nodded but without acknowledgement of her tragic personal comment.

"Look, I'll just take the two boys Phil Smith and Jake Jarrett to my house, I know it'll take no longer than a couple of hours." He assured them, but again Alison rigorously shook her head.

"I'm really sorry, but you can't ask those boys to go out there it's just too dangerous." She replied. Jason immediately offered her a look of mocking confusion.

"Who exactly put you in charge of my staff?" He asked with frustration in his tone. Alison stared back at him as she considered what he did on Friday morning regarding the five women who all sat around a nearby table and she managed to briefly put her own heartache aside.

"You did, when you sent those women outside to die and actually quoted health and safety to them, you conceited little idiot." She retorted, but still in a quiet and very calm tone, before Amelia again glanced up at him.

"If that store isn't there anymore they're not actually *your* staff, are they?" She asked him. There was suddenly a highly intense atmosphere around the table as Jason and Amelia stared straight at each other, but the uncomfortable moment was suddenly interrupted when wine bar owner David Wells also took a seat.

"So, what's the plan, do we have a plan?" He asked with an optimistic smile.

The snow continued to heavily fall outside when Reg stood beside David Wells inside the canteen and called for everybody's attention before the din began to fall silent. He eventually explained to all that down on the second floor promenade was a large, fully equipped camping store and that he and David would head down there soon to open it, to organise temporary bedding for everybody just until they were better organised.

He then explained that he was certain that they would all be living beneath the ground for weeks if not months. His statement caused everybody to glance at everybody else, as he also informed them that a large storage facility was situated across from the overhead car park and that a few work details would have to be organised.

One of those tasks was a path to be kept cleared of snow from the workshop and delivery area roller shutter, across the car park to the storage facility and for that, cold weather clothing from the same camping store and two sports shops would be supplied. Jake Jarrett slowly shook his head with a sigh and caused both Reg and David to chuckle.

"It looks like young Jake has volunteered for the first shift." Reg said. With that, sixteen year old Martin Sharpe raised his hand to show that he wanted to volunteer. Phil Smith then nodded to offer his services too before Reg and David glanced at each other and both smiled. At the same moment, Amelia discretely leaned forward and gently nudged Amy Vinton before the teenager turned on her seat to face her.

"What do you think, should we let the boys do all of the manual work so that we can do the cooking and cleaning for them like good little girls?" She asked in a whispered tone. Beside her, Alison Dixon watched as Amy and Amelia stared at each other for a few moments before Amy again suddenly turned on her seat and raised her hand.

"I'd like to go and dig in the snow too." She told Reg. When Amelia sat back in her seat, she and Alison glanced at each other.

"That was quite devious." Alison whispered, Amelia smiled back at her.

"Thank you very much." She just as quietly replied. Reg performed a head count of volunteer snow clearers who were so far Jake Jarrett, Martin Sharpe, Phil Smith and now Amy Vinton, but he needed one more so that they could use work rotations of two hours of shovelling snow and eight hours off around the clock, before assistant manager Alan Robbins stepped up and volunteered.

Reg then explained that the shopping centre had two brand new, state of the art diesel generators down at the basement maintenance level and enough fuel to run them both non-stop for two weeks, but he intended to switch them off at every available opportunity because he had no idea of how long they would all be living at the centre.

He also explained that to minimise the use of the suddenly precious diesel, he would switch off the heating and lighting, but inside the fully stocked supermarkets on the second and third floors, were large chest freezers that were filled with frozen food because the centre was due to open today.

He went on to inform everybody that one generator would be switched back on for six hours each day to keep that food partially frozen and edible and they would use it up first so that he could eventually switch off the freezers too, if they were in fact all still down there for that length of time.

The announcements suddenly caused everybody to grasp the reality that the situation wasn't a temporary one, that they were in fact going to be down there for quite some time and without help from the outside world. They had all seen the carnage and the bodies outside although none of them could know that this wasn't only a national catastrophe, that the entire world was in complete chaos, but they did know that no help or even signs of any other life had been seen in five days.

Everybody in the room wanted to discuss the possibility that their families were maybe still alive out there, but by now at the back of their minds they all knew, which meant that nobody really wanted to talk about it at all.

"Anita and I could do the cooking for everybody, but how can we cook if we're not going to have any power?" Gwen Vella enquired. Reg and David again glanced at each other and it was David that answered the first question at hand.

"We'll use up gas bottles from the camping shop and the storage facility until they run out and then re-evaluate the weather situation, when the snow stops we can send out scavenger parties to find more fuel for the generators." He informed her. Emma Todd then raised her hand and Reg smiled before she spoke.

"I know this is probably going to sound really stupid, but you saw us and then we saw Amelia from up top, shouldn't we have a lookout up there in case anybody else is walking about in the snow?" She asked. She glanced around the canteen to see if anybody was about to make fun of her suggestion, but when she eventually returned her stare toward Reg, she saw that his smile broadened and he raised a thumb in her direction.

"That's actually a really good idea, well done." He replied. When Emma turned back to face the table, Amelia beamed a smile at her before she winked.

"Good call." She whispered. Reg then turned his attention to young Martin Sharpe.

"Your stepdad tells me that you were about to start college and wanted to become a journalist." He began again. Young Martin stared back at him although he didn't reply.

"I have a really good idea in mind for you, we might at some point need a record keeper." Reg added, before the seemingly agitated night shift manager, Jason Moran suddenly stepped forward and interrupted.

"I think we need to form some kind of management committee, to discuss things before making decisions like the ones that you just made for all of us, such as turning off the heating down here." He said. Reg took in a long deep breath and sighed before he opened his mouth to respond.

"No we don't." Alison Dixon abruptly interjected, Jason turned his stare at her.

"We've been here together for less than five hours and I'm in no rush to vote just to make sure that you don't get to make decisions for all of us." She replied. Amy Vinton glanced down at the table in front of her to display a wry grin, but she glanced up when Alison spoke again.

"You're not thinking straight, because of that I think you're incredibly dangerous and while I do trust Reg with my life, I certainly don't trust you with it." She continued, but she wasn't quite finished.

"And let me tell you something else, there isn't going to be any kind of power struggle around here, you're all guests and we're going to work together, if you don't like that concept you're more than welcome to leave whenever you like, but you'll be taking nobody with you." She added.

Reg Simmons again stood beside the grey steel door, he watched the heavy snow fall when Amelia joined him and she pointed ahead toward the overflowed riverbank.

"We should put a Christmas tree right there." She suggested with a quiet chuckle. Reg laughed until they stood in silence for a few moments and both watched the heavy snow before Amelia spoke again.

"At least the snow will put the fires out and settle this dust down." She said. Reg nodded with agreement, there was more silence before she eventually continued.

"So, do you think this is like the end of the world or something?" She asked. Reg turned to glance at her before he returned his stare toward London, where he could no longer see the orange burning glow or even the grey silhouette and he took in a long deep breath.

"People are funny things, fifteen of you somehow found us at a brand new, undamaged underground shopping centre that's full of food, clothing and anything else we might need to survive for the next two years if we're sensible." He reminded her.

"We might need to organise more work teams." He pondered. He then stared up at the grey cloud filled skies and the heavy snow falling all around, he then glanced toward a large corrugated steel building around one hundred metres to the right from where they stood. They both watched young Martin Sharpe shovel snow as he very slowly made his way toward it, dressed in bright orange thermal clothing.

"I'm glad the younger ones like Martin and Jake volunteered, that storage facility is full to the rafters with more supplies and it has five giant freezers that are full of more food, that's why we need to keep a path cleared to it, but keeping those youngsters busy so that they don't sit around and overthink this situation is more important at the moment." He continued. He glanced back up at the skies.

"We might be entering a new ice age or something, the irony is that five days ago it was boiling bloody hot for about six months and now it's snowing in August." He added. As he continued to watch the heavy snow, it was now Amelia's turn to take in a long deep breath before she blew it out but just then, they both turned when the grey door opened and Jason Moran appeared dressed in blue thermal clothing, as were Phil Smith and Jake Jarrett behind him. Jake glanced at Reg and discretely shook his head before Amelia spoke.

"What are you doing? She specifically asked Jason, as the three of them started toward the main road. Jason immediately told her to mind her own business as he continued to head out. Phil Smith sighed as he and Jake began to follow.

"We've got to go to his house to find his wife and kids." He replied on Jason's behalf. Amelia rigorously shook her head to dismiss the idea.

"No you're not, go back inside look at it, the snow's already two feet deep!" She angrily pointed out. Reg nodded as Amelia pointed toward the already snow covered, corpse ridden field toward the river not far from where unbeknown to her, Anita Stone once lived.

"You won't make it there and back I promise." Reg assured them. Jake and Phil briefly glanced at each other before they both turned their stares toward Jason.

"Come on, let's go!" He called out, but nobody moved. They all watched him continue toward the road that he now couldn't even see through the thick white snowfall that replaced the earlier haze of dust. The two young men returned their stares to Reg and then Amelia for more positive guidance.

"Don't be stupid, go back downstairs." Amelia quietly insisted. The two boys stared at each other before they both nodded, but Jason came marching back.

"Come on you two, let's move it!" He angrily snapped. Amelia reached for the handle of the grey door and pulled it open, she nodded toward the inside staircase that led back down toward the canteen for Phil and Jake to return, but Jason suddenly grabbed her wrist as she held the handle and with sheer frustration he tightened his grip.

"Who do you think you are?" He angrily snapped. Suddenly and seemingly without much effort, Amelia somehow turned her arm and took a hold of *his* wrist using the same hand. She then pushed his own hand as far inward as it could possibly go and as a result, Jason just as suddenly found himself on his knees beside the door, while Jake, Phil and Reg stared with wide eyed surprise. Amelia stared down at Jason as he winced with extreme discomfort.

"Don't ever let me catch you putting your hands on anybody here again." She calmly told him. Just for good measure, she gave his hand another gentle push inward toward his own inside wrist using only her thumb and watched him again wince with even greater pain as she held it there.

"I understand about your family, but I'm not going to let you get these two young men killed so if you really think it's that safe, go on your own." She just as quietly added. Jake and Phil again glanced at each other before they both turned to watch Amelia.

"Shit!" Phil very quietly uttered. Amelia glanced up, first at him and then at Jake.

"Go back downstairs, move it the pair of you!" She snapped. They both hurriedly returned to the canteen without argument.

A short while later, after Reg and David finished with the early organisation, the small groups again began to congregate and quietly talk amongst themselves around the canteen. It was when Amelia privately revealed that she was in fact a Karate black belt fifth Dan and taught two classes at Oxford city centre, as Amy stared wide eyed at her.

"Could you teach me to kick arse too?" She asked. Amelia almost chuckled but not quite, before she replied.

"If we're going to be here like this indefinitely, all of you youngsters are going to learn to defend yourselves properly." She replied.

When they once again sat alone, out of curiosity Alison quietly asked Amelia why she thought it would be important to teach self-defence to the younger generation, Amelia stared back at her.

"If Reg is right and the whole country or maybe the entire world is like this, there are going to be other survivors, there's going to be no law and no police out there, so are we going to be the ones that everybody comes to take from, just because we have what they want?" She asked in response.

"We've got to survive this, Reg is right we have to be sensible and when we're both old women, those youngsters will have to become our protectors." She added.

All seventeen ate hot food for the first time in five days, before Reg took David Wells down to the lower basement level. Once there, he showed David how to switch on and off the heating and lighting throughout the entire multi-storey complex, everything was then shut down and turned just two floors into candlelit near darkness.

That night, almost everybody would lie on that long narrow dimly lit second floor promenade where it was warmest, in sleeping bags and in several thick layers of clothing from the various shops, but nobody really slept. They all lay in silence thinking about their own loved ones knowing deep down that they were gone, they had to be gone just like every person that they had seen.

Most quietly sobbed now that they were left alone to think. Those that didn't, they lay and listened to them. Outside the snow continued to very heavily fall, Phil Smith shovelled that path in the darkness as Alan Robbins watched holding a powerful spotlight on him as he prepared for his own turn and later, Amy Vinton would take to the torch, Alan would turn to the shovel to keep the path cleared.

Five Weeks later

Friday September 22ⁿᵈ

It was still snowing after thirty seven days and almost, but not quite as heavily as the day that it first started. Jake Jarrett stood at the top of the staircase and stared to his right from the grey steel door where he watched Phil Smith shovel around halfway along a wide, one hundred metre cleared pathway toward the large storage facility. He could see that the solid compacted snow on the ground was at least five deep against the corrugated shiny silver walls of the storage shed.

Phil Smith wore a bright orange thermal jumpsuit with a black woollen hat and he also wore clear plastic ski goggles so that he could see what he was doing. He stopped shovelling as he stood between the very wide seven feet high white banks, first at where he had already cleared for the third time in almost two hours and saw that it was again already lightly covered, but Jake would soon walk behind him and sprinkle salt right up to where he stood before he took to the shovel.

"This is still fun!" Phil called out with a chuckle. Jake laughed as he held up all of his gloved digits to show that he would take over in ten minutes. Phil raised a thumb in response before he continued to shovel snow.

Amy Vinton would soon climb the steps, where she would wait with Jake for a short while before she became the lookout at the door, he would step outside to take the shovel from Phil, who would in turn head down to the canteen for something hot to eat and drink.

Phil was due to return to start again at six that evening, when he should take over from Alan Robbins who would usually take over from Martin Sharpe. None of them would make those shifts because in a very short while, Jake Jarrett would become the last of the initial volunteers although others would later have to continue their work.

Down at the second floor, Emma Todd pushed a large stainless steel shopping trolley along one of the freezer aisles inside the huge, very dimly lit superstore. Thanks to advice from truck driver Paul Richards, she wore three pairs of thick socks inside one size too large white training shoes, two pairs of black jogging bottoms and a chunky red pullover beneath a dark blue padded thermal jacket.

Five weeks ago, Reg switched off everything and left no heating and for now there was only minimal lighting along the freezer aisles, but it would soon be switched off again. In front of the trolley walked Charlotte Strickland who was dressed similarly, she loaded food that they would take up to the canteen to thaw so that Gwen Vella and Anita Stone could cook it for everybody tomorrow, today's partially frozen food was taken up yesterday.

"Do you still think about your family?" Emma quietly asked. Charlotte glanced back at her before she nodded.

"I'm always thinking about them, what about you?" She asked in response. Emma appeared to stare down into a long freezer and pretended to study food that Charlotte had already loaded into the trolley.

"I know they died, I know they definitely did so in my head I pretend that they never woke up during the storm and didn't feel anything, now they think they're still asleep." She replied with a croaked tremble in her voice, Charlotte smiled at her.

"I really like that and you're right, that's exactly what happened." She assured Emma. They continued to privately confide for the very first time and both with tear filled eyes.

Three shops along the same darkened promenade, Reg Simmons worked alongside David Wells and Paul Richards inside a large, emptied greetings card store where they busily fitted the last of the plasterboard walls to create four separate personal living spaces similar to bedrooms, with real single beds from the vast third floor furniture shop and some minimal bedroom furniture, as opposed to where everybody still slept on the hard shiny floor outside on the promenade.

This first shared living accommodation was intended for Amy Vinton, Emma, Charlotte and Wendy Jones and when the room was completed by the end of the day, the three men would begin again at the slightly smaller chemist shop next door that would be converted into quarters for Gwen Vella and Anita Stone. Two shops along was where Reg, Alan Robbins, Jason Moran and David would eventually reside and this arrangement would be for the foreseeable future, maybe forever, nobody really knew anything for certain.

"Yeah good luck with that, I'd want to kill him within a week of sharing a room with him." Paul chuckled when he heard the plans three days ago inside Alison Dixon's fourth floor office. He would eventually share with Phil Smith, Jake Jarrett and Martin Sharpe after they finished the quarters for Alison Dixon, Amelia West and Vikki Annis at the far end of the promenade which was currently a just as spacious shoe shop.

"Who thinks it's time to go up for a cup of tea?" Reg asked, as he hammered the final nail into the pale grey plasterboard wall, his co-workers both rigorously nodded.

Inside the canteen that also currently had only minimal temporary lighting, Anita Stone and Gwen Vella worked behind the serving counter where they prepared a meal for the entire group. Seated around one table were Alison Dixon, Amelia West and Vikki Annis, at the table behind them sat Martin Sharpe who read yet another book from the third floor bookstore.

Alan Robbins sat at a table at the opposite end of the canteen with Jason Moran, they all briefly glanced up when the door opened before Reg, David and Paul entered for that tea break. They would later return to work on the next project down on the warmer second floor, but more importantly, the first four would tonight sleep in real beds.

For now, Gwen poured stewed tea for them before they chose to sit with Alan and Jason, but just then, the canteen door suddenly burst open and scarlet faced Phil Smith stopped and bent over out of breath thanks to the severe difference in the air outside, fewer trees worldwide equates to less oxygen.

"Reg, it stopped!" He gasped. Everybody glanced at everybody else before they all returned their confused stares toward Phil.

"It just stopped snowing!" He blurted as he continued to catch his breath after running from outside and down into the canteen.

All seventeen survivors soon stood outside on the deep, snow covered car park roof to see that Phil was right, the heavy snowfall had suddenly stopped. According to Jake Jarrett, who leaned on the shovel at the centre of the partially cleared path with his goggles now place on top of his red woollen hat, it was as if a tap was suddenly switched off.

"I was shovelling snow and when I turned around to look at Amy at the door, it just stopped dead!" He excitedly exclaimed. Reg then stared up at the completely cloudless bright blue sky that was dark grey just an hour ago. He shook his head before he returned his stare to Jake who stood with huge solid white snow banks on both sides and that was when Reg had a sudden engineering epiphany.

That's a hell of lot of snow.' He told himself, as he continued to think his new concept through before he glanced back at Jake.

"Hey Jake, how would you like to learn some engineering?" He called out. Jake stared back at him with confusion as he bit into a chocolate bar that he removed from his jacket pocket, he shrugged his shoulders and eventually nodded.

"Before I agree to anything, the last time you volunteered me to volunteer for something I ended up doing this, does engineering beat shovelling snow?" He asked, to stifled laughter from Amelia West and Paul Richards who watched him eat the chocolate bar as he stared back at Reg.

"What do you want me to engineer?" He then asked with a mouthful, while everybody watched and listened to the somewhat bizarre conversation as it took place.

"I thought you and I could build a distillery together." Reg eventually replied. As Jake continued to eat, he stared and waited for that response.

"We're going to make whiskey or something?" He asked with more confusion. Reg immediately shook his head with chuckle of his own.

"No, I thought we might turn all of this snow into clean water." He replied. Jake glanced down at the ground all around him before he returned his stare to Reg.

"All of it?" He asked.

Because most of the community spent the past five weeks below ground, an hour or so later they held an announcement meeting outside where they breathed the considerable thinner, cold fresh air. It was revealed by Reg that if it hadn't snowed again by tomorrow, David Wells, Phil Smith and Paul Richards would find the home of Jason Moran. In truth, it was merely to confirm the worst case scenario on his behalf, but they kept that information to themselves because it was highly, highly unlikely that his family could still be alive.

It was also agreed that the three men would take with them full camping equipment, regardless that Jason's home was a mere seven or eight miles away. After five weeks of constant heavy snowfall it was going to be no easy task, but they were all willing volunteers to make the trek in one day and probably return the next depending on the truth of the terrain.

"The snow isn't going to feel as deep as you'd think because it's so compacted, but this isn't going to be anything like just taking a walk down the road, you're going to have to be particularly careful because you'll have no idea of what's under your feet." He assured them. To everybody's surprise, Jason shook his head.

"Don't do it, I know my wife and kids are dead just like all of your families, they couldn't have made it through the past five weeks, don't put your lives at risk just to come back and tell me what I already know." He insisted.

"If we're all going to do this for others, let's at least wait until it's safer to go walking about but I already know we're the only people left alive, at least in Oxford." He added. Everybody stared at Jason, many nodded with reluctant agreement because they all knew deep down that his words were the truth. Alison Dixon managed a half smile because Jason was at last beginning to think about others and less about himself and his own needs, Reg eventually nodded.

"Alright, if you're absolutely sure, we'll wait until it's safer." He said, before Paul Richards turned to him.

"Maybe you should start digging up maps from the book shop to show us where all of the fuel stations are around here, we can go out and start bringing diesel back." He suggested. There was a pause as Paul glanced across at Jason.

"Like Jason said, when it's safer to walk around out there, we can then turn the bloody heating back on downstairs so I can stop sleeping in a coat!" He laughed. Reg nodded with a chuckle of his own, he then pointed toward the main road directly behind Paul.

"Well, there's the first one just a couple of miles up that road, that one shouldn't be much trouble to get to even now, we know that beneath your feet will be just a straight road." He replied.

Three Days later

Tuesday September 26th

At around ten in the morning, Paul Richards and Alan Robbins returned after two days and nights from that nearest fuel station, just two and a half miles to the north on the main road. The walk itself wasn't as treacherous as they expected, the snow just like Reg suspected was so compacted. They made it all the way back today in less than four hours, although they didn't go out to simply walk there or to test the lie of the land. They now sat inside the canteen with steaming coffee and informed everybody of why they had been away from the underground haven since early on Saturday morning.

On that first day, they marked the width of the road as they trudged there using whatever they could find before they investigated the fuel station. Over the next two days they also managed to clear the road by hand, of the seven hundred and twenty six frozen bodies of men women and children that now lay on the far roadside, from the entrance of the Ellington centre right up to around sixty feet south of the fuel station.

"When we go out again tomorrow, we're going to cremate the bodies using petrol from the fuel station, we already doused them once on our way back here, but we'll do it again before we light the fire." Paul announced.

He then turned to Reg and continued to explain, everybody listened in anxious silence as the reality of what they already understood once again dawned on them. That reality was that there were seventeen people seated inside the canteen. Sixteen of them would at least have known some of those people on the roadside or were possibly, in fact more than likely blood related to some, but exposed dead bodies bred serious infection and disease and they also understood that.

Paul Richards was the only outsider, he came from Maidstone one hundred and fifty miles south-east from Oxford at the county of Kent, he wouldn't know or recognise any of those people, but nobody else inside the canteen could say the same and that included Alan Robbins. Alan's mother however died several years ago and his sixty nine year old father was placed into care some thirty miles away with dementia long before the storm, but he could still possibly recognise faces of people that he once knew.

"How dangerous is it to walk out there?" Jason Moran enquired. Paul turned to him and shrugged his shoulders.

"If you're careful and concentrate on where you put your feet, it's not as bad as I expected the snow is so compact Reg was right, it's four or five feet deep and really solid, but that's just a main road and not much to worry about like other places will be." He replied. He then returned his attention to Reg.

"Tomorrow while the bodies burn we're going to find something big to drive down, I saw an old flatbed truck buried under crap inside what's left of the garage beside the fuel station, I want to see if I can get it started to carry drums of fuel now that we've got the road lined and pretty much cleared." He added.

"The underground tanks at the fuel station are full of diesel and petrol and we found another eighty full gas bottles, it looks like they had deliveries sometime just before the crap hit the fan." He informed Reg, who nodded with acknowledgement. He pondered for a few moments before he responded.

"So, if you can get that truck started to carry the diesel here in the few forty five gallon drums that I've got downstairs, we could switch a few things back on like the showers, the heating and some of the lights, you could maybe then get started on clearing a path to the next one." He thought out loud. Paul nodded before Reg turned his attention to the rest of the group.

"While they work at the fuel station, it's going to be back to shovelling snow for some of you, Jake and I are going to start building the distillery tank." He informed them.

"The tank isn't going to be difficult to build and we can soon turn the snow into clean water to store it, but more importantly we need to clear the entire overhead car park of the cold white stuff and it all needs to be shovelled right over to the river bank." He explained. There was a pause before he continued.

"We live underground, if the snow really has finished our new enemy would be rain if that decided to happen right now." He added. There was another momentary pause as everybody considered what he was trying to explain, it was Amelia who let out a sigh.

"It would turn all of the snow into a giant lake right on top of us." She quietly said. Reg nodded to confirm that she was correct. He estimated that there was around sixty or seventy tonnes of snow on the roof right above where they slept. Alison Dixon then shook her head with a sigh of her own.

"Then let's *all* get up there and deal with it, rain is the only weather that hasn't been thrown down at us yet so we're probably due it!" She uttered.

Wednesday September 27th

At six in the morning, everybody but a few stood on the car park roof in light thermal clothing. They used shovels and brushes to push heavy snow toward the narrow Oxford Thames river bank.

Paul and Alan returned to the fuel station on the road and because it was already cleared, they would reach it soon. When they arrived, their first task would be to begin the mass cremation of seven hundred and twenty six men women and children that were piled in a long, long line at the far roadside, after they once again thoroughly doused the bodies with petrol.

Down inside the dimly lit basement maintenance area, Jake lifted his welding visor and stood beside Reg where they both stared at a three inch thick, solid steel rectangular shaped tank that measured fourteen feet in length, four feet in width and was ten feet deep inside. Reg explained to Jake that two narrow trays would be welded along the entire length, five feet from the base floor inside the tank on both sides, before two stainless steel water pipes would be fixed just above the trays. A heating element would then be fitted between two, four inch thick solid steel base plated floors and the project would be ready for a test run in a few days.

He went on to explain that the two steel pipes would be filled with rotating chilled water from the toilet and shower systems as the water was already so cold, in fact more than chilled. When it was melted inside the tank by the heating element beneath, the snow would obviously turn to water and the water would turn to steam. Jake nodded with acknowledgement as he tried to keep up and so far he understood.

When the snow was melted inside the tank and that steam rose, in theory it would reach only as far as the chilled water pipes. Evaporated, clean distilled water would then drip from the pipes into the two tilted trays beneath and would in turn, run out from the tank via a clear plastic pipe, into large containers.

"Only the steam can rise, so any crap stays at the bottom of the tank and remember, the whole point to this is that soon, we're not going to be able to simply turn a tap to get water." He informed Jake who again nodded with acknowledgement.

"I've got a rough idea about the answer to this, but who gets volunteered to clean that out?" He enquired, as he ate a biscuit although like he said, he already knew the answer so Reg didn't need to reply.

"You're the assistant engineer now mate, you get all the good jobs it's the way you learn how everything works from the bottom up!" He explained, as he continued to chuckle.

At just after seven that evening when daylight began to fade, the eleven snow pushers all stopped shovelling and carrying snow in wheelbarrows toward the riverbank when Gwen Vella and Anita Stone brought up trays of hot drinks for everybody. There was now eight feet of visible wet pale grey car park from the centre toward the riverbank across the entire roof of the Ellington centre.

As she stood beside Alison Dixon and sipped steaming hot coffee, Amelia turned to see thick black smoke that just started to billow up from where she knew was the road. She nudged Alison and nodded toward it, they both now knew that Paul and Alan had started the petrol induced fire to begin the mass cremation.

Everybody else turned and watched in solemn silence as the line of thick black smoke slowly became longer and higher. The funeral fire spread down the road toward their general direction and they all knew that except for Reg, Anita, Alison and Paul Richards, those burning bodies could possibly be their own family members. The almost unbearable rotting stench soon drifted toward them although nobody said a word about it, some used their hands to cover their own noses and mouths but nobody complained.

"If anybody else is still alive anywhere around here, they're definitely going to see that smoke." Alison whispered. Amelia nodded as everybody continued to watch the funeral fire in tear-filled silence, but nobody else would see the smoke, that's how vacant the world had become.

That evening, Reg Simmons stood inside the dimly lit, smoke filled maintenance workshop. He watched Jake Jarrett slowly and very carefully weld those narrow trays as he stood inside the large tank, before David Wells entered and he also watched for a few moments.

"He's coming along with that." He said, Reg nodded.

"Jake was the one that I could see would be able to replace me one day and of course he's still young, I just have to teach him as much as I can." He replied. While Reg continued to watch Jake, David studied Reg.

"What do you mean, replace you?" He asked, before Reg turned to face him.

"I'm sixty five and no young man let's not live under any illusions, somebody needs to learn to weld and repair things around here because I'm officially now an old aged pensioner and retired!" He chuckled in response. He again turned to watch Jake. David continued to stare at Reg before he spoke again.

"After listening to Paul and Alan, I was thinking about taking a walk myself." He said. Reg again turned to face him and he waited for David to continue.

"I think somebody should go down to London, just to confirm that the situation is the same down there and see what's what." David eventually said. For a while, Reg continued to stare at him. He returned his attention to Jake before he took in a long deep breath.

"Jake, get the other side welded when you finish this one, I'm just going for a ten minute walk with Dave!" He called out. As Jake continued to weld, without removing his darkened visor he nodded.

"You know you can't do this walk alone, don't you?" Reg asked, as he and David walked along the darkened shiny second floor promenade, David nodded.

"I was thinking that maybe we ask for a volunteer to go with me and then pick one of the names out of a hat." He suggested. Reg nodded before he stared back at him.

"And you know that's a seventy mile hike in deep snow, you'll have to stick to the main roads?" He asked. Again David nodded. He also fully understood the risks involved, but he believed that they needed to know for certain and to gather facts, nobody had been in or out of Oxford since it all happened and Reg in turn understood that.

"We're going to need to plan this idea of yours, so let's get the last living quarters finished tomorrow I still need your help with that, but the planning for the walk to London will need to be meticulous, if you break a leg or anything else out there, you'll probably die from it and no help will be coming." He pointed out.

Thursday September 28th

Reg called a meeting inside the canteen, where he informed everybody that Jake's distillery tank would soon be built and operational. Alison Dixon playfully raised her hand and displayed a somewhat sarcastic smile.

"Reg, am I right in thinking that you intend to turn as much snow as you can find into water to store for future use?" She asked. Reg nodded to confirm that she was correct. She continued to display that wry smile.

"I don't know if you're aware, but there's quite a lot of snow out there and I'm just wondering how much you think we all need, taking into account that we have over two thousand bottles of drinking water in storage already." She reminded him. From the very first day that they met, Reg and Alison had a very playful, humorous relationship and they teased each other often. He immediately returned a sarcastic wry smile of his own before he replied.

"And would you, your ladyship like to still flush the toilets?" He asked. Alison rigorously nodded.

"That would be lovely, yes." She replied, with that same wry smile. Reg beamed a broader grin before he playfully winked.

"I thought as much and I only ask because the water storage tanks here are just about empty and obviously with no running water available." He continued. There was a brief silence other than stifled chuckles from almost everybody else, but Reg wasn't quite finished.

"And would you, your ladyship like to start taking hot showers when Paul and Alan return with fuel so that we can fire up the generators more often?" He just as sarcastically asked. This time everybody rigorously nodded with more stifled laughter. Anita Stone pointed out that she and Gwen would like to be able to cook using the ovens as opposed to the small gas stoves, Reg nodded with that same grin.

"He's such a smart arse." Alison whispered. Amelia beside her giggled before she leaned closer.

"You started it, *your ladyship*." She whispered in response. There was another silent pause before Reg continued.

"Dave is planning to take a walk down to London in a few weeks." He announced. The room suddenly fell silent and he watched everybody stare at David for a few moments before they all returned their attention to him.

Reg went on to explain the obvious, that nobody had been in or out of Oxford since the storm, the hailstones and then the earthquake that occurred almost two months ago. He also explained that they needed to verify that this situation was in fact a national one. He then pointed out that David couldn't make this trip alone although nobody would be expected to go with him, not unless he or she was a willing volunteer.

"Take a couple of days to think it through, he's not going for a few weeks and if you're considering going with him, come and find me and we'll talk about it and if you'd still like to throw your name in you can, but we only need one volunteer." He added.

Thursday October 12th

After a few minor glitches and leakages, Jake's distillery tank was now fully operational. Over the past two weeks, a total of nine hundred and eighty one barrows filled with snow had been turned to reasonably clean water and stored after the water tanks were completely refilled. Paul Richards with Alan Robbins had so far loaded onto the flatbed truck, eighteen large drums filled with diesel that were very slowly driven down the main road and parked on the overhead car park roof.

The drums were then unloaded and carefully rolled down the delivery ramp and now surrounded the two generators. The overhead car park itself was almost completely cleared of snow, which removed the immediate threat of flooding inside the Ellington centre, should rain decide to fall as heavily as the snow.

Gwen and Anita moved into their smaller shared room on the second floor, but that was some time ago and the larger accommodations for everybody else were also completed. They now all slept in beds, in their own private areas instead of on the cold hard floor or on camp beds on the shiny promenade, people were in general at last beginning to feel a little more settled, the general feeling was however that this situation was a permanent one.

Inside Alison Dixon's fourth floor office, she sat behind her desk with Reg, Amelia, David Wells and Jason Moran in front of her, where they all discussed David's proposed seventy mile trek south-east to London that would begin next week. On this day, one of four volunteers would be chosen to accompany him.

Paul Richards and Alan Robbins had their own project underway that involved the scavenging fuel runs, they also planned a second mass cremation which meant that they were not even considered for the long walk. Jake was also denied a spot as Reg's appointed trainee engineer after he volunteered, as were Gwen Vella and Anita Stone who were responsible for feeding the group although they didn't volunteer.

The youngest of the group, Martin Sharpe also discovered that as the recently appointed record keeper, he could not go after he volunteered to walk with his stepfather. The willing volunteers from that remaining group were Amy Vinton, Vikki Annis, Phil Smith and Charlotte Strickland. Before one of that four were chosen to accompany David, the discussion inside Alison's office continued.

"It's really difficult not to sound a bit sexist here, but the sled that I've nearly finished building for the walk is going to be heavily loaded with camping equipment, food and other supplies and I seriously can't see any of those young ladies being able to pull it in the snow with Dave." Reg explained to a solitary nod of agreement.

"The only one that could realistically do it is Phil Smith." Jason agreed. While Amelia and Alison appreciated that Reg wasn't in any way undermining any of the three volunteer women and understood his point, they both believed that a woman should also be with David during the long walk.

"Forget sexism, let's just say that whoever does go, encounters other women during this walk and offers them a new home, having a woman with Dave would make it much easier to convince them that they'd be safe to come back here." Amelia insisted and Reg nodded.

"So, are you suggesting we send three people instead of two?" He asked. Amelia shrugged her shoulders before she and Alison both nodded.

"If you were a young girl still alive somewhere out there on your own confused, terrified and surrounded by dead bodies, would you go off with two men you just met?" Alison asked him, Amelia agreed.

"There's no law out there to stop one person from doing whatever they want to another, I know I wouldn't come back here with them so yes and I think Amy should go with Dave and Phil, she's the one that could definitely do it." She added. Alison reluctantly nodded with agreement before Jason shook his head and quietly chuckled.

"You could always volunteer to go if you like, I'm sure you could do it." He sarcastically suggested. For a few moments, Amelia stared back at him.

"So could you Jason, we're talking about sending a girl with two men after all, but let me explain, the only reason I'm not going is because you're not." She replied. Jason's smug grin suddenly disappeared while Alison stifled a giggle.

"Do you really think I'm going to wander around miles away in the snow and leave you here to throw your weight around, just to get what you want?" Amelia then asked him, to no response whatsoever.

Friday October 20th

Paul Richards and Alan Robbins stood on the car park roof dressed in thermals ready to begin another slow drive in the flatbed truck. This time they would park at the fuel station to begin to clear more frozen bodies for a further half mile north, to a large roundabout where they would at a later date head right and then travel south for just another half mile to the second fuel station to scavenge more diesel.

For now, they stood with everybody else because David Wells, Phil Smith and Amy Vinton were about to begin their seventy mile trudge in the snow all the way to the capital city of London. The trio would initially head north in the same direction as Paul and Alan on the main road, but they would turn right around half way and head north-east on the Eastern Bypass Road for a little more than six miles until they reached the first planned checkpoint at Headington. There, they would pitch a tent and camp for the night, that walk was in fact a very long uphill six miles on deep snow.

They would make just one mile per hour, sometimes more sometimes less depending on the terrain. Tomorrow an even longer and more perilous unpredictable walk would begin from Headington, from where they would this time head south-east and downhill on a dual carriageway that would eventually merge onto what was back then known as the M40 motorway.

On that second day, they would arrive at Tetsworth to pitch up again, but by then already on the motorway. That single, very long road would eventually take them all the way into the outskirts of west London, hopefully around two weeks from today, again terrain and unforeseen circumstances permitting. Their final destination into the centre of the capital would take them at least an additional week, rest days not included at the rate that David and Reg meticulously planned although it was in truth theoretical, nobody knew what or who they might encounter along the way.

Everybody in turn hugged David, then Amy and Phil and wished them good luck because they all knew that the three would be gone for at least two months and that this was the most dangerous task that any of the survivors had undertaken to date.

The two men began to pull long thick ropes that were attached to the front of a large very sturdy steel sled while Amy pushed it from behind. It was laden with seven tents, additional cold weather clothing intended for possible survivors and enough food and bottled water to last them for more than two months. The remaining fourteen dwellers watched them make their way toward the main road, where they would soon take that right turn and disappear out of sight as they headed for the Eastern Bypass Road.

Later that day, Jason Moran leaned against the doorframe at a large, emptied shop down on the second floor that would later become spare living quarters. He watched Amelia for the very first time lead a beginner karate class with Emma Todd, Charlotte Strickland, Jake Jarrett, Wendy Jones and Martin Sharpe as her students, before Alison Dixon soon surprised Amelia with her attendance. She then glanced toward the opened doorway where she saw Jason standing with his arms folded in front of him.

"Do you want to join in?" She called out. He immediately shook his head with a chuckle.

"What are you doing, planning to invade Cirencester with ninja warriors if and when the snow clears?" He asked. There was a pause before he sarcastically spoke again.

"You know, when it's safer for you and your trained killers to go outside." He added. The group of six completely novice students continued with the stretching warm-up exercises that they had been shown when Amelia casually walked toward Jason, he stood defensively upright.

"I'm teaching them to defend themselves for when an obnoxious little dickhead tries to put his hands on them because as you know Jason, I know how to do that." She calmly and very quietly replied to his question. She then turned and headed back toward her class. Just then, from behind on the promenade, Vikki Annis turned sideways and edged past him in the doorway and briefly smiled, but she then laughed.

"I thought I'd come and learn how to kick your arse too." She just as quietly informed him. She joined the group of new students to make it seven. Jason watched her walk toward the others.

'When I get around to dealing with a few of you here you'll be the first, big mouth.' He thought to himself, as he continued to watch Vikki in particular as she joined the group.

David Wells and Phil Smith struggled to pull the two long and thick ropes over their shoulders as Amy Vinton continued to push the heavily laden sled from behind. They all knew to ignore that they guided it around snow covered corpses although that was easier said than done. They finally stopped at the beginning of the dual carriage just past their objective, which was at a roundabout beside the destroyed remains of a fast food restaurant at the first checkpoint.

"That's it for today we're at Headington, let's get a tent unpacked and a fire going and start something to eat." David gasped as he stretched his limbs. Phil slumped down onto the snow covered ground out of breath and he nodded, as Amy removed her black woollen hat and shook out her long auburn hair.

"Dave, I was just thinking on the way here." She gasped from exhaustion. David and Phil stared up at her.

"If we've got seven tents with us and we're going to pitch one up beside one of these ruined buildings, can't we just leave it here for when we come back and start to lighten the load as we go?" She asked. Phil watched David and waited for his response, to him it made good sense to lighten the load and to save them from having to pitch at least one tent during the return trip, it wasn't like anybody was ever going to steal it. They both watched as David thought Amy's idea through before he eventually stared back at her.

"We could leave a tent ready to climb back into let's say every other day, so tomorrow when we get down to the next checkpoint at Tetsworth we pack that one away the next morning, but when we make it to Stokenchurch, we leave that one up and ready to use for when we come back too, each tent we leave makes the sled lighter." He added. Amy and Phil glanced at each other with beaming grins as

David continued to think the concept through, he again stared at her.

"That's not a bad idea for you, Vinton." He said with a tease in his tone. Amy poked out her tongue in response.

"But we always keep two tents on the sled, just in case we do manage to pick up stragglers along the way." David suggested. Amy nodded with agreement before he displayed a smile of his own.

"Great idea, let's get set up for the night and eat something hot." He suggested. Phil stared beside them at the remains of his former favourite fast food restaurant.

"I could just kill a cheeseburger right now." He quietly uttered. David and Amy laughed.

"That's where we'll set up behind that wall so we know where to find the tent when we come back and behind there is whatever's left of a supermarket, maybe we should raid it on the way back and fill the sled up with whatever we can find." He suggested.

"We know where the supermarket was, we both used to work there." Phil reminded him.

Saturday October 21st

It was at around three in the afternoon when Reg Simmons sat alone at a table inside the canteen. Several others also sat quietly chatting amongst themselves, but he very discretely watched two in particular who sat alone and appeared to whisper. At the far end of the canteen, his appointed trainee engineer Jake Jarrett sat in his dark blue coveralls and very quietly talked with Charlotte Strickland. They sat away from everybody else, but Amelia and Alison suddenly interrupted Reg's discrete observations when they both sat with him, they soon followed his glances toward Jake and Charlotte.

"Something looks very cosy over there." Amelia whispered. She sipped coffee and continued to watch them. Alison nodded as she just as discretely watched the couple.

"We might have to keep an eye on that budding little romance." She whispered. Reg glanced across at her with raised eyebrows.

"Or maybe we should just leave them to it?" He suggested. Both Alison and Amelia stared at him for a few moments before he spoke again.

"Think about it, as far as we know the world's population is down to seventeen people all living in Oxford, which means that we might actually need this sort of thing to happen." He reminded them. They again glanced at each other before their stares returned to Reg.

"And do you by any chance know how to deliver a baby, Reg?" Amelia asked. Alison quietly giggled.

"I doubt it there are no nuts, bolts or manuals involved so he'd be scratching his head for ten hours while Charlotte screamed with her hands around Jake's throat." She replied. Reg poked out his tongue before Amelia whispered again.

"We might need young Martin to read up on it and learn how to become a midwife." She again quietly laughed, as Reg shook his head with despair. They all continued to very discretely observe Jake and Charlotte until they both climbed to their feet to make their way out of the canteen, they knew that they were being watched.

"It looks like they're going for a romantic walk, probably hand in hand down on the dimly lit third floor promenade." Amelia quietly chuckled. Reg again shook his head before Alison commented again.

"I so want to shout out that condoms are in both supermarkets." She quietly giggled, as did Amelia, but Alison then glanced back at Amelia and then at Reg.

"I wonder how David, Amy and Phil are getting on." She said. Amelia offered a genuine look of confusion.

"Wait, condoms made you think of those three, what do you think they're actually doing out there?" She asked with more laughter. As Jake and Charlotte left the canteen, Reg sat and watched Alison and Amelia quietly laugh and joke. It suddenly dawned on him that today was the very first one that he had seen or heard genuine laughter in weeks. He also realised with a smile of his own that simple laughter, that he once took for granted was now something that he could sit and watch all day.

He recalled how distraught Alison was on the day that he had to tell her that his wife Marcie and her own entire family had been wiped out by the storm. He also considered everything that Amelia went through to somehow even reach the Ellington centre on the same day. He continued to discretely smile to himself because here they were together, making it through everything that they had endured. He wondered if these two contrasting personalities would have ever been friends before August when both of their worlds came crashing down around them. He doubted that they would, in the old world they had absolutely nothing in common, but the catastrophic disaster forced them to become the friends that they were today, purely because just like everybody around them, they now needed each other.

At the far northern end of the deep snow covered main road, with scented scarfs covering their noses and mouths, Paul Richards and Alan Robbins continued to carry preserved frozen corpses of men women and children to the roadside. So far, the second count stood at two hundred and fifty eight as they finally neared the large roundabout. They now knew from experience just as David, Phil and Amy were quickly learning, to pay the dead no attention in order to carry out this dreadful task.

Something was however about to change that near failsafe philosophy, it was the reason that nobody else could do it. When they eventually laid the final body down onto the roadside which made number two hundred and sixty one, they both stared fifty metres to the north at the roundabout where they saw a lone, partially snow covered corpse lying face down in the centre of the road. Paul suggested that it join the others before they started the funeral fire, it somehow didn't seem right to leave what was obviously a man out there alone and Alan agreed, so they both trudged toward the roundabout.

After they carefully turned over the body that was dressed in pale green pyjamas, Paul took a hold of the dead man's frozen blue feet while Alan lifted his shoulders and stared down at the pale face with obvious stunned shock.

"Remember what I told you, don't look at the faces." Paul reminded him, but it was already too late. Alan very slowly glanced up at him and eventually nodded, but Paul could clearly see that obviously nothing was alright as they started to carry the man toward the line of corpses. As they walked, Paul continued to watch Alan and he could just as clearly see that something was very, very wrong and not even close to alright.

"What is it, mate?" He asked. Alan glanced up at him, again he said nothing as they very carefully laid the frozen body down at the end of the line, bringing the new final count to two hundred and sixty two. Paul then walked toward several large red jerry cans that were filled with petrol to begin to douse the corpses. He turned to see that Alan now sat on the deep snow covered ground beside the last body that they carried from the roundabout, where he gently stroked the elderly man's frozen face.

'Shit, he knew him!' Paul thought to himself. He trudged back on the snow to where Alan sat and now quietly sobbed. It was always a concern for everybody but Paul as the only person within the group that this couldn't possibly happen to. Alan had done so well to this point to pay no attention to the dead and in fact to no longer even view

them as people, but this was obviously something else. When Paul reached where his friend still sat and stroked the dead man's face, Alan glanced up at him with tear filled eyes.

"I don't understand how, he was in a care home thirty miles from here." He quietly croaked. Paul stood in stunned silence and stared down at the old man, he didn't know what to say or how to comfort Alan, who returned his stare back down at his deceased father Malcolm Robbins, as he continued to gently stroke the old man's frozen pale blue cheek. Paul slumped down on the snow beside him where he placed his arm around his friend. For a while, they sat in silence until Alan wiped his tears as he continued to stare down at his father's contorted face.

"I don't want the others to know about this, I don't want my dad to be the subject of idle chat around canteen tables." He quietly croaked. All Paul could do was to nod with acknowledgement.

"I'm so sorry." He eventually uttered. As they sat in silence, Paul considered that there was one person in the entire world who should never have been exposed to the body of Malcolm Robbins in this way. That one person now sat beside his corpse and tenderly stroked his frozen face.

It was around four hours later when David Wells, Phil Smith and Amy Vinton manoeuvred the heavy sled as daylight faded. They now thankfully travelled downhill on the motorway heading south-east and very close to the second checkpoint at Tetsworth, almost nine miles from Headington. Phil stopped, stood upright and stretched as he stared north-west at black smoke that slowly billowed up toward the skies from some five miles away as the crow flies, he then nodded toward it.

"They started the second cremation." He uttered, as he regained his breath.

"Let's stop here for the night." David suggested, as he also stretched. He stared across rolling, untouched snow covered fields at the rising black smoke. For a few moments, the trio watched it slowly climb toward the sky as they all regained their breath, but they of course had no idea of the significance of the second mass cremation.

From the back of the sled, something caused Amy to turn one hundred and eighty degrees, an instinct suddenly distracted her away from the funeral smoke. She stared at a field behind them at the other side of the wide road and her eyes suddenly widened with stunned disbelief before she let out a gasp.

The small enclosed field right in front her was of course still covered with snow, it was partitioned with completely undamaged short wire fencing all around with a still intact small closed wooden gate on the left side. There were dotted darkened patches in the not so deep snow like small circular footprints, unlike the surrounding paddocks that were all covered with at least a thousand snow covered corpses for as far as the eye could see and dead animals lay absolutely everywhere.

There were also around one to two hundred vehicles that on that dreadful night, heavily smashed down to the ground around or on top of the corpses inside every other enclosure. The small field that she stared at with utter disbelief at the centre was completely clear and as she stared, her heart pounded.

'How can they be there?' She asked herself in absolute shock. Phil glanced at Amy to see that she stared mesmerised at something behind them. He turned before his eyes widened with as much surprise. He grabbed David's forearm and shook it without removing his startled stare. David then turned and he also stared at the eight living, breathing black and white cows that chewed frozen grass at the far end of the completely enclosed, undamaged small paddock.

"What the bloody hell…" He blurted.

"How..." Phil began to ask, but David immediately shook his head to cancel out the question at hand.

"Look, they dug out all of the snow at the far end to get to the grass." Phil pointed out. All three super hurricanes, two of which they still didn't know about along with millions upon millions of giant four kilogramme hailstones that they did know about, miraculously missed every one of the cows that stood in an open field just north of the small town of Tetsworth, followed by five weeks of very heavy snow and until this moment, no life than fourteen other people had been seen by the trio since that night of terror almost two months ago.

There wasn't a single dead or even harmed cow in that particular field unlike all of the others around it, everything else was either dead or landed there. The animals stood and grazed on frozen grass as if the events of early August never happened. As David continued to stare with utter disbelief at the mere sight, he realised that there were no corpses lying inside the enclosure unlike every other around it. He then realised that at the centre, a single large oak tree remained also completely untouched, not to mention that all of the surrounding fences remained intact.

"Maybe there is a God after all, somebody has definitely been looking out for them." He quietly said. Both Amy and Phil nodded in awestruck silence.

Ella, accompanied by LMS twinned with the Viking, even together when they directly passed each other at middle England not far from Oxford and Tetsworth, somehow completely missed just one small paddock that was surrounded by many others during the purge of life on that terrifying night. This wondrous sight gave new hope. If eight cows still stood untouched in an open field and somehow made it through everything that followed, more people could have also made it elsewhere.

Hope was again suddenly there.

Thursday October 26th

Hurst

Five days after the discovered cows at Tetsworth, David, Amy and Phil left the sled at the roadside and carefully crossed a small wooden bridge that passed over a narrow but vastly overflowed river at the side of the motorway. They made their way onto what would be a winding dirt track beneath the deep compact blanket of untouched snow as they headed toward the first isolated building that they had seen, that from a distance appeared to be only partially damaged.

"Follow my footprints in the snow, you know it'll be safe to walk on them." David insisted. The roof of the farm building appeared from a distance to be heavily damaged, but the rest of the house especially the stone walls seemed to be intact and gave the trio hope that maybe somebody, possibly a family that lived there just outside of Handy Cross could have possibly survived.

From sheer exhaustion after they manoeuvered the vast sled around scattered frozen corpses for six days, the trio spent much of the day before on the motorway at Stokenchurch, where they drank coffee and periodically ate hot food to regain their strength, but they all now suffered from fatigue. David made a point since this trek began, of trying to keep morale high by encouraging his two younger friends to talk about what they did for fun prior to what they still believed was a single vast storm.

They eventually left Stokenchurch at around two o'clock yesterday afternoon and stopped after just four hours to sleep for the night before an early start this morning. They made it to the old farmhouse at Handy Cross at just after midday and as they neared, they could now see that most the roof was in fact missing.

In eerie silence, they began to search the darkened ground floor where they all hoped that maybe there were survivors although it was now very doubtful. Those doubts were soon confirmed as they searched amongst the scattered ruins and rubble and found nobody dead or alive. They then slowly and very carefully climbed an old winding solid oak staircase toward the upper floor.

"At least downstairs will keep us out of the wind if we're staying here tonight, why does everything in here echo?" Amy asked.

"Because it's just an empty house, it's not anybody's home anymore." Phil replied. As Amy followed him, he followed David up onto the first floor where they all stood and stared around in more eerie silence. Although they were technically still inside the building, with hardly any roof and only one remaining inside wall, they once again stood outside where the same cold breeze stroked their tanned faces.

"Whoever lived in this place must have been up here when it happened." David quietly uttered, as they all stared around at what remained of the devastated, internal wall-free carnage.

"Like Amy said, at least we'll be out of the wind downstairs tonight." Phil said, to change the uncomfortable topic of conversation. The reality once again dawned on them all as they stared around, that people once lived inside the house, but nobody lived there anymore.

Phil guessed that David was right, during the early hours of that terrible night back in August, those people probably lay in their beds and waited for the storm to pass over. Now there were no beds or anything else to speak of, only broken and smashed wooden beams and strewn rubble remained. Everything else along with everybody must have joined the entire roof when it was violently wrenched up to join the turning carnage while they lay terrified in their beds. He also considered that their beds were where they should have felt safe, but Mother Nature, Mother Earth and Karma obviously had other ideas.

The trio would spend that night and much of the next day down at the ground floor, they again used the time to rest and recover. That day was when David realised that the long walk wasn't going to be anything like the mere incredibly difficult one that he and Reg optimistically envisaged.

It was in fact much more physically demanding and mentally draining than any of them could ever imagine, although so far the three walkers had over the past seven days, dragged and manoeuvred the heavy sled for forty three miles since they left the Ellington centre. David congratulated Amy and Phil for that achievement alone, although they were now managing on average just five miles per day as opposed to the eight or nine that was originally planned, but the younger pair didn't need to know that.

They spent the rest of that day at the farmhouse eating hot food to store energy and drinking coffee. They talked about the astonishing sight of the eight cows back at Tetsworth, David's wine bar and his stepson Martin Sharpe's studies. They all laughed about the fact that Jake Jarrett's pockets always seemed to be filled with chocolate bars.

"He's like a walking vending machine except he never gives anything out!" Phil laughed.

They discussed what they did for fun and enjoyment prior to the days leading up to the terrible disaster that still unbeknown to them, had already changed the face of the entire planet forever and in more ways than any of them could possibly comprehend. They couldn't know that entire great land masses such as Norway, Denmark, Japan, Australia and Florida were not merely decimated like everywhere else, but completely submerged and gone, while closer to home Ireland clung onto her very existence by the mere skin of her teeth with just fifty four survivors from more than five million.

David continued to keep the conversations light and positive whenever they sat, even though he and Reg believed that the catastrophe that they all survived, purely by being in the right places at the right time could well be a global one.

They both also believed that surely even if Westminster really was gone, they would have heard from somebody by now even from abroad after almost two months. They would have seen or heard aircraft or helicopters, but there had been absolutely nothing in the sky or on the roads for that matter since it happened and they were yet to encounter another living person on their travels after seven days.

The stark reality was that the entire world had fallen almost lifeless and completely silent, more than seven billion corpses lay scattered and frozen on the ground around what was left of the entire world.

"We all definitely needed these rest days, this is much harder than I thought it was going to be." Amy commented, as she sipped steaming hot coffee. Phil nodded with agreement as David glanced around at what remained of the battered old farmhouse.

"Why don't we leave a few things here to drastically lighten the load of the sled?" He asked. Both Amy and Phil glanced at each other and returned their stares to him before they both eagerly nodded.

"I like that plan and we could do this place up a little bit at some point, maybe when we come back whenever that is, then use it as a stopover for future casual strolls to London." Phil replied with a chuckle.

Later discovered records reveal that Lawrence Hurst aged thirty five at that time, owned and lived at the farmhouse just outside of Handy Cross prior to the end of the known world, with his wife Amanda Hurst, nee Gregg aged thirty one. The couple had three small children Caitlin Hurst aged eight, Michael Hurst aged six and Daniel Hurst aged just two years.

It is probable, due to the severe damage to the roof and entire upper floor of the building, that the family joined the horror in the skies during that night in August, although no bodies were ever identified. No more details regarding the Hurst family have been discovered, but history will remember them, the same cannot be said for so many others.

Sunday October 29th

At around eight in the evening, two days after they left the farmhouse at Handy Cross and again as daylight rapidly faded, the three walkers passed a bent and battered signpost, showing that they were entering the Borough of Hillingdon at the outskirts of west London. Beneath it a smaller, yellow sign showed that Hillingdon underground train station was one mile directly ahead on the same snow covered road.

They left supplies, including two of the remaining four tents along with some spare clothing and non-perishable food inside the farmhouse. Yesterday, they reached Gerrards Cross after another exhausting full eight mile trudge in deep snow. Today, they reached the very first London checkpoint although there were still many, many days of walking ahead before they would reach Westminster at the city centre.

"If we can get in there, why don't we just sleep in the underground station tonight to save us putting a tent up?" Phil asked. Amy pushed the much lighter sled from behind and she nodded.

"We could just get into sleeping bags on benches without having to put another one up." She agreed. David also nodded as they guided the sled around more snow covered corpses which was becoming almost nonchalant to them. They didn't know it, but over the past nine days they had passed more than sixteen thousand frozen bodies on the roads alone.

They crossed the darkened street and headed toward what remained of the entrance at Hillingdon underground station, they all bent over out of breath after they released the sled.

"If we can get down onto the station platform, you're both right we won't need to pitch a tent and we can just get into sleeping bags on the benches." David gasped, before he stood upright and took in another long deep breath.

"Let's leave the sled here and see if we can actually get down onto the platform first and if we can, we'll come back up for the cooking equipment and sleeping bags." He added, as he continued to fill his lungs, his travelling companions again both nodded.

"We'll need to take torches with us." Amy reminded them as she regained her own composure.

Inside the obliterated roofless station entrance, Phil hurriedly clambered over one of two heavily damaged rotating turnstiles. Amy more carefully negotiated her way over the other and after David watched them he followed.

"Phil, be careful, if you break a leg or anything else out here we're in big trouble, you could die from the infection of a single broken bone." He called out. Phil glanced back at him and nodded with a wry grin before he switched on his long black powerful torch and pointed a bright beam of light down into a black abyss past a motionless escalator. He started to clamber down followed by Amy who also switched on her torch, as did David behind her.

"I know everybody around here is dead, but this place is really bloody eerie." Phil called out. His voice echoed as he hurriedly made his way down the escalator, followed more cautiously by Amy and then David.

"Slow down!" David called out.

When Phil reached the bottom of the escalator, he turned left and stepped onto the pitch dark platform where a strong, ice cold gust brushed his face. He slowly shone his bright torch around the platform from left to right as Amy stopped behind him and David soon appeared behind her.

"Who came up bright idea to sleep down here?" David asked, before Amy and Phil both playfully pointed toward each other.

"It's actually windier down here than it is up top!" Phil laughed. He continued to slowly move his torch around the platform. He eventually pointed and stopped it on the pale white face of a still and lifeless young girl, who lay frozen to death on a blue platform bench. The three of them stared at her for a few moments.

"Do you think she starved to death or something?" Amy quietly asked. They continued to stare at the dead young girl, but only one would answer Amy's question. The girl suddenly opened her blurred eyes and she squinted up at the bright blinding lights before she very slowly began to sit upright, Amy let out a stifled gasp.

"She's alive!" She squealed.

"Who's that?" The girl quietly croaked as she shielded her eyes from the bright blinding torchlights. Amy immediately unfastened her thick black padded thermal jacket and removed it as she hurried toward her. She wrapped it around the girl before she sat and began to gently rub her arms in an effort to warm her. David and Phil continued to shine their bright torches around the darkened platform until another pale face appeared, then another and another.

"There's more here!" Phil excitedly yelled. The frozen young woman sat trembling in Amy's arms on the bench, as more people climbed to their feet and appeared from the darkness, as the trio stared around at them all in stunned silence.

There were in total twelve, they had been barely surviving on the underground station platform where they ate and drank whenever and whatever they could on a daily basis. They had been down there since the catastrophic events of early August, it was by now late October.

"Phil, get up to the sled and bring down the camping stoves and loads of food!" David called out. Phil nodded before he scampered out from the platform and back up the escalator as he headed for the sled. David called out and again reminded him to take care.

"You're going to be alright, everything's alright." Amy quietly assured the young woman on the bench. She then climbed to her feet and she also headed toward the escalator.

"I'm going up too, I'll bring as many blankets down as I can carry." She told David, before she also disappeared out of sight.

Harrison Bax, Deborah Lloyd, Karen Willis, Sue Cole, Lisa Betts, Zack Zimmerman, Umar Okur, Katie Chamberlain, Tess Morking, Jackie Nightingale, her stepdaughter Maria Nightingale and the young girl on the bench Joanna Simpson, all survived beneath the station. They somehow, albeit barely made it down there since the night that Ella,

LMS and the Viking angrily appeared in the darkness to kill every single one of them along with everybody else, that was however seventy eight days ago.

Around forty minutes later, the survivors all huddled around three burning gas stoves wrapped in warm blankets or opened sleeping bags. For the first time in almost eleven weeks, they sipped steaming coffee or hot chocolate while David cooked food for everybody. He turned to twenty six year old Hillingdon police officer Harrison Bax, a tall man with short dishevelled blonde hair.

"How long have you guys been down here for?" He asked. For a while, Harrison stared back at him as he sipped from his mug of steaming coffee.

"We were all down here when the storm hit." He eventually replied. David stared back at him with utter disbelief.

"That was weeks ago, how the hell have you all survived?" He asked. He briefly glanced across at the ailing Joanna Simpson who looked worse than any other. He wondered just how much longer she would have lasted, if they hadn't by chance chosen to sleep beneath the ground for the night and had walked past the station entrance to pitch a tent elsewhere.

Harrison explained that he and Umar watched from what remained of the station entrance when the giant rocks of ice slammed down onto the ground and completely pulverised what was left of the roof and the already ripped apart borough of Hillingdon. Since that day, everybody had taken their turn to venture outside in pairs to scavenge for food and water with the exception of Joanna Simpson, the clearly unwell girl on the bench.

"The body that you would've seen out on the steps at the entrance with no head, she was running to here when she was hit by one of the hailstones." Harrison explained.

"We were screaming at her to come to us and that's what she was doing, she was running to us until just one took her out." He continued.

"A single hailstone went straight through the top of her head and came out of her lower back, she didn't scream or let out a sound, she was dead before she even hit the steps." He added in a croaked voice and with tear filled eyes. He slowly shook his head as he vividly recalled the moment.

David considered that he hadn't even noticed a headless woman on the steps that led into the station entrance, or the obvious signs of footprints in the snow that would have been left by their daily scavenging runs. It led him to the conclusion that they had become so nonchalant to the sights of utter devastation and dead bodies that surrounded them on a daily basis, that they were missing obvious signs although daylight was rapidly fading when they arrived.

It gave him food for thought regarding the psychological effects that the long walk had to be having on the three of them, to make them so blinded to the those blatant and obvious facts, not to mention what was at the beginning of their trek, the almost unbearable stench of death that they now hardly noticed.

For the next couple of hours, they listened to each survivor's story of how they made it to the station during that first night, along with how many they had personally lost over those first few days. It was their turn to tell their own story of where they had walked from, what they had seen over the past week and of course the fact that there were another fourteen survivors at Oxford living in reasonable comfort inside a brand new underground shopping centre. David also sold them the concept that they now even had refurbished, separated accommodation and slept in real beds.

The trio learned that none of the Hillingdon survivors, even during their local scavenging travels had seen another living soul since the night of the storm followed by the terrible entire day of those giant hailstones that took the life of the young woman out on the steps. She was in fact the very last living person that had been seen by any of them until now.

"I thought we had it bad." Phil quietly uttered, before Amy interrupted the conversation.

"We've got a tent up on the sled, another back at the farmhouse and another one at every other checkpoint, thermal clothes and enough food for everybody here for the next three weeks." She informed them all and there was a momentary pause of silence.

"You're all coming back to Oxford with us, right?" She asked. She stared at each Hillingdon survivor in turn. She then breathed a sigh of relief when they all started to slowly nod their heads. David also nodded with thankful acknowledgement.

"Good, so my plan is that we stay here for a couple of days to get everybody properly fed and strong enough for the walk back to Ellington, the one to Westminster can wait." He said, before he glanced at Phil and quietly chuckled.

"It's a shame we can't just give Reg a call or hit him up on the internet anymore to tell him not to stop building bedrooms." He said.

"He's going to love you!" Phil replied, as Amy quietly giggled.

"Hit him up on the internet, how old do you actually think you are?" She asked. David poked out his tongue in response before a few Hillingdon survivors also began to quietly chuckle for the very first time since August.

Tuesday October 31ˢᵗ

At just after six in the morning, Phil Smith left the underground station with twenty seven year old Hillingdon survivor Corporal Zack Zimmerman, who it transpired was a soldier on leave from the Royal Anglian Regiment when the terrifying storms impacted. Zack was a well-built man of five feet nine with short brown hair that was in fact cropped eleven weeks ago.

The two fit and strong young men left Hillingdon with enough food, water and a few extras to last for five days along with the last sleeping bag. They departed Hillingdon a whole day earlier than the main party to make it to Ellington, to inform Reg and the Oxford dwellers that more people were coming, so that plans and preparations could be made for the main group's later arrival.

Phil and Zack would pass through the checkpoints at Gerrards Cross and nearby Woodburn Moor, they would hopefully make it to the partially destroyed farmhouse at Handy Cross that the original trio discovered on their way to Hillingdon, although that one was doubtful. The main party consisting of David, Amy and the other survivors would leave tomorrow morning when their own preparations were completed.

Phil had already made this trip once albeit with rest days and at a much slower pace, although on the way to Hillingdon he and David pulled the heavily laden sled while Amy pushed it from behind and Zack was a physically fit soldier, so the pair would make much quicker time hopefully passing through two checkpoints to pitched tents each day, while the considerably slower, main party would make just one.

Tomorrow, they hoped to pass through Stokenchurch and later reach Tetsworth where the eight black and white cows were discovered and finally stop at Headington, just six miles from the Ellington centre before arriving there on Thursday morning. Phil knew only too well that the theory of this faster walk was one thing, completing it on the same time schedule was something very different. The walk to Hillingdon was proof of that, so Thursday's arrival at Oxford was very dubious at best, not to mention that much of this walk would be uphill.

This plan theoretically meant that when Phil and Zack reached the Ellington centre, the main party would, or at least should be at the farmhouse, or maybe Stokenchurch with at least seven more days of walking and another rest day or two ahead before they also arrived at Oxford, giving plenty of time for the Ellington survivors to prepare for their arrival.

At just after nine that night, Zack stared into burning flames while he and Phil sat outside in front of the camp fire that they rebuilt when they arrived at the farmhouse at Handy Cross a little more than an hour ago, they held plastic camping mugs of steaming coffee after they ate a hot meal. They both now realised that the faster walks through three checkpoints would be much more difficult than they anticipated, in fact the extended walks would be too difficult, but they made it just this once, they made almost twelve miles in one day on deep compacted snow.

They were unaware that because more than seven billion people lay dead across the entire planet and those corpses were no longer breathing, there was an abundance of considerably richer Oxygen in the air and of course fewer trees, the result was that one, or often both men felt light headed whenever they travelled too quickly.

"I'm never doing that ever again, not even without snow on the ground." Phil quietly uttered. Zack chuckled as he rigorously shook his head with absolute agreement. They eventually finished travelling for fifteen hours without stopping even once, although they should have both passed out.

"I ache in places that weren't even there yesterday, tomorrow let's think of this as a really good head start and stay at Stokenchurch, we left a tent there on the way down." Phil added. Zack nodded without protest or argument.

"The others aren't leaving until tomorrow, they definitely won't make it even this far with Joanna." He replied, Phil nodded as he sipped coffee.

"So how long have you been in the army for?" He eventually asked. Zack glanced up at him and displayed a smile.

"I joined up in the January seven years ago, but something tells me I'm not going to make the twenty two or get my pension." He replied. Phil this time shook his head with another chuckle as he sipped more coffee.

"Have you lost many family?" He asked. Zack returned his stare to the camp fire before he shook his head.

"I'm an orphan so I suppose that makes me the lucky one, what about you?" He asked in response before he glanced back up at Phil.

"I lost my mum, dad and two sisters." He quietly replied, before Zack nodded with a sympathetic half-smile.

"I'm sorry about that, mate." He uttered. Phil raised his thumb in response as he continued to stare into the flames.

"I make a point of never thinking about it and I haven't since it all happened, it's a bit like all of these dead bodies around us, if you think about it too much, that stuff can drive you mad." He replied.

At the Ellington centre in front of the grey steel door, Paul Richards and Reg Simmons stared to the south-east with some confusion, they could see a defined orange glow in the otherwise pitch black darkness.

"It's got to be on the motorway, but that means they're on their way back because we haven't seen one of their fires in days." Reg uttered. Unbeknown to either of them, Handy Cross where Phil and Zack sat was exactly where they last saw a fire from Oxford, it was in fact the same rebuilt fire.

"What do you think could've happened?" Paul asked. Reg shrugged as he continued to stare at the distant orange glow from around twenty five miles as the crow flies. Due to the fact that since the storms there had been no streetlights, no vehicle headlights or any other light pollution whatsoever. All around them with the exception of that single orange glow, was nothing but pitch-black darkness, with the moon and stars in the sky that all seemed bigger, brighter and clearer than ever before. Since August, they had also witnessed so many shooting stars that they would have never seen when the world was so hectic and illuminated.

"If they're still heading this way the day after tomorrow, I'll get one of the others to come for a walk with me to meet them, just to make sure that this fire actually belongs to our three." Paul said as they both continued to stare and Reg nodded.

"That's a very good point, you never know it might be somebody else." He agreed. He turned to head back down into the Ellington centre.

"I'm going to go down to finish the next bedroom now that Jason wants to live alone." He added. Paul continued to stare in the general direction of London, in particular at the bright orange glow.

"I'll come down to give you a hand in a minute." He replied.

Wednesday November 1st

At around eight thirty in the evening Reg, Paul, Alison Dixon and Amelia West stood on the roof at the Ellington centre, again in darkness. This time they stared at not one, but two separate orange glows in the distance that Reg assured them were both on the motorway that led to London.

"If we can see them both from here, they can definitely see each other." Amelia commented. Everybody nodded although none of them knew exactly where the two fires were other than probably on the same road. Unbeknown to them, Phil Smith and Zack Zimmerman now sat at Stokenchurch after a much more casual walk compared to yesterday, to just the one checkpoint and were now seven miles south of Tetsworth where the eight cows were discovered. Tomorrow, they would stop there although only for a break and for something to eat before they continued for another nine miles to Headington, the very last checkpoint and arrive at the Ellington centre on Friday or Saturday.

The main party led by David Wells and Amy Vinton, with the one one already pitched at Gerrards Cross, camped for the night. Ailing Joanna Simpson would never have made it to the next checkpoint at Woodburn Moor like David optimistically hoped. She would however be full of surprises from tomorrow.

"Let's just presume for a moment that they're both ours and they can obviously see each other right now, if they are ours, one of them has to be sitting out there alone, why would they split up?" Alison wondered out loud. Paul had now heard enough.

"I'm going down to load up a backpack and start walking to the first checkpoint." He said. Reg stared at him.

"You're going out there tonight?" He asked, as Paul turned to head back inside.

"Wait, I'll come with you." Amelia insisted, as Paul headed down the flight of steps and onto the fourth floor, she followed him as Alison turned to Reg.

"Isn't walking about at night going to be even more dangerous?" She asked. When Reg turned to her he shrugged.

"They'll be sticking to the main roads, they can follow footprints and sled runs in the snow to Headington tonight, Paul knows what he's doing he used to be in the army." He replied. They both then returned their stares toward the two distant orange glows in the darkness.

"I don't like this at all." Alison quietly uttered. Reg nodded with acknowledgement.

"Like you pointed out, if they're our three, somebody has to be sitting out there alone, what's to like?" He asked in response.

A little more than two hours later, Alison, Reg and this time young Martin Sharpe stood outside in the darkness. They watched Paul Richards and Amelia West head toward the main road wearing thermal clothing and carrying loaded back packs. Both held bright torches pointed down toward the snow-covered ground.

"We've got to be bloody mental." Amelia uttered. They turned right and headed north along the main road that was completely cleared of bodies and other objects. Paul glanced back at her and laughed.

"I already knew I was this stupid but I didn't realise you were." He replied, as they trudged north. Alison, Reg and Martin watched the moving torchlights eventually dull and fade into the distance before they returned their stares to the orange glows to the south-east. After a short while, the young stepson of David Wells turned to Reg.

"Are we hiding or something?" He asked.

"We can see their fires, so if we're not hiding why can't they see us?" He asked. Both Reg and Alison stared at him for a few moments before his question began to register and slowly sink in.

"Do you mean we should build a fire too?" Alison asked. She immediately considered that Martin was just sixteen years of age, he turned to her and nodded.

"If those people are coming here, they should be able to see where we are just like we can see them so that they can't get lost." He explained.

"They already know to stick to the roads, anybody else wandering around would know we're here too because bonfires don't light themselves." He added. Alison and Reg glanced at each other, but they both returned their stares to Martin when he continued.

"I've been reading a fiction novel about an apocalypse to get ideas and to see how the survivors found others, one group in the book had a fire constantly burning so that other people could be guided to them at night." He informed them. Reg and Alison now stared in stunned silence, the strange young man again glanced at Reg.

"Some of them built great big radio masts and they had people listening for others around the clock, somebody was awake all the time so the place didn't burn down while the others were all asleep." He added. Alison turned her wide-eyed stare toward Reg while he chuckled.

'I've never heard him say so many words at one time!' She thought to herself.

"I did tell you he was one smart kid." Reg reminded her. Alison slowly nodded before her stare returned to Martin.

"So, are you saying that we should build our own radio, to listen out for other survivors?" She asked. Martin again nodded.

"To listen out for anybody or any news because if other people are still alive, somebody will already be listening out by now, there are set radio frequencies for this kind of situation." He explained.

"I researched two electronic shops up on Oxford road, one of them specialised in amateur radios so maybe we could find bits and pieces around that area, if anything's still there." He explained, before he returned his attention to Alison.

"We could use your old office to set it up because it's up on the fourth floor close to where the mast would need to be, which is out here." He added. Alison continued to stare at the teenager, she eventually displayed a smile and again slowly shook her head with wondrous awe before she headed toward the grey steel door and as she passed him, she playfully ruffled his brown hair.

"Being a clever little shit is one thing young man, stealing my private office to find other people just so they survive is something completely different." She informed him. Reg burst into laughter before Alison stopped and turned to again face the youngster.

"Would you know how to build this radio thing?" She asked. Martin shrugged his shoulders.

"It's only radio waves it can't be that hard, I could learn to." He replied. Reg nodded, this time with agreement, he continued to chuckle as a result of Alison's response regarding the loss of her office.

"I know the basics of transmitting and receiving, so when you have twenty minutes would you mind clearing out your office for us?" He asked. He then playfully mocked a gasp of horror when Alison produced a single finger in response.

"You want it, you clear it out." She replied, before she headed down the staircase, Reg continued to laugh.

"I'm building living quarters!" He called out as he stared at the now vacant doorway.

"You already finished I checked earlier, I still check on everything you do!" Alison replied, as she made her way along the narrow corridor and back toward the canteen.

At just after two in the morning, Paul Richards and Amelia West finally reached the first checkpoint at Headington. They were now around six miles north-east from the Ellington centre and sixteen miles to the north of where Phil Smith and Zack Zimmerman were camped for the night.

Paul and Amelia pitched a tent and both climbed into it and inside sleeping bags after their arduous trek in the dark. Amelia's bright torch pointed at so many frozen corpses that were partially covered with snow from the moment they left the main road. A plan was hatched as they walked, to leave in six hours to head south for the second checkpoint at Tetsworth and to hopefully later tomorrow meet with whoever was camped closest to them on the motorway.

"Those bodies are a reminder that I'd almost forgotten about, I don't know how you did those cremations." Amelia uttered. They lay inside the tent where Paul stared up into the darkness. He eventually turned his head and glanced toward her.

"It's different for me, I didn't know anyone around here." He reminded her. Amelia nodded with acknowledgement.

"I get that, but they're still bodies, they used to be living people." She replied. It was now Paul who nodded.

"I prefer to look at them in a different way, I burned them because they didn't deserve to be left there to rot in the snow especially the kids, besides we needed that road cleared." He replied. There was a silence before he spoke again.

"I hope you'd do the same for me one day, if we ever find my family." He added. He lay in his sleeping bag and considered the probable fate of his own back at Maidstone in the county of Kent, more than one hundred and twenty miles to the south-east, way past London. There was another silent pause before Amelia spoke again.

"Let's get some sleep, we've got an even longer walk tomorrow." She eventually said. Her thoughts turned to Elms Road where her own partner Mark's sister once lived. She now wished that she had somehow found the courage and strength to climb through the rubble to find them. She believed that it would have at least given her some kind of closure even though it would have been incredibly painful at the time, but she also knew that Alison, Reg and Anita were slowly managing to get through the experience.

Thursday November 2nd

At around one o'clock in the afternoon, Phil Smith and Zack Zimmerman sat just north of Tetsworth where they drank coffee and ate cold baked beans straight from the cans. They both stared at the eight black and white cows that stood in the small enclosed field. Zack again shook his head with disbelief as he pointed toward the fields on the left side of the enclosure in question.

"The thing is, there are seventy or eighty bodies in the snow there, about sixty cars and trucks and even a crushed upside-down bus!" He pointed out, to more chuckles from Phil.

"I've already had this conversation several times with Amy." He replied. Zack continued regardless and still with absolute amazement.

"In all of the fields behind the cows, there are more bodies and cars and also on the right side of it, but that one field has got nothing, just eight bloody cows standing there chewing frozen grass." He continued.

"Don't forget the tree, there's an untouched tree still standing bang in the middle of it." Phil added to Zack's statement. Just then, they both heard a faint shuffling sound that came from their left, they instinctively turned their heads and saw two figures that trudged toward them, they both immediately climbed to their feet.

"That looks like Paul Richards." Phil uttered, he turned to Zack.

"They're from our place." He explained with confusion. He returned his stare toward Paul and Amelia and as they neared, he realised that she was the second walker.

"If this is your first date, you got lost!" He called out, Paul immediately shook his head.

"It's not, I just found out she snores like a pig!" He laughed in response, to a playful nudge from Amelia.

After Paul and Amelia were introduced to Zack, who was more than welcomed at Ellington by both, the story regarding the Hillingdon survivors was revealed. It was also explained that the two young men left the underground station a day earlier than the main group to make quicker time back to Oxford and that David and Amy were bringing eleven more with them, as the four sat around a small gas burner and drank steaming hot chocolate.

"Now the two fires make sense." Paul said. Amelia still stared at the field in front where the eight cows grazed frozen grass inside the partially snow cleared enclosure.

"I just can't see how they…" She began. Zack rigorously nodded.

"Yep, we've done that one a few times now." He interjected. Amelia stared at him, she slowly shook her head and returned her stare toward the cows before Phil spoke.

"On the way down here, that one was named Amelia and the one next to it Alison, that one there is Gwen and that one is Anita." He informed her, as he pointed toward four different cows. The three men chuckled when Amelia glared back at him.

"Exactly *who* named them?" She asked, as Phil continued to laugh.

"Alright, I can't lie, it was Amy." He lied. Amelia nodded with her own version of a mocking playful glare before she turned her attention to Paul.

"That's fresh milk standing in that field, is there any way we could get them over to Ellington?" She asked.

"They're also beef burgers in waiting." Phil added. Amelia then returned her attention to Zack.

"So, tell me about the people coming this way with David and Amy." She said. Zack glanced back at her and he seemed to ponder for a few moments, but there was good reason for his delayed response.

"I think Harrison is, or at least was a copper and Umar was an underground railway engineer." He began. He then seemed to again consider for a few moments. He went on to explain that Katie and Lisa were both nurses from the same hospital as Sue, a Psychologist and Deborah was a florist. Jackie and Maria were both care workers and Tess was a social worker or something, but he believed that she also did Karate, Karen was a cook at the same hospital. There was one more pause, this time an anxious one before he continued.

"Jo was a student, but she's pregnant." He finally revealed. He then glanced at Phil who stared back at him with disbelief before Zack returned his stare to Amelia.

"Nobody said anything in case she was left behind." He revealed, regarding the ailing young girl on the platform bench. Amelia raised her eyebrows with stunned surprise.

"She's the most important person in the world if she's carrying a baby, so David and Amy don't even know she's pregnant?" She asked. Zack shook his head before Paul then turned to Phil.

"You haven't got a tent here, where have you been sleeping?" He asked. Phil informed him that at every other checkpoint was a pitched tent, that there was one down at Stokenchurch where he and Zack stayed last night and another up at Headington where Paul and Amelia spent the night. Amelia stared at him with confusion.

"I know we didn't build a fire last night, but I didn't see a tent up there." She insisted. Phil shrugged before he sipped hot chocolate.

"It's definitely there behind a broken wall." He replied. Amelia and Paul glanced at each other before they both returned their stares to him.

"We put a tent up in front of a broken wall last night." Paul assured him. Phil again laughed.

"If you walked around to the other side of it, you could've climbed straight into ours." He assured them. they both continued to stare at him.

"I'm very quickly beginning to hate you." Amelia uttered. Phil playfully mocked a defensive karate stance using his hands while he sat.

"I'm ready, bring it." He teased, before Amelia smiled back at him.

"I already started teaching my karate classes on the day that you lot left, so when all we get back I'll be bringing it alright." She replied with a grin. She then playfully winked at him.

"Guess who's going to be my first volunteer for unarmed combat." She chuckled. Phil stared wide-eyed back at her.

"Oh crap, is it Jason again?" He asked, to laughter from both Paul and Zack while Amelia rigorously shook her head in response.

"Foot, mouth and filled." Zack then said and Paul nodded.

A short while later, Phil and Zack were told to make their way north to Headington, then tomorrow back to Ellington to inform Reg that more were coming. Paul and Amelia would continue south toward Stokenchurch where a pitched tent awaited them. They would hopefully meet up with the main group tomorrow at somewhere around Handy Cross, they also now knew about the farmhouse on the right side of the motorway.

Friday November 3rd

Reg Simmons sat inside the canteen with Alison Dixon, Vikki Annis and Emma Todd where he explained the reason that Paul and Amelia left very late the night before last, due to the mystery of the two burning fires some distance away on the motorway.

"Why would the three of them split up?" Vikki asked. Reg could only shake his head, he simply didn't have any answers until at the very least Paul and Amelia returned. Everybody else sat around other tables and quietly chatted while Gwen Vella and Anita Stone stood behind the serving counter and quietly talked between themselves.

The canteen door suddenly burst open and Phil Smith stood in the doorway and displayed a beaming grin, as he removed the clear plastic goggles that he had worn every day since they left. Zack Zimmerman stood beside him, everybody now stared in silence at the stranger, as Jake Jarrett who again sat with only Charlotte Strickland, suddenly burst into hysterical laughter.

"Look in the mirror, you idiot!" He cackled. He then climbed to his feet and walked across the canteen where he hugged his best mate. Phil eventually turned his attention to the table where Reg climbed to his feet and he also walked toward them as everybody else began to do the same.

"This is Zack, we found him at Hillingdon underground station with eleven more." Phil announced. Reg immediately shook Zack's hand and officially welcomed him to the Ellington centre as everybody surrounded them and almost all welcomed Zack too. Reg returned his attention to Phil, when he revealed that they met with Paul and Amelia yesterday. He also told Reg about the eight cows at Tetsworth and that Paul and Amelia were now heading south to meet with the main group.

"We saw three fires last night and we knew that one belonged to Paul and Amelia, so Dave is bringing the rest of them up here too?" Reg asked. Phil nodded while others continued to greet Zack with open arms.

"Zack will get you up to speed on who's coming back with Dave and Amy, but one of them is pregnant." Phil revealed. Reg and Alison stared at each other because they both immediately recognised the importance of Joanna Simpson, Alison leaned a little closer to Reg.

"It looks like young Martin might have to learn to become a midwife after all then." She whispered. Zack turned to her after he heard her whispered comment.

"Two of them heading up here are nurses and one is a Doctor, she's in good hands." He assured her, before all conversations were suddenly interrupted.

"Are you telling us that we're going to have twelve more mouths to feed and then a bloody baby?" Jason Moran asked, before Alison glared back at him.

"Yes, that's exactly what we're telling you, they're coming here like you did and they'll be welcomed just like you were!" She angrily snapped. She slowly shook her head with disbelief. Phil Smith turned to his best friend Jake who passed him a small handheld mirror courtesy of Gwen Vella and he stared into it. He suddenly shrieked with horror when he saw that his face was very, very tanned due to the exposed time spent on glaring white snow, but he had been wearing goggles for most of it and they left two large white defined circles around his eyes. Jake bent over with more hysterical laughter.

"You'd think one of those sods would have said something a week ago." Phil quietly uttered, as he slowly shook his head before he turned to Zack.

"Some new mate you're turning out to be, why didn't you tell me?" He asked. Zack shrugged his shoulders as he also laughed.

"You didn't ask and besides, Dave and Amy, then Paul and Amelia asked me not to." He replied. Reg turned to his apprentice Jake.

"Put her down, we've got more bedrooms to build." He said, to more stifled laughter from everybody.

With her arm linked through Joanna Simpson's, Amy Vinton trudged at the back of a very long staggered line on the deep compacted snow. They walked at a much slower pace than David, Umar and Harrison who all pushed and pulled the sled around bodies way ahead in the distance with everybody else in the long staggered line behind it. Every hour on the hour, everybody would stop at the sled so that the two at the very back could slowly catch up.

Twenty three year old nurse Katie Chamberlain cautiously stepped around frozen bodies back to where Amy and Joanna also briefly stopped. She checked the young student's pulse before they all continued to walk together.

"The sled has stopped again that was a bloody quick hour, how are you feeling?" She asked. Joanna nodded as she took in another long deep breath through her nose and exhaled it through her mouth with pursed lips just like she was taught.

Way ahead at the halted sled, David Wells and Paul Richards embraced before Amelia hugged him too. They both then shook hands with Harrison and Umar. Paul informed David that they met with Phil and Zack yesterday and that the two young men would by now be at the Ellington centre.

"Which one of this lot is Joanna?" He asked. David nodded south down the staggered line that very slowly headed toward them.

"She's right at the back, Amy's staying with her so that she doesn't get left behind, she's not well so they're walking slower than the rest of us." He explained and Paul nodded.

"She's not ill son, she's pregnant." He replied. David's eyes widened with stunned surprise, as Umar and Harrison knowingly glanced at each other.

Paul and Amelia made their way toward the back of the line and as they walked, they both stopped and shook hands with each individual until they eventually reached the last three. Amy and Amelia embraced while Paul took Joanna's hand in his, he began to walk her toward the sled. As they passed other Hillingdon survivors, they all stopped and watched in anxious silence until Paul finally sat Joanna down onto the top of the laden sled.

"She's pregnant, Zack told us as soon as he knew she wouldn't get left behind." Amelia revealed. She then turned to Katie.

"She's the most important person here, we'd never even think about leaving her and the baby." She assured the nurse, whose eyes began to fill with tears as she smiled back at Amelia.

"Thank you." She quietly croaked, before Amy interrupted the conversation.

"Why didn't she tell me?" She asked, again Amelia smiled at her.

"This lot all vowed to stick together no matter what, they thought she might get left behind as a burden, but that's not important she hasn't lied to you, she just didn't say anything and you have no idea of how proud of you I am." She replied.

"I can walk, why do I have to sit here?" Joanna nervously asked. Paul and Umar joined Harrison and David at the front of the sled and all four began to pull on the long thick ropes.

"We're taking you home faster so that you can be pregnant in comfort." Paul replied with a chuckle. The other three men laughed before Sue Cole and Tess Morking joined and started to push the sled from behind and just like Katie Chamberlain a short while ago at the back of the line, Joanna gasped as her eyes filled with tears of utter relief.

"Reg should be having a cow about now if Phil and Zack are there, the poor old sod only just finished building

Jason's private accommodation." Paul chuckled. David laughed as they all manoeuvred the sled northbound.

"Talking of cows, did you meet them?" He asked, as six now pulled and pushed the sled with much more ease, even with Joanna seated on top of it.

"Amelia fell in love with one of them, I think Phil named it Alison." Paul replied. The main group with help from Paul Richards and Amelia West, who walked at the back of the line with her arm through Amy's but at a much better pace, would now make it to Stokenchurch during the early hours of that evening.

That night back at Ellington, Reg concluded from the single distant glowing fire, that they had obviously all met up and were now heading back together.

"It's funny now that there's no internet, no mobile phones and you can't take a simple drive down there, we still managed to communicate messages to each other." Reg quietly said to Alison. There was a brief silent pause before he spoke again.

"That was a real mission, they didn't make it to the city centre, but we're going to have a baby here, I'd swap that any day of the week." He quietly said as they stood and stared. Alison passed her arm through his as they both watched the single orange glow and she eventually nodded.

"You're going to make an excellent great, great, great grandad, you'll be able to bore the baby to sleep every night reading it engineering manuals." She replied with a chuckle. Reg nudged her using his shoulder.

"Shut it." He uttered. He shook his head to more giggles from Alison while they both continued to stare at the burning orange glow in the distance.

Monday November 6th

Alison Dixon sat behind the desk inside her office with only Jason Moran opposite and it was at her suggestion. She felt that they both needed to clear the air after his most recent outburst when Zack arrived three days ago. Nobody sat with them because they definitely needed to clear that air in private.

"So, what exactly is your problem with other people here?" She calmly began. She sat back in her chair and stared straight at him. Jason appeared to ponder for a few moments before he turned his own stare toward her.

"As we're clearing the air, do you mean with people in general or just you?" He asked. Alison raised her eyebrows before she opened her mouth to speak, but he cut her off and continued because today, Jason would have much to say to her.

"I don't have a problem with anybody else, it's just you and your bitch of a friend." He informed her. Alison correctly assumed that he referred to Amelia because he always spoke to Reg and most others in a civil way.

"Do you remember the day we all arrived here?" He then asked. Alison almost nodded in response.

"Of course I remember, but your problem with us, is it because you can't dictate everything like you used to, or because we're women who dare to answer you back, or is it maybe that Amelia can kick your arse whenever she likes?" She sarcastically asked. It was now her turn to continue.

"I have a massive problem with you too as we're clearing the air, mine is that when the storm hit us that night, you sent those five women outside but then hid in the underground car park yourself and to me, that means you knew how bad it was out there to go and hide below ground to survive it." She pointed out.

"And what was all of that crap about twelve more mouths and a baby to feed, on the day that Zack arrived here?" She asked. They again stared at each other for a few moments.

'Ok, you're not being very constructive.' She told herself, before she eventually continued.

"At some point in the future, we're going to have to send more scavenger parties further and further out and now we have more people to do it." She added and Jason actually nodded.

"Yep I get that and in truth, I don't have a problem with them coming here, my only real issue is with you and that other slut." He replied. Alison took in a long deep breath and sighed.

Name calling, really?" She asked, but Jason wasn't finished.

"On that first day when we all came here, my wife and kids might have still been alive but you stopped me having any help to go and find out, so you might see why I think that every breath you two take is just wrong." He quietly and calmly informed her.

"We'll never know for sure, but as far as I'm concerned you're both probably responsible for the deaths of my entire family along with almost everybody else's here." He still very calmly continued.

"What if any of these people still had living family members, family members who desperately needed help when the snow started to come down?" He then asked. Alison's heart pounded against her chest. She stared back at him with a combination of anger and guilt as she listened, although the sudden rush of guilt that she felt wasn't from any belief that she was responsible for anybody's death like he claimed, but because she could see that he genuinely believed what he was saying.

"That's a ridiculous thing to say, everybody here lost everybody they knew that day including me!" She angrily reminded him. Again he very calmly nodded with acknowledgement.

"You don't think you killed at least some of their families when you stopped anybody from going to find out?" He asked.

"I'm only asking because I definitely do." He assured her. Wendy Jones suddenly appeared at the opened doorway, Alison glanced up to see her there, which told Jason that somebody now stood behind him.

"Reg asked me to come down to let you know that Dave and the others are walking down the road." She informed Alison, who nodded. Jason climbed to his feet, he passed Wendy in the doorway without saying another word, the teenage girl stepped inside.

"He could've gone to his house to find his family on his own without putting anybody else at risk if he really wanted, but he didn't and nobody else thinks what he just said." She quietly assured Alison.

"If it wasn't for you and Reg, we'd all be dead by now." She added. Alison smiled up at her for a few moments as she fought back emotional tears for her own lost family.

"Shall we go up and welcome our new housemates?" She asked with a croaked voice, as she also climbed to her feet.

Saturday November 11th

Five days after seventeen became twenty nine, the flatbed truck very slowly rolled northbound along the deep snow-covered main road toward the roundabout, where back in September Alan Robbins discovered his partially buried father. A third mass cremation was planned for today, this time on the Southern Bypass Road from the same roundabout, but in a south-easterly direction for around three miles to what remained of the superstore where Alan, Jason Moran and other survivors worked on the night shift prior to the storms.

Tomorrow, a shorter run and cremation was planned for around a mile to the next roundabout and the same on Monday for another three miles and so on from roundabout to roundabout, until seven cremations would lead them to the eight cows at Tetsworth. A plan was formulated to bring the cows back to Ellington, which was of course surrounded by fields for them to graze on that would at some point soon also be cleared of the dead prior to their arrival.

Seated on the long flat wooden bed at the back of the truck was David Wells because his partner Ruth, young Martin Sharpe's mother travelled to Shropshire before the storms which meant she couldn't possibly be one of the corpses up on the roads, although again, he could possibly recognise some of the patrons from his wine bar, but he was prepared and willing to accept that.

Alan Robbins sat beside him as he had already discovered and cremated his only living relative, the soldier Zack Zimmerman who was an orphan, not from the area was seated with them as was the Hillingdon police officer

Harrison Bax. Because of the somewhat eerie task ahead that all but one of them had never undertaken, they sat in silence as the truck travelled northbound at a much, much slower speed than usual during the now more frequent scavenging fuel runs.

Inside the cab, Paul Richards sat beside the passenger side window with Hillingdon florist Deborah Lloyd, a very nervous Emma Todd sat on the driver seat and stared wide-eyed at the absolutely cleared, snow-covered road ahead.

"How the hell do you drive these bloody great big things in traffic?" She asked. Both passengers chuckled before Deborah leaned closer and glanced at the speedometer, she turned her stare to the eighteen year old completely novice driver.

"You sped up, we're nearly doing five miles an hour now!" She giggled. Emma nodded without removing her terrified stare from the vacant road ahead.

"Yeah, we'll see how you do later when you have to drive the bloody thing back!" She replied, with a giggle of her own.

"You'll both get used to it over time, but we need more people than just me and Zack to be able to drive them just in case something happens to one of us." Paul reminded them.

"Emma, I wouldn't worry too much about traffic." He then added. The two women nodded with more giggles before Emma nervously spoke again.

"How do I turn the windscreen wipers on?" She asked with more panic in her tone. When Paul glanced ahead, he saw that right in front of him was a single wet splatter that he watched slowly trickle down the windscreen.

"Stop the truck!" He suddenly instructed. As soon as Emma slammed both feet down onto the brake and clutch, Paul opened the passenger door and jumped down onto the deep compacted snow where he stared up at the greying sky.

'Well this might be really, really good or really, really bad.' He thought to himself as he studied the heavens.

"Is everything alright?" David called out. Paul walked to the back of the truck where he stared up at him.

"I think it's about to rain." He replied. David stared up at the darkening sky as did everybody else seated on the flat bed. A single ice cold splatter then landed on his cheek, he again stared down at Paul as he wiped it away and with that, Paul walked back and around the front of the cab and opened the driver side door where Emma stared down at him.

"Move over, we're going back." He told her. As he climbed up into the cab, Deborah slid across so that Emma could sit between them.

"I thought we wanted it to rain." She quizzed. Paul nodded as he slammed the door shut and immediately drove the truck forward.

"We do, but we need to be back at home when it happens, rain is the only weather we haven't had and if it's going to come down anything like the snow did, it's going to be all hands on-deck because we live underground." He reminded her.

"At least this time we've been able to plan for it." He added, as the truck headed north at a faster speed toward the large roundabout.

Sunday November 12th

At just after nine in the morning, most of the larger community stood on the earlier cleared wet grey car cark roof. It hadn't heavily rained although it had been very lightly 'spitting' since the first splatter on the windscreen of the truck yesterday, but still nothing more.

"It would be great if it kept doing this for the next ten years until the snow was all cleared." Tess Morking uttered. Almost everybody agreed with her wishful statement. They all however believed that lady luck disappeared never to return back in August, on the day that the picturesque town of Porthleven was completely ripped apart by Ella.

Since that fateful night, everything that happened to the world did so with a vengeance and with absolutely devastating consequences. Nobody believed that the very first rainfall would be any different or that they would be that lucky, they just waited for it to come and they waited with dread.

"How do we know it's going to come down like never before?" Psychologist Sue Cole asked, Reg turned to her.

"We don't, but I'm of the belief that what happened back in August was finally the result of global warming and this extreme weather aftermath is Mother Earth correcting herself, but of course nobody is a scientist." He replied.

"Yesterday was a day completely wasted." Paul Richards sighed. David Wells beside him nodded with agreement.

"We could always go back and start again if you like, just remember to put your foot down if it comes down hard while we're up there." He replied. There was a momentary pause before he spoke again.

"To be honest if I'm going to drown, I don't really care if it happens here or up on the road, we might as well be constructive while we wait for it." He added with a chuckle.

That same evening, Reg, Jake Jarrett and railway engineer Umar Okur stood in front of the grey steel door. They watched the long bright orange burning glow of what they would soon discover was another two hundred and sixty eight burning bodies that would later turn to ash up on the Eastern Bypass Road. The bright headlights of the truck could be seen as it slowly trundled down the main road on its way back toward Ellington while the rain continued to merely spittle.

"Maybe we should take turns to watch from out here through the night, just in case it decides to come down while everybody's asleep." Umar suggested. Reg turned and he studied the line of dirt filled sandbags that were stacked twelve high in front of the large, closed roller shutter door that led to the sloped delivery area and maintenance workshop.

"The three of us can do watches for four hours each tonight, those five mad buggers can get some sleep because if I know them, they'll be going back up there early tomorrow to get the next one done." He replied, he then turned to Jake.

"You do the first four hours from now and wake Umar up and I'll do the last four, if it starts to come down hard, wake everybody up and get them all up to the canteen." He said. Jake nodded as Umar studied the same sandbags for a few moments before he again turned to Reg.

"Surely this place was designed to handle heavy rainfall." He interjected, Reg nodded.

"It was and you can't see it, this car park very gently slopes toward the river, but that's already overflowing even without all of this snow turning to even more water, if the storm, the hailstones and the snow are anything to go by, the rain probably isn't going to be merely heavy, is it?" He asked in response. Umar returned his stare to the headlights of the truck as it trundled down the main road toward them.

"Good point, none of us have been that lucky so far." He uttered. This time Reg shook his head.

"So for the first time, this time we're ready for it." He replied.

Sometime later, Reg, Paul and David stood around two joined tables inside the canteen where they stared down at a large map of Oxford and the surrounding areas. Paul reached forward and placed his forefinger down onto it.

"That's where we're up to." He informed Reg who nodded with acknowledgement.

"Dave you're local, do you know where the two hospital buildings used to be?" He asked, before David stepped forward.

"The Churchill was just up on the left of where we start tomorrow and the Warneford right behind it." He replied.

Once again Reg nodded before he glanced up from the map.

"It might be a good idea to raid whatever's left of them both, to see if you can find medical supplies for Katie and Lisa to use." He suggested, David agreed.

"We can do that while the bodies burn all the way up to the first walking checkpoint at Headington." He suggested. The conversation then turned to the ground conditions considering that no torrential downpour had yet occurred, but it was still lightly 'spitting' more than twenty four hours after it started.

"The main road outside here is getting a bit slushy because we're driving up and down it every day, but the rest of them are so compacted they're still ok to walk and drive on." Paul explained, as the canteen door opened.

"I just wish it would pour down for a couple of days solid and get it over and done with." Amelia West said with a chuckle, as she entered with Tess Morking. Everybody nodded because they all thought the same after they had anxiously waited and waited for the next catastrophic event to occur.

"So tomorrow, let's get the bodies cremated right up to Headington and while they burn, we'll have a look around whatever remains of those two hospitals." David suggested, as everybody again stared down at the large map.

Tuesday November 14th

The very light rainfall abruptly stopped during the early hours of the morning. It didn't pour like everybody expected with utter dread, although thanks to the continuous driving up and down the nearby main road along with the light rain, there were vague dotted signs of what looked to be black tarmac beneath the snow. On this day, the skies were clear and bright blue like never before due to a distinct lack of pollution in the atmosphere as Mother Earth continued to correct herself.

At around three in the afternoon, nurses Katie Chamberlain and Lisa Betts walked arm in arm on both sides of the pregnant student Joanna Simpson around the snow-free car park roof. She was now showing a small bump, they believed that she had to be at least four months by now maybe even five, but the previous technology to determine anything with precision was no longer available and she of course earlier suffered borderline malnutrition, but they could determine that the baby's heartbeat was thankfully very strong.

As the three women casually strolled and chatted at the far end of the car park near to the main road, maintenance duo Umar Okur and Jake Jarrett worked to fix mountings into the concrete beside the grey steel door, to attach a triangular shaped sixty feet tall radio mast that was already constructed, mostly from scrap metal in twelve feet sections down at the basement level workshop. Reg drilled holes into the wall inside Alison Dixon's office to connect it when it was later erected.

As they all busied themselves with the early stages of construction and the three women walked for exercise, the other younger women Amy Vinton, Emma Todd, Wendy Jones, Maria Nightingale and Charlotte Strickland clothes shopped on the third floor, just to reinstall some sense of normality at the suggestion of Alison Dixon. They all tried on outfits that were approved or disapproved by the others and of course there were no spending limits. Emma Todd in particular would later leave with twelve new pairs of shoes amongst many other items.

Martin Sharpe sat alone inside the dimly lit bookshop, where he meticulously hand drew maps with detailed landmarks and specific buildings, copied from a larger map in preparation for a plan that Reg still pondered upon.

The glowing fire up at Headington was started early in the morning, after the remaining bodies were last night laid onto the roadside, where pitch-black smoke now billowed up toward the skies. The two nurses with their priority patient watched the truck as it rolled down the main road toward them and as it neared, Paul Richards flashed the headlight three times. To prove a point regarding that nonchalance, you no longer gasp at the thought of yet another mass cremation.

An hour or so later, Katie stood on the third floor promenade with her arms folded in front of her. She watched Paul, David, Zack, Harrison and Alan push shopping trolley after shopping trolley taken from the supermarket. The seemingly endless flow were all completely filled with medications and other supplies that were retrieved from the remains of Oxford's Churchill and Warneford hospitals, after it was discovered that both had completely undamaged underground medicine vaults.

"There wasn't even any dust on the floor of either of them, once we got the steel doors opened!" David exclaimed. Katie stared at a once empty room that would gradually fill almost to the ceiling with all kinds of boxed medication and various types of equipment.

"That's us busy sorting through this lot until Jo has the baby and right up to its eighteenth birthday." She quietly uttered. Deborah Lloyd and Sue Cole stood beside her and chuckled.

"I've got something for you as well." Paul informed Deborah.

"Because the snow has almost cleared in patches up there, we found a massive allotment full of planted vegetables." He informed her. Deborah nodded but with a dismissive frown.

"It'll all be damaged by the snow and no good." She assured him, but he already also nodded even before she finished her reply.

"It's right next to the university botanical centre and there are samples, seeds and all sorts of stuff in their vault and the allotment is on the grounds, I thought you might be able to work it if we clear it up." He suggested. He grinned when he watched her eyes light up.

"I thought that might shut you up for five minutes." He told the somewhat talkative florist, with a playful wink of his eye.

Sunday November 19th

Outside, beside the grey steel door stood a fully fitted although as yet untested rusty sixty feet tall, triangular shaped radio mast with a ten feet tall, thin radio antenna at the top that was now connected to several items of equipment inside what used to be Alison Dixon's office. Her desk and chair remained and one of the tables from the canteen now stood beside it.

Placed on top of the tables was what looked to be highly technical electronic equipment that consisted, courtesy of the remains of the radio shack up at Oxford road, a repaired Ham radio system that could under ideal conditions possibly reach as far as the European continent.

Beside it and connected to the same system, was a long-range radio scanner that automatically alternated on the hour to pre-set emergency frequencies researched by Martin from literature also discovered around what was left of the radio shack. Inside the room was also Martin's single bed because he would now contently live alone inside the new radio room at his own suggestion.

When the Ellington centre was due to officially open ninety-six days ago, on the same day that the first seventeen initially met, all of the thirty shops were to be issued with a two-way radio handset for security and crime prevention purposes, they were linked to a system that was already installed inside what was then Alison's office. The system of forty handsets in total remained, the range would be greatly boosted because it was also now connected to the tall mast outside. At times, some of the survivors would later be issued with one, but the completely flat batteries were still charging in preparation.

The mast was still untested although white noise could be heard from the receiver inside the office but as yet no voices, but at best it meant that if a future long walk was planned, the walkers might be able to communicate with the Ellington centre from out on the same motorway that led into London.

Wednesday November 22nd

At four in the morning, Phil Smith woke everybody and urged them all to meet inside the canteen because outside it was absolutely pouring with torrential rain, less than twenty four hours after the largest mass cremation to date was ignited. He explained to Reg as he woke him, that the rain was so heavy that he could no longer see the river at the edge of the car park from the grey steel door, but the conditions outside were in fact much, much worse than he explained.

The cremation up on the road consisted of eight hundred and twenty eight counted bodies with some identified names and was undertaken from Headington, all the way down the dual carriageway and onto the motorway to the eight cows at Tetsworth, but it would now be completely extinguished thanks to the very sudden, almost impossible downpour.

Most dwellers nervously sat huddled inside the dimly lit canteen and sipped tea or coffee while Paul, David, Phil and Zack stood outside in the pitch dark dressed in wet weather clothing and goggles from the camping store. They frantically pushed water away from the line of now soaked, mud filled sandbags, using brushes that Reg prepared for this particular event more than a week ago when the rain merely drizzled.

Umar Okur, Alan Robbins, Jason Moran and Amy Vinton would take over outside at eight that morning. At midday, Amelia West, Emma Todd, Vikki Annis and Deborah Lloyd would take their turn to be thoroughly soaked through. Those teams along with two more, consisting of everybody with the exception of Joanna Simpson, Anita

Stone, Gwen Vella and Karen Willis who, as a cook now also worked behind the serving counter with more mouths to feed.

Reg with help from Jake, placed twelve open topped blue plastic water butts outside along with eighteen cut-down steel drums that could each hold forty five gallons of rainwater for later distillation and purification. Another thirty seven drums that Paul Richards collected during scavenger runs were ready to join them and would do so very soon, just to minimise the amount of pooled water on the roof itself.

The incredible downpour hammered vertically and so hard that Phil could not see David beside him. The first four manically pushed the continuous growing pools down toward the river and away from the sandbags, to prevent it from running down the slope to flood the entire storage and maintenance areas along with the drainage system. The already overflowed river would however, eventually burst its banks and begin to send the water back. After Reg placed the first water butts, he stood at the opened doorway and watched as he dried his face with a towel.

'The drains aren't going hold out if it keeps coming down like this.' He anxiously told himself. He searched for David in the incredible downpour. David should be almost directly in front of him, but the rainfall was so heavy that Reg couldn't see him.

He knew that if the water reached the emergency drains down inside the sloped loading bay, the water would be sent down to the riverbed, but only after it completely flooded the entire drainage system inside and after that, the river would eventually send the additional water back up the car park toward them and possibly flood every single floor inside the entire centre. It was all dependent on how long this impossible downpour would last.

The Ellington underground shopping complex was of course designed to withstand heavy rainfall, but what they experienced as of now wasn't mere heavy rainfall. It was almost impossible to comprehend and if it continued for too long, Reg knew they would all be in very serious trouble.

The teams worked non-stop throughout the entire day and night with those work rotations turning to six hour shifts to give people proper rest breaks to recover. The incredible deluge didn't look like it was going to ease up at any time soon and because of that, Anita Stone, Gwen Vella and Karen Willis turned to eight hour individual shifts behind the serving counter to feed people around the clock, as the relentless rain continued to hammer down.

Sunday November 26th

The torrential rain just as heavily poured straight down throughout the next day and night, all forty water butts were completely filled and spilling as the exhausted rotating teams continued to urge large pools down toward the river, that by this time completely flooded the field at the opposite side. It was the same field that was cleared of bodies in preparation for the arrival of the eight cows that still stood at Tetsworth.

At around two o'clock that morning some ninety hours after it started, the downpour began to ease off just a little, eventually into an almost normal very heavy rainfall, but everybody outside at the time felt the difference.

At just after nine that same morning Reg, Paul and Amelia stood in front of the grey steel door after the last team was sent inside for something hot to eat and drink. The trio studied the field opposite that was now mostly cleared of snow although it looked more like a lake halfway across because the river in front burst its banks long ago. It was still raining heavily although not as heavily, but many more rotting corpses now floated there. The three of them knew only too well the renewed, almost unbearable stench of death that they had over time become accustomed to.

"Let's have a couple of people out here, just to keep an eye on the river and manage the water back down and away from us when needed." Amelia suggested. The two men nodded before Paul turned and walked toward the main road. Amelia watched him for a few moments before she turned to Reg.

"So how does this affect us when the rain finally stops?" She asked, he shrugged his shoulders.

"Jake's been keeping the water containers downstairs topped up with distilled snow, that water has only been used to fill the cistern downstairs for the showers and toilets so we still have plenty, but when it eventually stops raining there isn't going to be much snow left around here, but as you can see there will be a hell of a lot of water." He added, he then turned to face her.

"I've been giving that some thought, thankfully Oxford has lots of rivers so there's going to be water for years, we just have to adapt and start purifying after we distil and then boil it, but that's still a few months away and I'll figure it out." He added. Amelia then returned her stare toward the flooded corpse ridden field in front of them.

"I know it's been terrible over the past few days, but it feels like the weather's starting to break in some way." She quietly commented. This time Reg didn't glance back at her.

"Let's just hope it stops breaking soon and we don't have to build a bloody Ark next." He just as quietly replied.

Those vague patches of black tarmac that began to appear on the main road a week ago as it slowly turned to slush, were not tarmac at all, Paul soon discovered what they were. He recalled that on the day that they first walked toward Jason's house before the snow fell, that particular road was in fact made from white concrete as he could now see.

Around ten minutes later, Reg and Amelia walked to where he stood in the pouring rain. They also stared, the cleared road only now revealed more corpses that were previously buried beneath the deep compacted snow.

"Oh crap!" Amelia uttered. She stared to the north along the road that Paul had unwittingly driven and walked over so many times. It looked as though there were around two to three hundred additional thawing bodies up to the fuel station alone.

"I wondered about this." Reg quietly commented and Paul nodded.

"It dawned on me as soon as it started to turn to slush because of how deep I knew it was, it's why I just walked out here to look." He replied. He turned as he took in a long deep breath before he sighed.

"As soon as it stops raining we'll start burning bodies, I'm just wondering how many more we're going to find by the time we get to Tetsworth again." He added. He then started back toward the underground complex to inform his team.

The heavy rain finally petered down to another light drizzle on Tuesday November twenty eighth and almost all of the snow was suddenly gone, although every waterway in and around Oxford of which there were many, burst their banks as a result of the incredible downpour that turned the deep snow to even more water. Much of the city centre itself, was thanks to the River Thames just like at London, now flooded.

Paul, Alan, David, Zack and Harrison started a new mass cremation of another four hundred and seventy four bodies on the main road up to the service station, not the two hundred that was initially guessed. They used petrol from there to light the fire and so bodies once again slowly turned to ash on that first road.

They would later burn another one hundred and twenty two corpses from the fuel station right up to the roundabout. A day later, on the Eastern Bypass Road to where Alan once worked at what remained of the supermarket. They would raid another fuel station for more petrol to continue with the dreadful task that they earlier believed was already completed.

By this time, everybody concerned was used to the task and again almost nonchalant, the bodies were no longer people. They had all seen corpses for as far as the eye could see from wherever they walked on any given day, but that renewed stench of rotting death was almost unbearable. Everybody used scarves to cover their noses and mouths as they burned more of the dead.

Thursday December 7th

The stationary truck faced north on the motorway at Tetsworth on a cold bright cloudless day. Eight black and white cows were tethered to four small solid steel eyelets that were recently welded to the back. Standing around the animals were Paul, David, Amelia and Deborah Lloyd.

"So, we're taking them up to Headington and you'll stay there with them for the night and when we come back in the morning, we'll take them down to Ellington." David said just to confirm. Paul glanced back at him.

"We take them down the main road and throw them in the field opposite the one they were supposed to go in, I'll walk beside the cab so shout or let me know on the radio if Emma's driving too fast and I'll slow her down." He replied. He then patted the rear of the nearest cow named 'Gwen' as he walked toward the front of the truck.

"They desperately need milking." Deborah informed Amelia, who initially smiled at her but not for long.

"And only you know how to do that!" She replied with a snigger. Deborah smiled back at her.

"I can teach you, if you like." She sarcastically replied. Amelia rigorously shook her head before Deborah had even finished her suggestion.

Back at the Ellington centre, Reg Simmons sat inside the radio room with Martin Sharpe, where he worked on a revised work rotation when the radio system quietly crackled before Amelia's voice informed Martin that they were about to begin the journey with the cows.

Since the rain stopped two weeks ago, Paul Richards and his team worked tirelessly to clear the roads from Ellington all the way back to Tetsworth at the rate of one, sometimes two additional mass cremations per day. The body count stood at more than thirteen hundred corpses that were previously buried beneath the deep compacted snow. At Tetsworth where they stood, the dark grey ash was still warm and smouldering on the concrete roadside. Emma Todd very slowly drove the truck forward as Paul walked beside, the cows had no option but to follow.

"Keep the speed to your usual two miles an hour." Paul jokingly called up to the cab. Emma showed him a single finger in response after the truck began to creep forward, her eyes remained transfixed on the completely cleared road ahead.

When they reached Headington some five hours later, everybody but Paul and Amelia walked back to Ellington, but they remained with the cows and the truck. They would all begin again tomorrow to reach home in around the same length of time and the cows would settle in a brand new field.

Monday December 11th

Amelia and Alison stood outside where they faced the main road, they stared at the eight cows inside a much larger enclosure than the one that they came from at Tetsworth, the cows still seemed to happily graze as if they never witnessed a thing.

"So, which one of them did that little sod name Amelia?" Alison asked with a teasing giggle, with reference to Phil Smith. Amelia turned to stare at her for a few moments before she shook her head.

"I have no idea how somebody as thick as you managed to get a job as a manager, it's standing right next to the one he named Alison, you moron!" She sarcastically replied. Alison's giggles immediately stopped, Just as Reg suddenly appeared.

"The one closest to the fence is Alison, I recognise her straight away she resembles somebody I know." He informed them both as he passed them on his way to the water butts, the two women watched him for a few moments.

"He's a horrible old bastard." Alison quietly uttered. Amelia chuckled before she mocked a gasp of utter horror.

"Your language is becoming awful, *your ladyship!*" She replied in a mocking upper-class tone, Alison immediately nodded.

"Blame it on the company I have to keep these days." She retorted.

Later that morning, Jason Moran climbed the steps up to the grey steel door and stepped outside onto the car park roof. He immediately headed for the main road wearing a black woollen hat and thermal clothing, he carried a large empty red back pack. When he reached the road, he turned left and headed south for what remained of his house at Abingdon some eight or nine miles away, although the main road south of the Ellington centre was still strewn with thousands of the dead.

That morning when he announced his intentions, he was offered help from several others, but that help was immediately refused because as he pointed out, identifying whatever was left of his family was his responsibility alone.

Some three hours later, Jason stared at a completely obliterated pile of grey and brown rubble at the beginning of Crossland's Drive, it would have been his own and two neighbour's terraced houses, he slowly shook his head.

"You should've gone back to your mother like I said." He quietly uttered. He then walked back to the main road and made his way to the rear of his former home at the centre of the three and stepped into what would have been his back garden, where he stared around at the ground for something particular, if he was in fact inside his own garden, the damage was so extensive that he didn't really know for certain.

'Where did it used to be?' He asked himself. The truth was that he hadn't stepped inside his garden since long before the storm. He lifted rubble and rocks from the ground and tossed them aside. At the first attempt he searched in the wrong place, but at the second he found what was left of

the concrete slabs that were once the floor of his large wooden shed. A short while later, he lifted one of the heavy grey square shaped slabs and found what he was looking for.

Buried beneath, wrapped in clear plastic sheeting was a sawn-down shotgun that Jason's younger brother used to carry out an armed robbery on Sunday April ninth, long before the storms. The weapon along with sixteen cartridges was hidden shortly after his brother Michael Moran shot and injured a police officer during the bungled attempted robbery.

Jason placed the wrapped gun with the cartridges into his backpack, he then searched around for any strewn items to conceal it and to fill the pack with memorabilia, although he recognised none of the additional items including two now filthy toys that may or not have belonged to the children. He made his way back to the main road without ever searching for his estranged wife. Sarah Moran, was in fact separated from Jason and had filed for divorce. He had not personally seen her or lived at the house since July ninth, almost a month before Ella appeared in the darkness.

Neither did he bother to search for the two children, they were not in fact his by blood they merely came as additional baggage when he and Sarah first met. None of the family meant anything to Jason, but the shotgun and ammunition were without doubt a game changer and the sole reason for his request to live alone in his own separate and isolated quarters.

He always knew that he would return to the house to retrieve the shotgun, it was the real reason that he so desperately wanted to return before the snow fell, which begs the question of what would have happened to Phil Smith and Jake Jarret, if Jason was suddenly in possession of a loaded shotgun on that day when Amelia stopped them all from leaving the Ellington centre.

Later that day, he would be the fourth to confirm without doubt that his entire family died during the storm because he found them all. He stared straight at Alison Dixon with tear filled eyes when he revealed the information with a laden backpack of personal possessions slung over his shoulder, possessions that would be taken to his new personal living quarters where nobody had previously, or would enter in the future.

Wednesday December 13th

All of the survivors sat inside the canteen for a meeting that Reg earlier called, they casually chatted amongst themselves as he quietly talked with Umar Okur before his speech began. He eventually climbed to his feet and called for everybody's attention and watched as the quiet din subsided, all eyes soon stared at him.

"Good morning everybody, I have a couple of announcements to make." He began and he glanced around at a few faces.

"Over the past week or so, Umar and I have discussed building a reinforced high wall around this place to protect us and our supplies now that the snow is gone, one conversation has led to another about where to begin building it because we now have cows in a field, but Umar's initial idea was to build it around the perimeter of the car park above us." He explained. Everybody listened in silence, he briefly glanced at Amelia before he continued.

"Some time ago, there was a discussion about the fact that there would be other survivors, that before now couldn't wander around because of the deep snow, but now they can and we obviously have everything that they'll all want." He explained.

"I think we've been ironically lucky up to this point because of the snow and because you're all decent, but not everybody else is going to be like you lot, they'll all be desperate by now." He informed them, he briefly paused.

"None of what I'm now talking about seemed relevant at the time, but with the snow gone it suddenly does and I think Amelia's right, we need to protect ourselves." He said. There was another brief pause as he gathered his thoughts, he then glanced at the Psychologist Sue Cole.

"I had a chat with Doc yesterday about what these dangers might be because she obviously knows how people think, one of the things she told me was that it's human nature to cluster and form groups just like we have, I'm now sure Amelia was right, we do have what they want and there's no police or law out there to stop them from taking everything, especially if they come heavy handed." He added.

"We've got it good here compared to what others will have and we're defenceless, so Umar wants to start building this wall, two miles south of here to run from east to west and he wants it to be sixteen feet high and ten of brick courses wide, it'll be two miles long with a large reinforced gate in the middle, that one will eventually become the known as the south wall." He informed everybody.

He went on to explain that when the south wall was completed, hopefully in around eight months provided no new natural catastrophes occurred, the construction of an identical west wall, again with a large reinforced gate at the centre would begin, followed by a north wall and finally the east wall, Umar then climbed to his feet.

"Think of a square shaped castle or a fortress with a walkway around the top, so that we can keep lookouts up there and if we have to, defend this place on all sides, but still be able to transport things in from any direction." He added to Reg's statements.

"Defend it with what, exactly?" Jason Moran enquired with a new air of confidence since his distraught return from his destroyed home, Reg turned to him.

"Are you going to throw sticks, stones and harsh language down at them?" He asked with a chuckle, Reg continued to stared at him.

"Paul, Zack and a couple of others are going to raid Dolby Barracks down at Abingdon because they'll have an armoury, those two will know exactly what to look for." He replied. Jason shook his head, he knew that right now he could beat anybody, including Amelia.

"When we all first came here you lot only wanted to help people, now you want to shoot them if they come near us?" He asked, Reg rigorously shook his head.

"We still want to help people, Jason you're missing the point we want to help people that need help not the people that will want to take everything we have." He replied.

"How is this wall going to be built and when do we start?" Amelia asked. She glanced across the canteen at Jason to show that unlike him, she obviously approved of the plan, Reg turned his attention to her.

"We're surrounded by bricks and rubble it's everywhere, but the foundation stones are going to be the remains of Oxford castle and between the fifth and sixth courses of brick, Umar want to reinforce it with whatever plate steel we can find around Oxford, but what we're really going to need is lots and lots of mortar." He informed everybody, although he still stared at Amelia and she nodded.

"Let's get started on it, as soon as possible." She insisted. Everybody then watched Jason climb to his feet and he headed toward the canteen door.

"Count me out, I thought we were here to give people help not kill them for coming to us." He uttered before he left the room. He headed for his private isolated living quarters. The hidden truth was that Jason wanted nobody else to be in possession of a firearm just like he now was. The game changer with ammunition was hidden beneath the mattress of his bed for when he had absolutely no choice other than to impose his will, in his opinion for the good of everybody. Paul Richards spoke up.

"I'll start searching around what used to be builder's merchants to find bagged sand and cement to begin with, but people were building walls long before any builders yard was open for business so we'll find a way." He said. Reg turned his attention to Anita Stone, Gwen Vella and Karen Willis behind the serving counter.

"On a lighter note, are we planning some kind of Christmas dinner this year?" He asked. The three women glanced at each other before they returned their stares to him. He was told to mind his own business, by all three in quite obvious rehearsed unison.

Monday December 25th

Just in front of the serving counter, Reg sat smartly dressed as opposed to his usual old dark blue boiler suit. He sat at the end of a table with Paul Richards to his left, Anita Stone to his right and seated at the same table were David Wells, his stepson Martin Sharpe and Alan Robbins. After a not so brief toast made by Reg regarding hope for the future, everybody began to eat a large feast. A short while later, he glanced around the table at people eating and talking, he stared at David and suddenly recalled that he actually walked all the way to the outskirts of London in deep compacted snow and even pulled a large, very heavy solid steel sled there and he then pulled it back, that was more than one hundred and forty miles!

'That was incredible!' Reg privately thought. He slowly shook his head with wonder, there was no way that he could have ever done that, not even his younger self could have done that. Young Martin seated beside David had already, purely because of the way that he thought outside of the box made his own unique place at Ellington. The youngest member of the entire group for now, was the source for more decisions and choices made than anybody knew.

Directly opposite Reg at the far end of the table sat Alan Robbins, who with Paul Richards cleared and cremated so many corpses of humans and animals from the roads. Reg did know the story of Alan's father Malcolm up at the far end of the main road although Alan was unaware and only Reg knew the story.

Anita Stone on his right side, was one of the few to discover her own family at what remained of her house.

Reg knew exactly how that felt as did Alison and now Jason, yet Anita had become one of the most valuable members of the community, a stalwart along with Gwen and now Karen Willis for feeding the entire group. None of the three once faltered, even when it rained continuously for a week, when they switched to eight hour shifts in turn, to ensure that people were *'fed and watered around the clock'* as Gwen described the situation.

Paul Richards in Reg's opinion was an absolute rock, not once had he ever complained or wavered from any task that needed to be undertaken and although he didn't know Paul before the catastrophic events of August, Reg today considered him a close friend and confidant. He then glanced across the canteen at his friend Alison Dixon and beside her Amelia West, he again considered that the two women had absolutely nothing in common and yet they were today the closest of friends, as usual they sat together talking and giggling and that sight as always brought a smile to his lips.

Also seated beside Amelia was the Hillingdon florist Deborah Lloyd, who was becoming a very important member of the team because after the bodies were cleared up at the university botanical centre, she was working the soil and because she was raised on a farm, she also milked the cows and was teaching others to do so, although Amelia was still decidedly not one of them.

Vikki Annis was also a close friend to Amelia, Alison and Deborah, she also helped up at the botanical centre. At the opposite end of the same table was the Psychologist Sue Cole, who had since her arrival set up a small office to sit, listen and counsel anybody that wanted to talk about their losses or anything else. Tess Morking sat and chatted with

'Doc' as Sue was becoming known, thanks to Reg. Tess was still something of an unknown quantity, she was just like Amelia a black belt at Karate although apparently not quite as qualified at second Dan whereas Amelia was a fifth, Reg again slowly shook his head.

'I have no idea what any of that means.' He thought to himself. He slowly turned on his seat and glanced at his apprentice Jake, who of course sat beside Charlotte Strickland who apparently preferred to be known as Charlie. Reg only recently learned that the two had in fact been seeing each other since long before the storm.

Seated opposite Jake was his best friend, the joker of the group Phil Smith who undertook that incredible walk in the snow with David. Phil then made it back with Zack who now sat beside him and they did it in five days. Once again Reg slowly shook his head in awe of both young men for that alone.

'That was incredible maybe that's it, nobody here is just ordinary!' He considered, as he glanced around the canteen. Seated with the four youngsters were the two other pillars of the community and particularly of the canteen, Gwen Vella and Karen Willis who quietly talked between themselves. Reg considered that they along with Anita always kept the entire family running.

'What amazing ladies you three are.' He told himself, as he watched them.

The nursing staff consisting of Lisa Betts, Katie Chamberlain, Jackie Nightingale and her quietly spoken stepdaughter Maria sat around a table with the pregnant student Joanna Simpson, where they all ate and happily chatted as a group. Joanna just happened to glance up to see that Reg stared at her and she displayed a smile, he immediately smiled back at her.

'Are you ok, fatty?' He silently mouthed. He watched her laugh before she nodded. Umar Okur sat at the far end of the canteen and Reg considered what an asset he was quickly becoming, he sat with his friend from Hillingdon the former Police Officer Harrison Bax and with them sat Jason Moran, who for once joined in with the conversation.

Amy Vinton also glanced up when Reg stared at her, she playfully poked out her tongue so Reg did the same. He absolutely admired Amy for the part that she played in bringing the Hillingdon group to Oxford and in particular what she did back then for Joanna. Seated at the same table, Emma Todd also poked out her tongue followed by Wendy Jones who did the same, Reg quietly chuckled.

'You're all horrible little brats!' He thought. Just then, he suddenly spun his head back to his own table with a startled look when he heard a knife gently tap on glass, he saw that David Wells stood and stared down at him.

"I want to make another toast, a much shorter one than Reg made." David called out to the entire group with a chuckle. The din eventually fell silent as he continued to stare down at Reg.

"Without you and Alison my friend, none of us would be here." David began. The sound of moving chairs was heard as the entire group slowly climbed to their feet.

"My toast is to you young Simmons and to you, *your ladyship.*" David informed them both. Everybody inside the canteen raised a glass in full agreement, with the exception of one. Reg slowly climbed to his feet and glanced behind at Alison. She already stared straight back and both now did so with tear filled eyes. she slowly nodded with a smile before she again raised her glass, but this time it was privately from her to Reg. They hadn't lost a single soul since after the catastrophic events of August.

Sunday December 31st

Forty minutes after they searched the city of London and banked the plane right to head north-west to fly over Birmingham, Steve and Hannah Madison saw nothing but more devastation and destruction for fifty miles after circling several vast areas just to be certain. They now approached the southern outskirts of Abingdon, they stared down at more of the same along with thousands upon thousands more scattered corpses.

"Do you think we're somehow the only people left alive?" Hannah anxiously asked through the microphone. For a few brief moments they stared at each other.

"I don't know what I think, we still haven't seen another soul." Steve eventually replied. As he began to bank the plane left to circle over Abingdon in search of survivors, Hannah spotted something incredible down on the ground on their left side. It was something that she hadn't seen since they left Cambridge Airport that morning and flew over Newmarket, Bury St Edmunds and in fact everywhere else, but it wasn't people dead or alive that she saw, she in fact saw none of either.

"Wait, that road's been cleared of bodies!" She excitedly said. She pointed down toward the main road, so Steve immediately levelled off the plane and stared.

"Where are you talking about?" He asked. Hannah again pointed down toward the main road that led toward Oxford. A little further north they both saw a flatbed truck that slowly trundled northbound.

"That truck isn't driving itself, we found people!" Hannah excitedly said with utter relief.

Due to the noisy engine of the truck, David Wells and Tess Morking who sat on the flat bed with the prizes raided from Dolby Barracks, couldn't hear the additional engine from above. Neither could Paul and Zack inside the cab, but when he glanced to the right, Paul saw with confusion that Reg, Alison, Amelia and Sue Cole stood on the car park roof where they stared up at the sky.

"I wonder where they came from." Reg uttered. The four watched the single engine plane very slowly head toward them at an altitude of around four hundred feet.

"I was about to walk up to the botanical centre to see how Deb and Vikki were getting on and I kept hearing this intermittent noise, when I looked up there it was in the distance." Amelia replied.

"We're not alone after all." Reg said, as he considered the situation.

"Oxford Airport is about six miles that way, but it's going to be covered with bodies they won't be able to land on the runway." He explained, as he pointed in the general direction of north-west.

"They're going to land there." Martin Sharped suddenly interjected. When the four turned toward the steel door they saw that he pointed to the completely cleared main road, he then displayed a smile at Reg.

"I just spoke to them on the radio, they're from Cambridge!" He yelled, as the noisy plane flew directly overhead and at the same time, Paul Richards drove the truck onto the car park roof.

The entire wooden floor of the eighteen feet long flatbed truck was filled with piles of rifles, pistols, hand grenades, landmines, and large brown steel rectangular shaped tin boxes that were filled with ammunition.

"What are those things?" Alison asked as she, Amelia, Reg and Sue walked to the back of the truck with Paul.

"They're called general purpose machine guns, they can fire seven hundred rounds a minute we used to have them back in my day." Paul replied, before Sue turned to Zack.

"What does he mean by rounds?" She quietly asked. Zack glanced up at the same twelve, heavy looking black machine guns that stood on the wooden floor on short bipod legs.

"Rounds are what you know as bullets." He replied. Alison stared up at them before she also turned to Zack.

"Those things can fire seven hundred bullets each, in a single minute?" She asked just to confirm that she heard correctly and he nodded. The flat bed was also filled with modern day rifles, pistols and other, smaller machine guns. Paul climbed up onto the bed and picked up a longer, much older looking black rifle of which there were just four.

"I'm having this one, we used these back in my day too, I don't know why they had them down there." He said, those on the ground stared up at him.

"It's called a self-loading rifle, I can't miss anything with this from three hundred metres once it's been zeroed, but it's got a kick like a mule." He added. Reg nodded, but not with agreement.

"We need to create a secured room like an armoury to keep this lot locked away." He insisted.

"Do you feel safer now?" Paul asked. He received no response from Reg because he wasn't a fan of guns as he earlier pointed out, but he believed that they were now a necessity because other people could just as easily have them and suddenly appear at Ellington to take everything.

"Why did you bring landmines and hand grenades here?" Sue Cole asked. Paul turned his attention to her.

"We stripped the place bare, that armoury is just a few miles from here and I don't know about you, but I don't want anything on this truck to be in somebody else's hands just down the road from us." He replied. He then glanced up at the sky toward the north and watched the plane bank to the right, he then returned his stare back down toward Sue.

"We know we're definitely not alone now, Doc." He reminded her.

At an altitude of fifty feet, the aircraft approached the cleared main road from the north. Steve and Hannah saw that many survivors stood on a car park around two miles away and watched their approach. The wheels soon touched down and bounced just past a destroyed fuel station on their right and began to roll down the wide road in the direction of the group.

"Thank God there are other survivors." Hannah blurted through the microphone. Steve nodded as he concentrated on slowing the plane.

"It looks like they've been quite busy." He replied.

London has fallen

An hour or so after Steve landed the plane on the road beside the car park roof, everybody sat or stood inside the canteen and listened to the story of how the couple survived the incredible storm beneath the destroyed tower at Cambridge airport. They all heard what Steve and Hannah had so far discovered today after they flew out for the first time since August. The group also listened to Hannah's vivid accounts of Newmarket, Bury St Edmunds and a broken beached nuclear submarine at Thorpeness on the eastern coastline, before she revealed the truth about the capital city.

"Before we even flew over London, we saw that the Queen Elizabeth Bridge at Dartford had been ripped to shreds, it isn't even there anymore." She explained to the entire group, to gasps of stunned disbelief, Steve nodded to confirm.

"London Bridge is gone too, so is tower Bridge and most of the others and the river is more than twice the width it was, the place is pretty much under water." He added to her statement of fact, Reg then spoke up.

"I used to sit up top when we were moving into this place and stare at the top of Canary Wharf from here, but I can't see it now." He interrupted. Steve stared across the table at him.

"You won't, it's gone there's about a third of it left, so is Big Ben and all other tall buildings and the place is void of life, we circled over three times but nobody survived there, London is definitely gone." He replied. His words were followed by another air of stunned silent disbelief.

"You're saying that everybody in London is dead?" Karen Willis eventually asked. Steve stared at her and nodded before Hannah spoke up.

"There are no Politicians left, the House of Commons is under the River Thames and Buckingham Palace is gone too, you're the first people that we've seen alive today and we've just flown from Cambridge, all the way down the eastern coastline, over London and then up to here." She revealed. Gwen Vella placed two cups of coffee down onto the table in front of them. Hannah glanced up at her and beamed a grateful smile because neither had even seen coffee or smelled that aroma since August.

Alison and Reg, along with Steve and Hannah slowly walked along the darkened shiny third floor promenade during a tour of the entire complex.

"Ali and I, we were already here when it all happened and another fifteen arrived in small groups on the first clear day after the hailstones, the others came up from Hillingdon just before the rain came down." Reg explained.

"If London's gone, we did the right thing back then turning this place into a haven." Alison interjected from behind them and beside her Hannah smiled.

"You've done incredible things here, we've been living in a small basement since August, we finally finished clearing the bodies from the runway yesterday and took off this morning." She replied.

During the guided tour, they were shown the converted medical centre where they were introduced to Lisa Betts, Katie Chamberlain and the pregnant student Joanna Simpson. They both immediately recognised the importance of her and the baby.

Down on the second floor promenade, they were shown the shared living quarters where Reg explained that it was warmer during the colder, darker days before Paul and Alan began to empty the nearby fuel station of diesel for the generators. He also explained that they had by now cremated more than five thousand corpses.

"We wondered how you cleared the roads, you've got a brilliant team here." Steve said. He glanced into one of the shared quarters, Reg displayed a smile.

"It was a simple case of fight or flight and we are a team yes, but we're more like a big family now and we're hoping you're going to join it." He replied. Steve then turned to stare at his wife and he waited for her to speak.

"We're most grateful, we'd love to join you." Hannah replied with a smile, before Steve again turned to Reg.

"Is there any chance we could get the runway cleared at Oxford Airport so that we can borrow whatever aviation fuel they still have? He asked.

Monday January 1st 2029

At the completely destroyed city of Manchester, forty three year old former pig farmer and life-long survivalist Robert Early scavenged at the remains of an obliterated supermarket with his daughters Arya and Hope, chalk and cheese as he often referred to them. At Wolverhampton where they survived the storms and the hailstones, the somewhat enigmatic family hid beneath the ground inside a fallout bunker that Robert built some ten years earlier because he was absolutely certain of an impending nuclear apocalypse.

He was a well-built man of five feet eleven inches with shoulder length wavy greying dark brown hair. Everybody back at Wolverhampton that knew him considered the man insane or at best incredibly extreme, although they were all of course now dead and he was still obsessed with living.

Back in August, when LMS passed over the country for the first time, Robert, Arya and Hope were comfortably safe inside the fully equipped two-tiered bunker beneath the ground at the bottom of his spacious back garden. His wife, the girl's mother Sara sadly died giving birth to Hope twenty two years ago on this very day. Robert raised his daughters alone and today, they were just as efficient and as ruthless in the art of survival as their father, possibly even more so.

Robert's vision and prophecy obviously included cities and towns in destroyed ruins after a nuclear fallout, he and his daughters were more than fully prepared for scavenging before they had consumed all of the stored rations inside the lead lined, bomb proofed bunker back at Wolverhampton. That was where they expected to spend at least two whole years beneath the ground, but this was a completely different type of apocalypse to the one that he envisaged.

He was dressed in a long dark brown leather coat, he carried in his left hand a Machete and strapped to his back were a very long just as sharpened broad sword and a black loaded rifle, both partially concealed beneath his backpack. It was just after eleven in the morning when Robert glanced up at his eldest, his dark haired daughter as she approached him.

"We've still got to make a safe home somewhere around here for tonight." Twenty three year old Arya informed him. His just as strange daughter casually stepped over a rotting corpse inside the destroyed dusty supermarket building, she watched her father nod in response. Her younger sister by just eleven months, twenty two year old Hope suddenly appeared from nowhere and on both sides of her stood two very large black Doberman dogs named Cain and Abel, the four stared at Robert as they all waited for instruction.

Hope was slightly shorter than her sister and in contrast she had long straight light brown hair that was pulled back into a ponytail, both girls were dressed from head to toe in similar, hard wearing dark brown leather.

Arya and Hope also carried what were before illegal, fully loaded rifles and Arya was also armed with a high powered crossbow while Hope favoured a very large razor sharp, double sided axe strapped to her back that she had practiced using every day over the past six years and was now incredibly proficient, not to mention unafraid to use it. She believed that practice made perfect. When her father first gave her the axe, she was too small and weak to even lift it from the floor.

"There's a house just across the street with no roof, but it does have a ground floor ceiling, I just threw four stinking bodies out of it." She informed her father. She walked to where Robert stood and just as nonchalantly stepped over the same rotting corpse that her sister earlier did, before she handed her father a gold wristwatch.

"A present for you pops, one of the stiffs in the house was wearing it." She said. Robert lovingly smiled at his precious daughter and thanked her. Hope then turned to her sister and handed her a gold necklace.

"I expect she was his wife, the other two must have been their kids." She nonchalantly added, while Arya appeared deep in thought, before she again turned to Robert.

"Explain again, what do we do if we meet somebody armed with weapons like us, we don't even speak to them?" She asked. Robert returned his stare to her.

"Let's go over it again, you send the dogs at them first as a distraction, while they're fighting off the dogs you shoot them in the face just to be on the safe side, never let them get the first shot in, always attack before they can." He replied. He then displayed another warm, caring smile that only his daughters ever saw.

"I thought we might head back to Wolves tomorrow, to rest up for a few days." He suggested.

Monday February 12th

At around nine in the evening, most of the community At Oxford sat inside the canteen where they waited for news. Nurse Lisa Betts entered and everybody stared at her before she shook her head.

"She only just started, it could take a day or two she's only a little dilated, she's actually sitting downstairs reading a book!" She informed them all, as she walked toward the serving counter where Anita made a cup of tea for her.

"I expect some of them will be waiting to put Jo and the baby to work by the end of next week." Anita quietly chuckled, she briefly glanced at Reg. The reality was that everybody viewed this event as a truly momentous occasion. When former student Joanna Simpson finally gave birth, the baby would become the first born anywhere as far as anybody knew, since the terrible life ending catastrophe that was August last year. For now, they all returned to quietly talking amongst themselves as they waited for it to take its seat in the table of brand new historical events.

At two thirty in the morning, Zack Zimmerman casually walked back to the centre of the main road to meet with Phil Smith who approached from the northern end, both were armed with loaded rifles although only one knew how to use his.

"Whose stupid idea was it to suggest four hour guard duties at night?" He asked, Phil chuckled.

"What was it again, foot, mouth and filled?" He asked. Phil's question in response was a playful one that he recalled Zack use on the day that they sat in front of the cows at Tetsworth, prior to his introduction to the rest of the community. The former soldier rigorously nodded because the suggestion was of course in fact his own.

"I'm an idiot I know, but at least this is all good practice." He sighed. Jackie Nightingale and Vikki Annis would relieve Phil and Zack in an hour and a half, but for now they both sat inside the canteen along with almost everybody else and waited for the baby to arrive.

Charlotte sat with her head rested on Jake's shoulder while he also slept with his head buried inside his folded arms on top of a table and almost everybody else snoozed, seated upright. Paul Richards suddenly opened his eyes and glanced up as did David Wells beside him, when the canteen door opened and this time, Katie Chamberlain stepped inside and glanced back at them before she shook her head with a smile. Both men returned to their seated sleeping positions.

Tuesday February 13th

At eight in the morning, Gwen Vella stepped into the canteen to relieve Anita Stone who immediately poured them both coffee, they stared around to watch everybody else still soundly sleeping at tables.

"They've all got beds, this baby is going to come when it comes." She quietly uttered. She slowly shook her head as Anita nodded hers with agreement.

"They're idiots the lot of them." She just as quietly chuckled in response, as Karen Willis then entered the food hall.

"Everybody decided to sleep in here then." She giggled, as she headed toward the serving counter. The three canteen workers soon stood and sipped coffee as they watched the rest of the community sleep. Karen pointed in the direction of Zack, Phil, Jackie and Vikki who all sat around the same table.

"Look, even they came back here instead of going to bed after they finished outside!" She quietly giggled, Anita again nodded.

"Unlike me, I'm going to bed so I'll see you two and these idiots in in a few hours." She replied. She passed everybody still sleeping and left the canteen.

At nine thirty that evening, Paul Richards slowly walked south along the main road with his older rifle pointed down toward the ground. When he reached level with Umar's long trench on his left, he would turn and slowly walk back toward the centre and would walk mostly backward to where Amelia stood with her rifle also pointed downward just like she was taught.

'I thought I was done with this crap twenty odd years ago.' Paul thought to himself as he patrolled. He quietly chuckled and shook his head, but that thought led to another which was of his family back at Maidstone. He knew that they were gone although he always tried to never think about that situation and always kept himself busy and his mind occupied. He also knew that solitude and silence with time to overthink were the worst enemies at times like this. He then stared up at the pitch black sky that was absolutely littered with bright shining stars, he took in a long deep breath before he thankfully heard a quiet 'crackle' from his radio.

"Come back to the middle, Anita brought us coffee." Amelia informed him. He immediately started back toward the centre to face south to keep an eye, once there and after coffee, Amelia would just as slowly head north to the fuel station and back while Paul would wait for her to return, always within his line of sight.

Regardless that Amelia had never fired a weapon of any kind, just like Phil Smith she was the deterrent against what Reg spoke of inside the canteen. Nobody that might be watching in preparation to attack the centre to take what they had would have a clue that she, like almost everybody else had absolutely no idea of what she was doing, other than how they stood and walked with confidence like they did know what they were doing.

Wednesday February 14th

"The baby has a very faint heartbeat, the contractions are weak and still twenty minutes apart, she's not even nearly ready to pop." Katie Chamberlain informed Alison, Amelia, Sue, Tess and Vikki inside the canteen, Alison shook her head.

"She's been in labour for nearly four days now, is that even normal?" She asked, Katie shrugged.

"I'm sure they'll both be fine, Jo's ready to go the baby obviously isn't, but we don't have the equipment to gauge anything." She added. She then walked toward the serving counter and was asked the same question several times and offered the same answer, before she eventually made it to Gwen and Karen.

"Hasn't she had it yet?" They both asked her.

That same early evening, everybody once again sat inside the canteen and waited because those contractions were down to eight minute intervals.

"If she doesn't have it within the next three hours I'm going to bed, I'm not sitting up waiting all night again." Paul uttered beneath his breath, to chuckles from Reg, David and Harrison Bax, who all sat around the same table.

Down inside the third floor nurse's station, the profusely sweating and scarlet faced Joanna sat upright on top of the small bed, she took in deep breaths and with pursed lips, blew them back out while Sue Cole sat and held her hand.

"Just get out of me you little bastard!" Joanna screamed, when another contraction began and Sue chuckled.

"I think somebody else should to teach this baby its first words!" She suggested, as Joanna again squeezed her hand. Amy Vinton and Emma Todd sat on chairs directly opposite and glanced at each other with wide eyed utter horror when Joanna let out another loud scream.

"Just get it out, now!" She yelled at Katie and Lisa. One checked her heart rate and blood pressure, the other checked the baby's heartbeat and they very briefly glanced at each other, Emma leaned closer to Amy.

"I'm never putting myself through this, stuff humanity!" She quietly uttered, before Amy rigorously shook her head with full agreement.

"You're nearly there, when the contractions are down to five minutes apart we'll get started." Katie promised. Shortly after, those contractions abruptly stopped and Katie could hardly find the baby's already very faint heartbeat. She again glanced across at Lisa who already stared back at her.

"I've never had anything to do with one, have you?" She asked, Lisa shook her head. They both then stared down at Sue Cole a Doctor, but in the field of Psychology, she also shook her head because she had also never performed or taken part a Cesarean Section.

"Just get it out of me!" Joanna pleaded.

At just after eleven that night out on the road, as Amy approached, she stared at Emma at the centre, both still in a state of horrified shock.

"If you ever see me even holding hands with a man, feel free to punch me in the face to remind me of what we watched!" Amy uttered and Emma giggled.

"Why did Alison and Amelia even suggest we go down there to sit with her?" She asked in response. Amy shook her head, they both then turned to watch Karen Willis approach carrying a large tray with coffees.

"Has she had it yet?" Emma called out. They watched Karen shake her head.

"Nope and as far as I know she's not even close, but something's definitely going on down there." She replied. The two young girls removed coffee cups from the tray and both shook their heads with disappointment.

"Charlie will be next I reckon." Emma said, to a chuckle from Karen as Amy rigorously nodded.

"Good for her, as long as it's not me I don't care." She adamantly insisted. Karen turned and headed back toward the car park roof.

"Or maybe Karen's next to have one!" Amy called out, to more giggles from Emma. Karen stopped dead in her tracks and turned to face them with a look of utter horror.

"I sincerely doubt that, but you younger ladies are definitely prime candidates, there are bets running on which one of you it might be!" She retorted. She then displayed a wry grin as both Emma and Amy rigorously shook their heads. Karen turned again and continued to head toward the car park as she quietly chuckled to herself.

'The best contraception known, let them watch somebody else in labour!' She thought to herself, as she continued to quietly giggle.

Thursday February 15th

At just after four in the morning, with a very heavy and exhausted heart, Katie Chamberlain slowly climbed the staircase from the nurse's station and headed toward the fourth floor with Maria Nightingale beside her. Both women sobbed, they knew that others waited for news inside the canteen, but there were several complications regarding the baby and they now headed there to deliver that news.

The baby's heartbeat had been weak for the past eighteen hours and surgery could not be performed because nobody really knew how to perform the emergency procedure. As they slowly walked from the staircase toward the closed canteen door, tears continued to stream down both of their reddened cheeks. Katie stopped and attempted to regain her composure because of what she had to now do and Maria stood beside her.

"Are you going to be ok?" She asked, as she wiped tears that ran down her own flushed cheeks and Katie nodded. For a few moments the two women stared at each other, both with streaming eyes before Katie again finally nodded.

"Let's just get this done, I'm already a complete mess and I need to sleep." She croaked. Maria slowly pushed open the door before Katie entered the canteen.

She carried in her arms the small, but reasonably healthy new arrival to meet the people that had been waiting to meet her. There was one in particular that she wanted to take the very recently delivered newborn to meet for the very first time.

Emily Dawn Simpson was born at three thirty eight on the morning of February fifteenth weighing four pounds and three ounces, mother and baby were both healthy and Joanna was currently recovering. Katie headed for that one person inside the canteen where she stopped and stared down.

"She's almost an hour old, Jo wants you to be the first to hold her, she wants you to be Emily's godmother." She quietly blurted, still with streaming eyes. She then carefully handed the baby down to the absolutely awestruck Amy Vinton, who also suddenly burst into tears. Amy very carefully took her brand new God daughter while Alison, Amelia, Vikki, Tess, Sue, Emma and Maria's stepmother Jackie all fought back tears, as they watched her stare with absolute amazement down at the newborn baby in her arms, Katie turned to them all.

"If it wasn't for her, Jo and Emily would never have made it here during that dreadful walk." She quietly blurted, as she wiped more tears from her eyes. She was of course talking about the young woman who now held the baby. Anita stood alone behind the serving counter and covered her own mouth with her hands as tears also trickled down her cheeks. Most of the men however slept through the entire incredible moment, or so the women initially thought.

"It's about bloody time!" Paul croaked without opening his eyes. Reg, David, Harrison and Umar all nodded while they also half-slept. They would meet the new arrival at a more convenient and reasonable time of day.

Sunday March 4th

Approximately two miles south of the Ellington centre, a trench inside a field was dug in turns by almost all of the thirty one survivors, but it was no ordinary trench. It was three feet deep, ten feet wide and was now mostly filled with hardened, still settling pale grey concrete mixed with tonnes of added shingle.

The long and straight hole in the ground travelled for two miles from east to west and piled three high beside and along it for around a quarter of a mile, were to date around three hundred large and very heavy dark grey square shaped stones that were once part of Oxford Castle. They would eventually become foundation stones for the sixteen feet high and eight feet wide brick wall.

Umar Okur had made one or two design modifications since the original plans, one of which was that because the two mile long wall would pass over the main road to the left of centre, the first of four huge gates would be situated there, as opposed to its original, centralised position.

The second adjustment was due to the obvious lack of mortar, to lay standard whole and half bricks on top of the grey stones of which they had in abundance, bricks and half bricks were absolutely everywhere. A large oval shaped pit was dug beside the trench and the pit was now lined with four inch thick hardened concrete and plate steel at its base. Beside it another, much smaller trench that ran beneath it where a burner would be positioned.

With young Martin Sharpe at hand, Umar researched the longest man-made wall in human history for the purpose of building methods and techniques for such an undertaking. Together, one of the facts that they discovered was that mixed with the mortar at the Great Wall of China was unbelievably, sticky rice.

It was tried and tested for centuries to strengthen, which was apparently the reason that the mortar between the bricks of the huge Chinese wall was so brilliant white. The pit was now ready to boil rice to add to and extend the use of valuable mortar, but Umar waited for the concrete inside the trench to settle and completely harden for a few weeks.

Three weeks ago, four more cremations were carried out by Paul Richards and his team of Zack, David, Harrison and Alan, to clear what was becoming Umar's building site. The cremations consisted of some six hundred plus bodies, which were by this time completely thawed and rapidly decaying and with them came that absolutely foul, almost unbearable stench of death.

To the south of Umar's trench, was now a home-made shooting range with eight positions where Zack had been teaching others to accurately fire the modern rifles and on a few occasions, the older general purpose machine guns that still astounded Sue and Alison. Fifty metres to the south from the firing positions were eight light brown, upright plywood rectangular shaped targets that were all by now riddled with small holes, as was the high mound behind them.

Back at the Ellington centre car park roof, Steve Madison's light blue stationary plane stood with Reg's large red tool trolley beside it for routine maintenance. Parked on the main road was the flatbed truck that was next in line because both needed to be kept in working order, Reg was now teaching Jake about engines.

Inside the canteen, Reg stood in front of Alison Dixon who was dressed in thermal clothing in preparation for a walk, although not as long as the previous one to London and there was of course now no snow. Others stood quietly talking and busied themselves at the opposite end of the canteen.

"You do realise that I've known you for longer than anybody else in the world and with that in mind, are you absolutely sure about this?" Reg anxiously asked. Alison nodded as she prepared herself.

"Everybody around here is doing something productive and we're talking about going for a walk here, I used to be a building manager I don't have any other skill sets like building walls or driving trucks." She reminded him.

"You can't keep me wrapped in cotton wool forever I have to toughen up, this is me toughening up." She explained, as Amelia approached them.

"If you break a nail come straight back here." She said with a chuckle. Alison poked out her tongue before Amelia began to fasten the zipper at the front of her black thermal jacket.

"I do know how to do my jacket up." Alison assured her, as Amelia continued to assist.

"All you're going to do is walk for twenty miles up to Bletchley with Tess and Amy with a great big trolley to pick up anything valuable, look for armouries, hospitals and fuel stations and find a building there to tidy up to use later, then you come straight back home." She reminded Alison, who nodded with acknowledgement.

"Remember what you've been taught, two of you pull the big barrow and the other one walks behind to keep everybody protected and don't stare at the bodies, Amy already knows how to do this walk from experience, so listen to her." Amelia finished. Alison picked up her modern rifle from the table and for a few moments she smiled back at her best friend.

"I'm good, please stop being such a girl." She eventually laughed. Amelia chuckled too before they hugged.

"I'll be kick-arse in no time." Alison said. Again her best friend nodded as they continued to hug. Amelia just as quietly assured her that, that was quite a scary thought.

An hour or so later, Sue Cole, Reg and Amelia stood on the car park roof and watched Alison and Tess pull a long, four wheeled caged wooden trolley by a modified T-Bar pole, north along the main road with rifles slung behind their backs. Amy walked behind them with her loaded rifle pointed toward the ground just like they were taught by Zack over the past weeks, while they also learned to properly use the firearms. In two hours, Amy would take to the barrow while Tess walked behind, Alison would take her turn at the rear two hours after that, before they stopped for the night to set up camp.

"How long do you think it'll take them to walk to Bletchley? Sue asked. Reg shrugged his shoulders and opened his mouth to speak, but he didn't get the chance to.

"Probably about three days at the slow pace they have to walk, they'll be fine they all know how to do this." Amelia insisted. She didn't glance back at Sue, she stared at Reg who immediately stared back at her.

"They'll be fine, they've got two radios if they do get into any trouble, ten of us will be straight to wherever they are to get them out of it." She reminded him. He eventually smiled before he nodded.

"It's the first time she's been out of here since August last year." He replied. This time it was Amelia who nodded and she suddenly grinned.

"If they do come across anybody dangerous, she'll nag them into submission long before Tess or Amy ever get near them." She chuckled. Reg also managed to laugh.

"That's true, she'll preach health and safety at them for about four hours." He replied. He turned to watch Alison, Tess and Amy now in the distance slowly continued northbound before Sue spoke.

"She desperately wanted to do this, she told me that she feels like a fifth wheel around here with everybody else so busy all of the time." She explained.

Monday March 5th

York

For at least twenty miles in every direction from the ruins that were once York city centre, large and small hand written posters nailed to anything available, could be found scribbled in bold red so that they could never be unnoticed.

'Food water and safety come to York Cathedral'

Six feet seven inches of Abraham Bridger stood beside his only real friend Clive Henderson outside York Cathedral where they watched two large, powerful motorcycles begin a fifty mile journey south-west to Huddersfield.

"They've been told to be back here no longer than two weeks." Abraham uttered in his deep northern accent.

Thirty one year old Bobby Michaels and twenty eight year old Daryl Pritchard were both already competent motorcyclists and intimidating, well-built men which were in fact criteria for the job of scouts, on the chance that they encountered anybody living and if necessary force them to travel to York, particularly women.

The two recently recruited men arrived at York with women, which was another reason for sending them out because if anything should happen to either on their travels, the woman attached to him would suddenly belong to Clive as a reward for his loyalty, this arrangement was privately made with Abraham.

When they eventually disappeared out of sight and the sound of the powerful engines subsided, Abraham and Clive turned to watch the third member of the original team Andy Clarke, who supervised twenty one physically strong men who all worked on repairs, rebuilding the vast Cathedral that would in the future become Abraham's personal palatial home. Unlike at Oxford some two hundred miles to the south, no corpses were cleared in or around York, there was no need because as Abraham pointed out, after the snow was gone they were already rotting to dust quite nicely.

The busily working, seemingly contented men were all very well fed and lived in comfortable, temporary accommodation inside the Cathedral building as payment for their services. The mostly destroyed old building behind it known as Treasurer's House was also a part of his expanding estate. He kept his personal spoils there because it now had a makeshift temporary roof and Abraham currently resided there almost, but not completely alone.

Inside the darkened basement beneath Treasurer's House, thirty two year old Rebecca Hamilton sat in the darkness only partially clothed in one of the corners on the hard cold grey stone floor. The large basement was ironically where the three women, along with the mild mannered Richard Wise survived the great storms followed by the giant hailstones only to find themselves back there, but this time there was no option to leave and there was no Richard, the giant monster was responsible for both.

During lengthy moments of silent solitude, Rebecca often thought about Richard Wise who she had known for three years prior to the storms that he also survived, only to be murdered by Abraham for merely being too small in stature in order to survive in *his* new world. She had come to terms with the fact that the grotesque animal would never pay for that or any other crime that he and his two friends committed because murder no longer existed, neither did rape of which was carried out on one of them every night by Bridger alone, the three women were his personal spoils.

Murder and rape no longer existed, there was no law to deter or punish for them, new laws of the land were being re-written on a daily basis by him and him alone and each night, the evil twisted bastard as they knew him, would unlock the heavy basement door to take one of them upstairs for the night. If any refused him they would be beaten mercilessly, often to unconsciousness and given no food or water for two days. Today their only role in life was to survive and one day escape him.

Kate Musgrove was three months pregnant with his first born child so he no longer had an appetite for her. Kate sat quietly sobbing, curled in the corner opposite Rebecca. Louise sat also curled up across the basement from them both on the same cold hard floor in silence, where she once again waited for her turn.

Rebecca thanked the heavens if those heavens existed, that tonight it would be Louise who would be dragged away and taken upstairs and not her. Tomorrow night would yet again be her turn until one of them also fell pregnant. The one that failed to as he put it, would be donated to the workforce. They both knew that because the evil twisted bastard promised it, as if they could simply make it happen.

Both Clive Henderson and Andy Clarke stood beside Abraham, who watched the wife of Bobby Michaels and the younger sister of Daryl Prichard head back inside the vast Cathedral building to the makeshift kitchen area where they both worked for their keep. Abraham eventually turned his attention to the twenty one man workforce who all sat around on the ground drinking tea and coffee as they stared up and waited for him to speak.

"Guys, you are all the best the strongest men in the country, if you weren't you wouldn't be here, you all know I've disposed of a few that didn't make the grade." He began. He stared down and around at each individual with a seemingly caring smile.

"This country is in ruins, so is the rest of the world and there aren't many people left, there's no law and no cops this is now ours to take and make our own, you will all become Lords of your own country, but we have to rebuild it first." He continued. The keen historian paused and watched men turn to others, some nodded in agreement, others with acknowledgement before they returned their stares up toward him.

"There are people still alive out there who need our help but they might not know it and they might not think they need it, this morning I sent two riders to start looking for them and anything else of value." He eventually continued. He again paused to allow his words time to sink in.

"I'm not one for speeches I believe action speaks louder than words, but as you know I keep to my word and you're all fed very well every day, just like I promised when you arrived here." He then reminded them all.

"You have a roof over your heads but I'll give you more, when this great building is finished we'll start on others and they'll be for you to live in wealth with power and land." He assured them. With each and every word that left his lips, Clive Henderson and Andy Clarke stood at both sides of him and nodded to confirm his promises.

"When we've finished rebuilding York, you'll be given that land, properties, women and servants in exchange for your hard work and loyalty to the cause, there is no other law now, as I speak we rewrite it as chosen men, you are all Lords of the new realm." He added.

"We were all chosen by nature, we're the biggest and strongest." He assured them. There was another pause before he continued. He glanced down at the ground and seemed to quietly chuckle to himself before he glanced back up at his so called chosen men.

"I used to watch the morning news on the telly and before all this crap hit the fan, the world went politically correct and mad, you had to mind what you said and did because you might offend somebody, but that's all gone." He began again.

"We can be as ruthless as we have to be, you lads with my help and guidance will rule this country and it all begins right here at York, you're already Lords and whatever you want is yours by right, nature chose you and I'll make sure you get it all." He continued.

"If there's a house you like the look of, a woman, a car to drive take it they're all yours, but let's get this new capital rebuilt and then go and take what's ours by right." He added. He then displayed a wry grin while those men all continued to nod.

"There's a smashed up Mansion just outside the city not far from here, are you saying I can have it to rebuild?" One called out. Abraham immediately stared down at him.

"When you finish work today, make a signpost and walk or ride out to your Mansion and put it up outside so that others know that building and the land around it belongs to you, I'll sign papers to say it's yours." He replied, there was a final pause.

"Ok, let's get this place rebuilt, get back to work you dogs!" He yelled with that same grin. The entire group, every one of those large, so called chosen men roared and punched the air.

Sarah Michaels was a petite woman of five feet three inches with long straight blonde hair, she possessed blue eyes that stared out from the makeshift kitchen window, where she watched the long haired giant finish yet another inspirational speech. She turned to stare to Claire Prichard who was of around the same stature with long tumbling brunette hair.

"We're not safe here he's a lunatic, did you hear what he just said to them?" She asked in a whispered trembling tone. Claire stared back at her and she slowly nodded.

"We can't leave yet because your husband and my brother are away, we can't get out until they come back." She whispered. Sarah nodded before she walked to where Claire stood at a large makeshift sink.

"Don't you find it strange that the two he sent out are the only ones that came here with women?" She very quietly asked.

"I heard him talking to the bald one this morning, there are other women locked inside a basement somewhere around here so we're not safe, you heard how he just spoke to those men and we're already serving them." She very quietly whispered, as both of their hearts pounded with renewed anxiety.

"If something ever happens to your brother or my husband, we're going to become somebody's property if we don't get out of here." She just as quietly added.

Nothing at Huddersfield but Hope

Tuesday March 6th

At the southern end of a road that encircled the centre of what used to be Huddersfield town, Bobby Michaels slowly weaved his powerful motorcycle to meet with the other rider, Daryl Prichard at a roundabout at the end of the wide road.

When they arrived at Huddersfield from Viaduct Street at the north of the destroyed town, he headed right and Daryl to the left. Bobby rode in an anti-clockwise direction while Daryl rode clockwise and they would eventually meet at the roundabout to exchange information.

The sound of those motorcycle engines would be heard for miles.

As he slowly weaved around decaying corpses, smashed vehicles and strewn rubble, something suddenly moved and caught his eye. He instinctively glanced to the right at Chapel Hill and that was where he first saw her as she just as quickly disappeared out of sight. He headed after her but she was suddenly gone, all he knew as she fled, was that she had long straight brown hair.

'If you bring a half-decent looking woman back here, she can replace your wife in the kitchen and you can have yours back.' He recalled. He knew that Abraham's promise and motivation was also offered to Daryl regarding his sister Claire, so Bobby needed to get to this young girl first.

He slowly rode south along Chapel Hill, but the young girl was nowhere to be seen until he finally reached the junction with Milford Street on his left where he spotted her again, just before she ran between two obliterated buildings on the right side around halfway along the street.

'There you are.' He thought to himself. At the same moment, Daryl Pritchard appeared on his own motorcycle at the top of Chapel Hill. The men stared at each other until Bobby motioned using his hands, first the curvaceous form of a woman, he then motioned for Daryl to turn around to ride south along Queen Street and to turn right and rendezvous at the centre of Milford to entrap her, Daryl nodded before he turned his bike around and rode away.

'Now I'll find you, I just have get to you first.' Bobby thought to himself.

Because there were only remains of partial, destroyed long grey factory buildings at both sides of Milford Street, he slowly headed toward the narrow alleyway on the right side where he watched the young girl flee to. He soon heard Daryl's motorcycle engine now slowly heading south and approaching the opposite end of Milford at Queen Street.

To ensure that he got to her first, Bobby steered to the right and very slowly trundled through the narrow alleyway that led into a small enclosed parking area behind what was left of a factory building. That was where he saw the same girl at the centre with her back facing him, he switched off his motorcycle engine.

"Are you alone?" He called out. She didn't answer but she was by no means alone, unfortunately for Bobby all that awaited him at Huddersfield was Hope. As he dismounted and stared at her with her back still facing him, she held her head in her hands and slowly nodded to confirm that she was alone and she appeared to quietly sob. Daryl Prichard appeared at the top of the alleyway, Bobby turned to show him a flat palm to indicate for him to wait where he was, Daryl nodded. Bobby then returned his stare to the young girl who still appeared to quietly sob with her back facing him.

From his motorcycle saddlebag, he removed a length of thick brown rope that he fashioned into a noose for her slender neck and another for her wrists so that he could walk her back to his motorcycle to then tie her to it. He knew that she would offer no resistance and when he returned to York, his wife would be given back to him. He glanced back at Daryl Pritchard who again nodded, so Bobby began to approach the fragile looking young waif.

Hope, the youngest daughter of Robert Early displayed no rifle and no huge double-sided axe, but that chosen weapon was there beside her, hidden behind an overturned car. Bobby simply couldn't see it or even imagine that she could possess or possibly be capable of using such a ruthless heavy weapon. Daryl Pritchard continued to watch from the end of the alleyway and he reached forward to switch off his own motorcycle engine, but thankfully for him, he didn't have the time to do that.

As soon as Bobby was close enough and without any warning whatsoever, Hope suddenly spun around and violently swung her heavy axe as hard as she could and sliced the razor sharp blade straight through the top of his right upper thigh, causing a long gaping four inch wound and a blood splatter that hit her own face.

"You taste like a mongrel." She calmly informed him, as she stepped forward. He screamed from a result of startled shock and incredible, unbelievable searing pain as blood pulsated from the wound and now continuously splattered onto Hope's left upper thigh. Bobby slumped to the ground in absolute agony clutching his wounded leg, as Hope stood over and stared down at him. She showed no emotion whatsoever as she slowly raised her axe high above her head to finish the job, but she then turned that stare toward the end of the alley at Daryl Pritchard, who stared back at her in a state of absolutely stunned shock.

"You're next, bitch!" She called out to him. At that moment, her father and older sister Arya suddenly appeared from nowhere and two large black Doberman dogs now stood where they stared, snarling and growling at the chosen man, Daryl Prichard.

"See him!" Robert yelled.

Without a moment's hesitation, the two ravenous looking dogs Cain and Abel hurtled themselves toward Prichard. With absolute terror in his eyes, he immediately wound back the throttle and his powerful motorcycle screamed into action. The front wheel lifted from the ground as he sped away toward Chapel Hill. The hounds chased after him, snarling all the way until he skidded to the right and sped north, back toward the ring road.

At the junction of Milford Road and Chapel Hill, the two huge dogs heard a single whistle and immediately stopped before they casually trotted back toward their Master. Prichard bumped over rotting corpses and around demolished vehicles as he sped back toward York without once looking back, but he left Bobby Michaels behind at the mercy of the strange and more than sadistic Early family.

The ruse began when the family scavenged and heard motorcycles from around three miles away as the riders approached Huddersfield from the north. They now wanted to know who the two heavily armed motorcyclists were, where they came from and more importantly, Robert Early was more than curious as to why this one thought it a good idea to tie a noose around his youngest daughter's slender neck. Unfortunately one got away, but the other screamed on the blood-soaked ground in agonising pain as Hope Early along with her father and sister stood over him.

"Let's not kill him, let's have a little chat with the young man." Robert calmly suggested. Bobby screamed in agony and held his gaping wound. Hope then turned to her father.

"Did I do good?" She enquired. Robert glanced back at her before he displayed a loving smile.

"You were very convincing, in fact it made me quite angry that he made you pretend to cry, so tie that noose around his own neck and drag him into what's left of that building, if he even tries to fight back just hit him with your axe again." He instructed, both daughters nodded.

Around forty minutes later, Bobby Michaels lay flat on his back on top of a large wooden dust covered workbench where he screamed in agony as Arya and Hope very, very tightly bound him to it using barbed razor wire while he pleaded for medical attention, as blood continued to pour from his open wound. He was bound by his bare wrists at his sides, his ankles to the foot of the table, his stomach, chest and purposely across the gaping deep wound across his right upper thigh. Every razor barb that touched, pressed harder as it tightened and eventually pierced into his flesh.

"Make him tell you everything!" Robert called out. He sat outside of the roofless building with the hounds where he lit a cigarette and studied Bobby's powerful motorcycle.

'That'll be a good trade.' He considered.

"I want to know his name, where they both came from, how many more are there and ask him why he thought it a good idea to put a noose around my youngest daughter's beautiful neck." He instructed.

From above Bobby's head, Hope tightened the noose around his neck before she pulled very, very hard, she then crouched down onto her knees to strangle him. Bobby spluttered and choked as she used all of her weight to hang from the end of the rope. He instinctively attempted to raise his hands, causing the barbs to pierce deeper into his flesh, before Arya leaned over and smiled down at him. She then glanced beyond him at her sister down on the floor.

"You've got to stop doing that, if you keep strangling him he won't be able to tell us anything, you heard what dad said." She uttered. She shook her head with a sigh before she returned her stare down to the choking, profusely sweating, scarlet faced Bobby who lay helpless in his personal living hell.

"Who are you?" She calmly asked him. After Hope reluctantly released her grip of the noose, Bobby coughed and spluttered in an attempt to regain his breath, Arya stared down at him with a wry smile. She pushed a single forefinger down hard onto the razor wire that as a result, pressed deeper into his opened wound, he immediately screamed with even more incredible pain.

"B…Bobby, I'm Bobby Michaels!" He yelled. Arya smiled and nodded although she continued to press the razor sharp barb deep into his incredibly painful, blood soaked wound.

"You heard my dad's questions Bobby Michaels, where are you from, how many more are there and what did you think you were going to do to my sister?" She enquired. She then leaned down and closer to him.

"In case you hadn't noticed, dad's really pissed off about that last part." She whispered.

Around two hours later, Arya smiled down at Bobby and nodded for the final time before she turned to her sister, as the chosen man continued to suffer in incredible, excruciating pain.

"We know everything he does, he's all yours, make it quick." She uttered. With tear filled eyes, Bobby watched Arya disappear only to be replaced by Hope, who now stared down at him although unlike her sister, she didn't smile.

"So let me get this straight, dickhead you thought you were going to tie me to your motorbike and take me all the way to York to give me to this giant nut job called Abraham in place of your wife, am I right?" She asked. She then considered his earlier intentions and shrugged her shoulders.

"I sort of get that, this is a dog eat dog world and we all have to look after our own." She eventually added. Bobby stared back up at her and silently pleaded with streaming eyes as he lay helpless and still in incredible pain. He had already lost so much blood since the interrogation began, but neither sister did anything to stem the flow, if anything they encouraged it.

"Well Bobby, here's what's actually going to happen, but it's obviously not going to be what you wanted." Hope continued in that same calm, quiet and articulate tone of voice, as both girls were educated.

"My dad wants me to chop your head off and stick it on a pole to leave as a warning for your giant nut job friend when he comes here looking and what's left of you, the dogs will eat." She continued. Bobby then watched her lift her huge heavy axe from the floor.

"N…No please, I've told you everything I know!" He pleaded, as he rigorously shook his head and fought desperately against the sharp razor wire that again pressed deeper as a result, but Hope merely nodded with acknowledgement.

'I know you have." She replied.

With terror-filled widened eyes, Bobby watched her slowly raise the axe high above her head and throughout, she stared down into his eyes but again she stopped in her tracks.

"Before I send you to wherever you're going, I want you to know that after what you tried to do to me, if I ever find your wife and I am going to look for her, I'm going to torture her for days and then kill her very slowly." She calmly informed him. She then launched the axe down with all of her might and sent Bobby Michaels straight to hell.

Those were the very last words that he ever heard, his lights were abruptly disconnected from the living world before his head dropped down onto the floor with a thud and slowly rolled toward the opened doorway where Robert and Arya sat outside.

Hope stared down at her blood soaked axe during a moment of silent contemplation. It was now embedded deep into the solid oak workbench as blood continued to pulsate from his neck. She contemplated only because prior to this day, she had only ever practiced chopping off the heads of live animals at the pig farm where Robert used to work. Bobby Michaels was her first ever human kill and she still wasn't quite sure how she felt about it, he didn't squeal like the pigs did.

"Shall we actually head home this time?" Robert called out to both daughters.

"I'd like to take that motorbike with us and store it for future trade, it'll be worth a lot of food." He added.

Friday March 9th

Abraham Bridger weaved south-west around destroyed vehicles along Viaduct Street, Huddersfield with one of his chosen men seated pillion on his Harley Davidson motorcycle. Daryl Prichard followed on his with another heavily armed chosen man seated behind him. He watched Abraham's bike slow to a stop before he pulled up beside.

At the southern end of Viaduct Street, all four men sat with both engines running and stared at a pale grey head with matted blood soaked hair that was mounted onto a steel pole. The disfigured face was that of Bobby Michaels.

"Show me where this happened!" Abraham angrily sneered with gritted teeth. The men stared at the removed head and contorted face of Bobby Michaels, that they now all realised was unceremoniously wedged down onto an upright damaged signpost.

A short while later, after Daryl Prichard slowly turned right at Queen Street and onto Milford followed by Abraham, both motorcycles turned left into the alleyway where the engines were switched off and all four large men dismounted.

"That's where it happened." Daryl pointed and there was a tremble in his tone. It felt to him like they were returning to the eerie scene of a very recent crime, his heart pounded against his broad chest. He nervously glanced around for the possibility of rabid dogs as Abraham walked across the car park and stared down at the darkened, now dried bloodstain on the ground, he then glanced back up at Daryl.

"You said a little girl sliced his leg with an axe, so where's the rest of him and where's his bike?" He asked with an irate growl, Daryl shook his head.

"I said she looked like a little girl, she obviously wasn't one though." He nervously replied. They both then turned their stare toward the opened doorway after chosen man Stuart Walker called out.

"Abe, you might want to come in here, I think I found Bobby!" He suggested. Abraham, Daryl and the fourth large man Thomas Barker walked to the opened doorway where they all stared inside. Behind him, Abraham heard both Daryl and Thomas gasp at the sight that awaited them. What they saw inside was what remained of Bobby Michaels partially bound to the large, blood soaked wooden table with razor barbed wire although his head was of course missing, they discovered that particular body part back at Viaduct Street.

"Why would they chop his hands and feet off?" Thomas Barker quietly asked. Abraham heard a tremble in his tone.

Thomas, Daryl and Stuart all stared with utter horror until two of them began to throw up on the blood soaked stone floor where three days ago, Bobby's head rolled. Abraham stood absolutely outraged before he stepped outside of the partial building and returned to the centre of the car park, he stood on the dried blood of Bobby Michaels. He then yelled at the top of his deep booming voice.

"When I find you bastards I'm going to crucify you so you die slowly, then I'll pike your heads from York Minster as a warning for all to see!" He hoped that they were nearby and heard his vow, but it wasn't heard, the Early family were long gone. He stepped back into what remained of the building where he stared directly at Daryl who continued to vomit beside Stuart.

"If you ever leave another chosen man behind I'll cut your throat and leave you to die slowly, now all three of you search this town from top to bottom and find these bastards!" He angrily sneered.

Sixteen miles south of Huddersfield inside the darkened Peak District Forest, two black Doberman dogs trotted around the trees that remained, Cain with a left foot between his sharp teeth and Abel with a pale grey left hand between his. Arya and Hope walked behind them, both with loaded rifles at the ready and they stared around for any movement as their father walked behind and pushed Bobby's large black powerful motorcycle that would be used for future trade.

The family headed back toward their underground bunker at Wolverhampton, to rest up and to add the motorcycle to their vast and growing spoils that were acquired as a result of the deaths of everybody else. As he pushed the heavy motorcycle, Robert considered that because the snow was gone and whoever was left could now move around and scavenge just like they did, wherever they travelled around the country would be just as he envisaged, an incredibly violent and dangerous place with no rules regarding what one person could do to another.

"Keep your eyes open, you never know what might be up ahead and keep checking behind us." He called out to his daughters.

Saturday March 24th

At the large roundabout north of Ellington, Alison Dixon followed Tess Morking and Amy Vinton with her loaded rifle pointed toward the ground. They were three miles to the north of the underground centre. The long caged barrow on wheels that Tess and Amy pulled was heavily laden with various items that were scavenged by the trio during both twenty one mile walks.

They also created a shelter for future walkers and scavenging runs that nobody could possibly miss, it was in fact the basement beneath the obliterated, historical and famous Bletchley Park itself, a building that nineteen year old Amy had never heard of. From there, a future, much larger team could camp inside the basement and begin to clear the entire area of all resources to later return to Oxford with more walking barrows that Reg was in the process of building, using parts from shopping trolleys at both supermarkets.

The three day walks were both uneventful, they saw nobody alive only scattered rotting corpses, although Amy did spot a single bird, a tiny Robin standing on a battered fence post that provoked a lengthy discussion as to where it could have possibly flown to and hid when the storm hit because as they could clearly see, the incredible vast storm hit absolutely everywhere.

David Wells and Zack Zimmerman frantically waved to the three women in the distance from the back of the truck as it slowly trundled south past the Ellington centre. The women had by now been away for two and a half weeks.

The flat bed was fully loaded with more large dark grey stones from where Oxford Castle once stood, piled on top of them were red or brown whole and half house bricks and the truck continued south, past the car park for an experiment to begin.

Some two miles to the south of the car park roof, beside the two mile long hardened concrete filled trench with large, very heavy dark grey stones placed on top, Reg slowly stirred boiling white rice inside the deep oval shaped pit using a long, bright orange plastic snow shovel. The water supplied to the pit came from the overflowed river just east from where he stood. Umar beside Jake watched with keen interest.

From the much smaller trench that ran beneath the pit, was a taut white electrical cable that was attached to another that was attached to another and so on all the way back to the fourth floor back at the Ellington centre. Beneath the much smaller trench was a large electric burner that heated and would boil the water inside the pit.

"I want to lay courses of bricks three or four high and ten wide on top of these big stones for about a hundred yards, using the mortar that Jake has knocked up with that sticky rice mixed with it, then leave it for a week to settle." Umar said. Jake turned to him with a little confusion.

"I want to test just how strong this mortar is with the sticky rice mixed in using a club hammer." He added. They all turned to see the truck leave the main road and head toward them on the same field.

"So this rice has to be boiled to mush?" Reg enquired. Umar nodded to confirm, Reg then turned his attention to Jake.

"So what do you think of my idea about building a cabin out here, but inside the walls when they're built, for you and Charlie to live in?" He enquired. Jake rigorously nodded in response as he watched Reg slowly stir the rice.

"Like you said, if people keep coming here to live, we'll have to eventually build a village around the place and Charlie likes the idea too, but she wants to know if it'll have Wi-Fi?" He asked and caused Reg to chuckle. When the truck pulled up beside the trench, Emma Todd switched off the engine before Paul Richards climbed out from the passenger side, David jumped down from the back followed by Zack.

"Alison, Tess and Amy are walking back down the main road." David announced. Reg immediately handed the snow shovel to Jake before he and the others headed back toward the Ellington centre to greet the walkers. Umar stared across at Jake.

"We'll just get on with this job alone then, shall we?" He asked with a chuckle.

A short while after the three walkers returned and were greeted by most of the population of Oxford, inside their shared private quarters on the second floor promenade, Alison and Amelia embraced while their roommate Vikki Annis watched until she also hugged Alison. The three women eventually chatted, Alison told them of the quite uneventful but also unnerving very slow walk to Bletchley, as Vikki and Amelia watched her sit on the edge of her bed where she began to unfasten and remove one of her boots.

"How is the baby doing?" She asked. They assured her that Emily and Jo were both fine before Amelia then turned to Vikki.

"We should organise some kind of welcome home party for all three of them." She suggested. Vikki nodded with agreement, but to no response from Alison.

"And we really should tell her that Reg and Jake made a cinema room upstairs that they're all going to love." Vikki replied, but again to no response from Alison. They both turned to see that Alison now lay flat on her back on top of her bed with one boot unfastened and removed, the other remained completely untouched and still on the floor. Both Amelia and Vikki giggled because Alison was suddenly, absolutely out cold and they both stared and smiled at the sight.

"Bless her, let's go back upstairs before she starts snoring." Amelia quietly suggested, Vikki rigorously nodded.

"I've really missed that, shall we take her other boot off?" She just as quietly asked before Amelia shook her head.

"No, leave the bitch as she is, if anybody deserves it she does." She replied with another giggle. They both left the room and Alison, absolutely unconscious on top of her bed.

Sunday March 25th

At around ten in the morning, Alison stepped into the canteen after a hot shower and carried a small grey rucksack, she headed for Reg who sat alone and glanced up at her.

"Did you sleep well?" He asked with a chuckle. He watched her nod, but then shake her head with utter disgust.

"Those two cows left me sparked out on my bed all night with one boot on!" She replied as she sat opposite him. She placed the small rucksack down onto the table.

"There isn't much left of Bletchley itself, but it's very close to Milton Keynes and there, they used to have a hospital, a university and a large builders merchant and there's lots more around there to scavenge." She explained. Reg nodded as he watched her rummage through the rucksack.

"How did you find going out for the very first time?" He asked, as Alison continued to search through her bag.

"It was terrifying all the time and I didn't sleep much, but I still did it." She replied, without looking up to see that Reg nodded.

"You did and I was thinking while you were away, with all of these weapons here now we need a permanent Armourer, somebody smart and sensible to keep control of those guns." He suggested. Alison very briefly glanced up at him before she returned her attention to the rucksack.

"I know what you're trying to do, there are still a few people here without permanent jobs and I'm sure you'll find somebody, so stop trying to protect me." She replied. She pulled from her bag one of the small items that she had been searching for. She handed Reg a small black, circular hand painted metal cog that he studied for a few moments before his eyes widened and he glanced back up at her.

"We only found three pieces of it, that's all that was left in what I'm guessing was their small museum area." She explained. Reg stared back down at the cog and particularly at a printed stamp that revealed what it was originally a part of. He read *'Enigma'* and Alison watched his eyes again light up.

"Amy didn't even know anything about Bletchley Park or what it used to be!" She giggled. Reg again glanced up at her and he displayed a grin.

"Then I'll be having words with that young lady, I feel a deep and meaningful three hour lecture coming on!" He chuckled. He stared back down at his new prized possession.

"We need to build an archive for the historical artefacts that we're going to find from these walks." He quietly uttered to himself. Alison shook her head and began to giggle.

"And there it is, we'll be able to stand you in there as one of them." She replied. Karen Willis placed a cup of tea down onto the table in front of Alison who glanced up and displayed a smile. Reg also stared up at Karen.

"Where's mine?" He asked. Karen displayed a seemingly innocent smile back down at him.

"She's a brave superstar, you still get up and walk to the serving counter like everybody else." She replied, to another giggle from Alison. She then promptly picked up her cup as Reg attempted to acquire that too.

Emily Dawn Simpson was now a little more than a month old. Seated inside Joanna's room was Amy Vinton, who sat and bottle fed Emily in her arms while Joanna sat opposite and watched as she sipped tea.

"So, what was it like going out with Ali and Tess with guns?" She asked with a giggle. Amy removed her doting stare from Emily.

"When we found you, there was ninety million feet of snow everywhere and it didn't feel so dangerous to be out there but now, when you know that people could be walking around or maybe watching you it's quite scary, but we still haven't seen anybody else yet." She replied.

"So, do you think you've become used to that fear factor now?" Joanna asked. Amy pondered on the question before she replied.

"We all somehow lived through the storm, before that I was terrified of dying but I'm not now because none of us should really be here anyway, but I still don't know if I could actually shoot somebody even if I had no other choice." She replied. Joanna nodded with acknowledgement.

"Well, you're back in the normal world now, so when she's finished her feed it's your turn to change her." She giggled. She nodded down toward Emily in Amy's arms. The nineteen year old glanced back up at her and cringed.

"This Godmother lark isn't all it's cracked up to be, I was tricked into it!" She chuckled. Joanna beamed a grin and playfully winked in response.

"So in reality, we're just picking up and moving most of Oxford Castle four miles that way by hand." Phil Smith suggested. He nodded south, as he and David Wells struggled to carry one of the large dark grey, very heavy stones toward the flatbed truck, David nodded.

"That's about the size of it, mate!" He replied with a gasp. They both struggled to hoist the large stone up to where Paul Richards and Harrison Bax waited to take it so that they could add it to others at the front of the flat wooden bed of the truck, that was parked where the castle used to stand.

"This load will be the last for a while, there's going to be enough down there to line the rest of the trench, it's all bricks from now on, until us four start digging out the trench for the east wall." Paul explained, as he and Harrison struggled to carry the heavy stone. Inside the cab, Emma leaned out from the opened driver side window and she beamed a wry grin.

"Hurry up, you lot are really slow!" She called out, to single fingered responses from both David and Phil. Paul stared toward the back of the cab with disbelief.

"Shut it Todd, like you know anything about being quick, we've all seen you drive!" He called out, to a giggle from Emma. She also produced a single finger before she sat back on the driver seat and suddenly stared directly ahead with horrified widened eyes.

"I'm turning into one of them!" She quietly uttered.

The thirty one survivors at Oxford continued with their rebuilt daily lives and now with a very young child. None had encountered the likes of the Early family who sat around one hundred miles to the north-east, who would kill anybody that they encountered in order to take whatever they needed or simply wanted just because it glistened. They also knew nothing of the Abraham Bridger's of this brand new lawless world who were around two hundred miles to the north.

The group at York continued to grow because simple hand written signs led those in need to York Cathedral, where the weak would be weeded from the strong, the strong would become chosen men, others would become servants or corpses. There were other threats that they at Oxford knew nothing of. Nobody could grasp the reality that those threats faced them from every direction and some much closer than others, some much, much closer than they would like.

What they couldn't see and knew nothing of couldn't possibly harm them or their reasonably comfortable way of life, in comparison to what others no longer possessed. The dwellers at Oxford lived within a very false sense of safety and security, they simply didn't know it.

Settled peace and tranquility reigned, although it was only a matter of time before they were discovered by others, others who would want and need what they possessed.

Three Weeks Later

Saturday April 21st

At around eleven in the morning, Reg Simmons and Steve Madison stood inside Martin Sharpe's fourth floor radio room where the seventeen year old sat at his desk and waited to hear more instructions.

"Shortly after they get started, we're going up in the air three times every day until they're all safely home in a few weeks, we'll keep in contact with you and I need you relay information that we give when it's needed to the team on the ground using their handset radios." Reg explained to the youngster.

Reg, Umar and Jake recently finished building much larger caged barrows in order to carry more with the same long double handled bars for two people to pull them. They firmly fixed ten of the larger, shopping trolley wheels beneath each, that were taken from the third floor supermarket and those five much larger caged barrows today waited outside on the car park roof.

Inside the bustling canteen, people prepared for the largest scavenging run to date, Amelia glanced around at many nervous faces regardless of the fact that they would be very well protected.

The original team that returned from Bletchley some three weeks ago consisting of Alison, Tess and Amy were included, as was Emma Todd, Deborah Lloyd, the Psychologist Sue Cole and Steve Madison's wife Hannah, along with Maria Nightingale and Charlotte Strickland, who both needed to cut their teeth so to speak and there would be no better time with so many others around them.

Everybody would be armed with personal rifles and would also be heavily protected by Zack, Phil and Amelia. The entire group would head this time to just north of Bletchley to scavenge the much larger town of Milton Keynes. The excursion was expected to last for three, maybe four weeks before they returned to Oxford with the heavily laden barrows and anything else that they could carry.

Zack, Phil and Amelia would all carry the larger, slung general purpose machine guns that each weighed twenty four pounds and could fire seven hundred rounds per minute. They carried those as a deterrent in case they were watched. Nobody out there could possibly know that none of the walkers had ever shot at another person, although the group as a whole did now possess some very heavy duty firepower.

A second, smaller walking team would travel and assist at Milton Keynes before they would walk for a further nineteen miles north, to the town of Northampton to survey that area, where they knew there was a huge builder's merchant warehouse if any of it still stood. The second team would comprise of Vikki Annis, Jackie Nightingale and after they both volunteered for the further walk to everybody's surprise, for the first time Jason Moran also volunteered.

"When we eventually get started, everybody leave your rucksacks inside the barrows, they're easier to pull on wheels than they are to carry on your backs with tents, clothes and food in them." Amy Vinton called out. Many nervous heads nodded with acknowledgement, at the age of just nineteen this was in fact to be her third walk into the unknown.

Reg, Steve and young Martin stepped into the canteen where everybody continued with their preparations. Reg handed one radio handset to Emma Todd with five spare, fully charged batteries and another to Jason Moran for the second team to continue communications after they split up and headed further north around a week from today.

The quiet din fell silent after Reg called for everybody's attention. He again explained that around three hours after the walk began, he and Steve would take to the air to check ahead of the team to ensure that no unexpected surprises awaited them.

He also explained that whilst in the air, they would remain in contact with young Martin who would relay relevant information to the team on the ground. This would regularly occur for every day that they were out, or until the radio signal on the ground failed due to distance and or atmospherics.

"Grab anything you think is going to be useful to us and load it into your barrows, in essence strip Milton Keynes bare of resources such as non-perishable food, bottled water and medical supplies, all of those are top priority." He explained.

At the early stages of the south wall, Jake Jarrett slowly stirred steaming rice inside the pit as Paul Richards continued to kick Umar's incredibly strong four, feet high wall to test the modified, now hardened brilliant white mortar from three weeks ago.

"That's not going anywhere is it?" He asked, as he studied it and Umar shook his head.

"I'm trying to imagine it sixteen feet high all around us." Paul added. Umar busily laid new bricks onto the existing build. He discretely displayed a wry grin as Paul stared across the entire two mile length and eight feet width of the trench, that was already completely filled with the large dark grey stones that were brought down from where the Castle once stood.

"Well as you can see, nobody will be kicking it down." Umar eventually replied with sarcasm in his tone. Paul shook his head with agreement. At the nearside of the trench where Jake slowly stirred boiling rice, the wall was now ten courses of house bricks wide by five or six high for around fifty feet in length and for a short while, Paul continued to study it with interest.

"Right, I'm on guard duty up on the road all day now that we're going to be fifteen people light, I'll see you two later." He said. He then made his way across the field and headed back toward the Ellington centre.

Around three hours later, Paul stood fully armed on the main road, he watched the large party head north toward the roundabout. Beside him stood Alan Robbins and Harrison Bax who would share the sentry duties for eight hours per day, with break days provided by David Wells and Wendy Jones, until the large party eventually returned.

"So why have we got one on guard during the day from now on?" Harrison enquired. Paul turned to him.

"There are going to be sixteen of us here, before it would be all hands to the pumps if anything kicked off but three of us are canteen workers, two nursing staff, one with a new born and that old fart." He replied. He nodded toward Reg as he approached.

"We need somebody out here all the time just to be on the safe side." He added. Both Harrison and Alan nodded with acknowledgement as Reg, Steve Maddison and the recently appointed Armourer David Wells crossed the car park to where the three men stood. They all watched the large party with five barrows continue north.

"It's going to be so quiet around here for a while." Reg commented and Paul nodded.

"From our point, that's what I'm hoping for now that we're this light on the ground, I like quiet and uneventful, I just want Umar to hurry up with that wall." He replied, as they all watched the heavily armed group of fifteen slowly head away from them.

The walkers headed toward the roundabout in a long staggered line with Zack at the very front with his heavy machine gun slung over his shoulder. Amelia positioned at the centre on the left side with hers and Phil Smith at the rear with his.

"How's the botanical centre coming along?" Amelia asked, as she walked beside Deborah Lloyd and Alison Dixon. The seemingly anxious Deborah turned her stare to her.

"We've got three long rows of potatoes coming through, but they're not for eating they're for replanting, it's going to take about two years to even start getting everything properly up and running." She replied.

"Aren't you nervous right now?" Deborah then asked. Amelia again turned to her and shook her head as she displayed a wry grin.

"Of course not, we've got Alison here to nag the crap out of anybody we meet." She replied with a chuckle. Alison laughed and shook her head as she and Deborah pulled a barrow together.

"We've got six hundred bullets between us and three machine guns with seven hundred each, so one of us must be able to hit something!" Alison laughed. Emma with Amy in front and Tess with Sue behind also laughed. Amelia's job of settling them all was suddenly done.

"We're going to stop every three hours for a break and the first time we do, Steve and Reg should fly over us to start checking ahead, I doubt very much that we'll see another living soul while we're out to be honest, these guns are just a precaution, but they do put us in charge of any situation." Amelia informed them all.

Jason Moran walked behind Zack with his rifle pointed toward the ground, although he refused any lessons at the makeshift range. Behind him walked Vikki Annis with Jackie Nightingale who both pulled a caged barrow with all four rucksacks inside.

Jason surprised everybody when he volunteered for the team to walk to Northampton after Milton Keynes, but he had a personal hidden agenda. After he finished with what needed to be done at Northampton, he planned to finally go it alone. He volunteered immediately after Vikki Annis in order to get himself onto the same smaller team because of a six month old vow, a vow that was back then decidedly aimed toward her.

'When I get around to dealing with a few of you here you'll be the first, smart mouth.' He recalled so many times since making the promise to himself, as he watched her walk away from him with a smug grin. He made the promise when he watched Amelia's very first Karate class during the October of last year, after Vikki chose to stop and make her own personal comment aimed at him purely because Amelia was there to protect her. Unfortunately for Vikki, Amelia who he despised most wouldn't be at Northampton.

A promise was a promise as far as Jason was concerned and he had been patiently waiting for the opportunity that finally presented itself. He knew that he couldn't get all of the housemates that he hated, but before he parted company with them he would at least take out one and one would have to do, with an additional parting gift to two in particular.

As he walked, he found it ironic and amusing that Vikki and Jackie pulled the barrow with his rucksack. Concealed inside it was his already loaded sawn down shotgun that waited in preparation for them, of course nobody knew that he possessed it.

One loaded cartridge was prepared for Vikki and the second was readied for Jackie Nightingale purely because she would also be there. He would patiently wait until just the three of them finally reached Northampton. The main group would be headed back toward Oxford from Milton Keynes, far enough away to do anything about it. When he was finished, he would then make his own way in this brand new lawless world, leaving Vikki and Jackie to join the long, long list of the dead.

He considered the death of Jackie a suitable, albeit unfortunate repayment to Alison and Amelia although she had never done anything to Jason personally, but he knew without doubt that those back at Oxford would at some point search for them at Northampton and discover the bodies with a note blaming those two in particular for her death. Whether he truly believed that or not was irrelevant, he simply wanted both to feel the consequences of their actions and behavior toward him, Jackie's death would surely provide that guilt. The handwritten note that he prepared blaming them was already hidden inside his jacket pocket waiting to be left with her cold corpse.

Sunday April 22nd

Alison Dixon was the first to climb out from her tent at the ruins of Bicester, some fourteen miles north-east from Oxford. Jackie Nightingale stood on guard duty after she was two hours ago woken by Zack. She watched Alison gradually wake herself up.

She quietly croaked a 'good morning' to Jackie as she lit a small gas burner and began to make coffee. Just like before, she hardly slept a wink because every faint noise outside of the tent throughout the night sounded like footsteps on sand or gravel.

Later, the large group would continue north-east to make it to Addington and camp there for the night. Throughout the day, they would all stare up at the clear blue sky to see the plane circle overhead wherever they were at that time.

Steve and Reg would later fly over them at Bletchley, then fly further to check over their final destination at Milton Keynes. Martin Sharpe would relay by two-way radio that there was absolutely nothing ahead of them, giving everybody a sense of security, Reg and Steve would see nobody alive on the ground and no movement there at all.

The rotting dead surrounded the group everywhere that they walked. The dead could harm nobody but there was always a strange, silent eerie sense throughout, a sense that they were being watched and everybody on the ground felt it.

At around midday, the plane flew overhead as the long staggered line of walkers headed toward Addington. Jason

Moran again followed Zack at the front where he continued to meticulously plan exactly how to execute Jackie and more importantly Vikki, who both continued to pull the barrow and unknowingly his loaded shotgun behind him.

Just like everybody else, Jason knew that their first port of call at Northampton would be the builder's merchant warehouse beside the River Nene. He already decided that it was there the deed would be done because when a search party much later headed out to find them, they would definitely search there.

The three would first assist the main group to scavenge at Milton Keynes until every one of the barrows was filled after a couple of weeks. The main party would then begin the three day journey back to Oxford when Vikki, Jackie and he would head to Northampton with their empty barrow. That walk would take them an additional two or three days which meant that the main party would be almost back at Oxford by the time that he was ready to carry out his plan.

He wondered as he walked, that because the entire country was now so silent, if the main group would hear the two loud gunshots from around thirty miles by then, although it was unimportant because even if they did, they would never find him. He would be gone as soon as the deed was done.

Sunday May 6th

Three days ago, the main party started their three day trek back to Oxford with four fully loaded barrows of mostly medical supplies from the remains of the hospital. Jason, Vikki and Jackie continued north to survey the town of Northampton. To the surprise of both women during the those three days of walking, Jason seemed remarkably chirpy and that wasn't like him at all.

They both witnessed it, in fact they were all getting along remarkably well considering that it was Jason, while he continued to secretly albeit now anxiously plan their deaths. At around eleven in the morning, the three approached Northampton on the wide dual carriageway formerly known as Nene Valley Way that would later pass directly over the River Nene.

"The builder's warehouse is just the other side of this roundabout up ahead." Jason called out. Both women nodded as they pulled the barrow behind him.

"Martin said there are quite a few building suppliers around here and a big hospital somewhere over that way." Vikki replied. When Jason turned to glance back at her, he saw that she pointed in the direction of north-west and he nodded.

"Why don't we have our lunch break down on the riverbank beside the warehouse and out of the wind before we get started?" He called out, both women agreed.

At the roadside just past the overhead roundabout, Jason removed his heavy rucksack from the large barrow before he climbed down a sloped narrow dirt track at the riverbank. The two women removed their own baggage and eventually began to follow him. Once directly in front of the river with his back facing them, he unfastened the rucksack and could hear their footsteps as they slowly climbed down some way behind him, he discretely reached inside his bag and felt both metal barrels of his sawn down shotgun.

'I'm feeling generous I'll make this quick for both of you, neither of you will even know you're dead.' He now very anxiously thought to himself. His adrenalin started to rush as he recalled that snide remark made by Vikki last year that brought them all to this point. He slowly nodded to himself although Vikki would probably never even remember the incident.

Just then, he felt something like a fly touch the back of his neck, he instinctively reached behind to move it away but there was no fly and suddenly no movement whatsoever behind him. He immediately felt a very eerie silence as his heart raced, he already knew that something wasn't quite right. His fingertips then touched something solid at the back of his neck before whatever it was, pressed a little harder and he realised that whatever it was, it was very sharp and made from metal.

"Move one inch before I tell you to and your head comes off before you even hit the floor." A deep male voice calmly and quietly assured him. Jason realised that he heard nothing at all from Vikki or Jackie, it was as if they were no longer there.

"Now turn around very slowly and let's have that shotgun out of the bag and down on the ground where I can see it."

The same voice instructed. With a pounding heart, Jason started to turn and he very slowly removed the shotgun from his bag and dropped it down onto the ground. His unknown visitor could clearly see that his entire body trembled.

"Turn all the way around and keep your hands where I can see them, now drop that bag while you're at it." The voice again instructed. Jason very slowly turned and as he released his rucksack, the first thing that he saw was that Vikki Annis stood near the top of the river bank, she was absolutely terrified and had urinated in her dark brown trousers.

Vikki uncontrollably trembled due to the fact that Hope Early's large and heavy axe was held and pressed against the side of her neck. Hope patiently waited for her to even flinch. Behind Vikki, Arya Early stood to the left side of Jackie with her high powered crossbow pressed onto Jackie's temple and of course she also visibly trembled. When Jason finally faced Robert Early, the tip of that long razor sharp broadsword pressed against his throat, Robert actually smiled down at him.

"Who are you, where have you come from and why were you trying to track us?" He calmly asked, as Jason continued to very anxiously stare up at him.

"Can I kill this one now, dad?" Arya called out, regarding to Jackie as Hope stared into Vikki's eyes with nothing but malice on her mind. They both saw that their father shook his head.

"Not yet, let's find out where they came from." He replied. Jason then saw that two very large, well fed Doberman dogs appeared and stood at the top of the riverbank, where they both seemed to watch the unfolding events. He very slowly returned his gaze back up into Robert's cold pale blue eyes.

"W…We're from Oxford, we're just scavenging we didn't even know you were here." He quietly blurted. Hope Early slowly stepped in front of Vikki and continued without any emotion to stare into her eyes with that razor sharp axe still pressed against her new enemy's slender neck.

"Let me torture this one to find out everything." She called out. Again her father shook his head without removing his stare from Jason.

"We'll take them back to the shelter and ask them a few questions before we decide anything, I do believe that they didn't know we were here, but that brings more questions than answers." He replied, still without removing his stare from Jason's terrified eyes and with the long sharp sword pressed against his throat before he quietly spoke again.

"An instinct does tell me to kill you right now and all I have to do is push this sword forward, but before I decide to do that, you're going to tell us everything about where you came from." He uttered. As Jason's heart pounded, he continued to tremble with uncontrollable fear. Hope then very briefly glanced down toward Vikki's crotch and chuckled before her stare returned up to the terrified brunette's tear-filled widened eyes.

"Didn't anybody teach you to go before you left the house?" She sarcastically asked. Arya pushed the tip of the sharp arrow that was loaded onto her crossbow a little harder into Jackie's temple.

"Slowly walk back up the hill with your hands where I can see them, bitch." She calmly and quietly instructed. With absolute terror, Jackie did exactly as she was told.

"You too, follow your friend." Hope insisted and without any hesitation, Vikki also did as she was told.

"Follow your girlfriends, young man." Robert advised. He didn't know it, but with his unhinged daughters, he had albeit unwittingly, just saved the lives of Vikki Annis and Jackie Nightingale.

At the top of the hill, Jackie continued to tremble in a state of absolute terror with her flat palms pressed together behind her back as instructed. Arya proceeded to tightly secure them using a wide black plastic cable tie around her wrists. Behind her, the same was happening to Vikki at the hands of Hope and to Jason by Robert, while the two large black hounds continued to stare at their master for instruction.

"We're not a threat to you." Jackie quietly blurted, as tears streamed down her face, only to receive a nudge from Arya to encourage her to walk forward.

"I'm a genuine threat to you so tell it to somebody that gives a crap, now walk before I shoot you in the face." Arya uttered in response. Jason walked behind all of them, followed by Robert Early who pulled the barrow.

"So, if you didn't know we were here but you were taking this shotgun out of your bag before I stopped you, who was it intended for?" Robert enquired. As he pulled the large barrow behind him, he glanced down at the loaded weapon along with the three rifles inside and as he walked in front, Jason momentarily turned to face him.

"I was just checking that I brought it with me." He lied. As Vikki was shoved forward, she suddenly began to work out Jason's true intentions, as did the just as terrified Jackie ahead of her and she very briefly turned to stare at Vikki to show that she had also figured it out.

"I get that, a sawn down twelve gauge shotgun in a world with no law is something that you wonder if you remembered to bring with you." Robert sarcastically replied.

'He was about to kill us!' Vikki realised as everything cascaded into place. That thought somehow turned her mindset from one of utter terror to pure anger. She then turned to stare at Hope, everything now suddenly made perfect sense.

"If you're going to kill us, can you do him first so that we at least get to watch it?" She angrily asked. Hope initially laughed in response.

"I really don't give a crap which order you go in you're all dog food as far as I'm concerned, would you like popcorn for that?" She sarcastically asked in response. Vikki then watched Arya in front shove Jackie through the opened doorway of a mostly obliterated, terraced house. Hope again pushed her although this time Vikki offered a little resistance.

"Do your best, you stupid little bitch." She sneered. Her comment caused Hope to again chuckle.

"I'll deal with you personally I promise and I'll even untie your hands first to give you a fighting chance, but you won't be my first or last kill, this is what my sister and I were born for." She calmly retorted. Hope genuinely believed that statement. As they walked toward the same doorway, Vikki mentally prepared herself to die, she knew and somehow calmly accepted that it was about to happen. She considered that after eight months of struggling to survive, her fight was finally over and for a very brief moment she actually smiled to herself, it all suddenly made sense, she finally found some peace as she neared her death.

Vikki sat with her back against a partial wall to the left of Jackie and with Jason seated the other side, inside a darkened dust covered room with no roof, only a dark blue tarpaulin cover. All three sat with their hands still tightly bound behind their backs when one of the large black dogs Cain, stood directly in front of and very close to Vikki and began to snarl and show his sharp teeth as saliva dripped down onto the floor from his mouth, after goading from Hope. Vikki immediately turned her head away from the hound.

"Not yet, boy." Robert instructed. The intense family stood and stared down at the Oxford trio, until Robert crouched in front of Jason and for a few moments stared at him with a half-smile. He then turned his stare toward Jackie.

"You see, I'm still trying to work out if this little toe-rag was waiting for us, did you know he had that shotgun tucked away in his bag?" He asked. As Jackie continued to tremble in terrified silence, she rigorously shook her head. Robert then turned his stare to Vikki and asked her the same question, she also shook her head.

"Whatever crap he tells you, it was us he was about to kill because that's the type of dickhead he is, none of us knew you were there." She angrily sneered in response.

"What's at Oxford?" Robert then asked. Vikki now completely calm and unafraid of her fate, stared back at him as Jason immediately opened his mouth to speak. Robert raised a single forefinger to silence him.

"I'm asking her, when I want to speak to you I'll stare into your shifty little eyes." He said in that same calm and quiet tone of voice. Arya then stepped beside Jason and kicked him very hard in his ribs and caused him to wince with pain.

"If my dad isn't speaking to you, shut your mouth or I'll nail it shut!" She angrily snapped, to another whimper from Jason and a quiet giggle from her younger sister. Robert then returned that cold stare to Vikki.

"So, what's at Oxford?" He again asked. She again stared angrily back at him.

"What do you want, I tell you everything and then you kill us?" She asked.

"Kiss my arse, I'm not giving you my friends so do whatever you want!" She snapped. Again Robert and his daughters chuckled. Without speaking, Jason made it clear that he was ready to tell them whatever they wanted to know, but instead Robert returned his attention to Jackie.

"Are you going to talk?" He asked. Although tears streamed down her face, Jackie rigorously shook her head.

"I've got a stepdaughter and there's a new born baby down there, I'm not going to tell you anything that'll get either of them harmed, I'll let you walk straight into that." She blurted. Robert raised his eyebrows.

"Let us walk straight into what?" He asked, to no response from Jackie. She now also chose to simply stare back at him.

"And do you also think this lowlife planned to kill the two of you before we showed up?" He asked. He watched Jackie rigorously nod, before Robert finally turned his attention directly to Jason.

"Why is it that everybody we've met that knows you, thinks you're a dickhead?" He asked, to more chuckles from his daughters. Terrified Jason stared back at him, but this time he didn't attempt to answer and so Arya again kicked his ribs very hard and caused him to wince with more pain. Just then everybody heard the low droning din of the aircraft as it approached Northampton from the south to circle over, Robert returned his stare to Vikki.

"Is that yours?" He asked. He displayed a smile when Vikki reluctantly nodded to confirm. Hope then kicked the sole of Vikki's boot and so she glared back up at her.

"Do they think he's a dickhead too?" Hope enquired. Vikki watched her nod in the direction of Jason, she then glared at Jason before her stare returned up toward Hope and again she nodded.

"That's all you're getting out of me." She vowed. Robert returned his focus to Jason and asked how many were at Oxford. Jason immediately informed him that there were twenty eight other adults and the one new baby. He also revealed that they were heavily armed with lots of supplies.

Robert nodded with acknowledgement, he glanced back toward Vikki and then Jackie before Jason spoke again.

"You would need to sneak up on them, but I could show you exactly where they are." He added. Robert again stared at him before he nodded and then returned his stare to Vikki and then Jackie.

"You young ladies are believe it or not a little bit like us you have honour, I understand that you're protecting your own because that's what we would do." He informed them both. He then returned his stare to Jason.

"You on the other hand have none and I don't trust you one little bit, these two would die to protect their own, you would sell yours out in a heartbeat." He uttered. Hope stared down at her father.

"Dad, can I kill this one now?" She asked as she nodded down toward Vikki, who again glared back up at her, but Robert once again denied her.

"Nobody's going to die yet, I've got to think this all through before I decide what to do with them." He replied. His stare once again turned to Vikki.

"Tell me, do your twenty eight friends down at Oxford trade with others?" He enquired.

Jackie, Vikki and Jason remained seated and bound inside the dusty darkened room when Robert and his daughters stepped outside because they had much to discuss.

"The game with these people has changed." Robert quietly said. His daughters waited for him to continue.

"You heard what the dark haired girl in there said, those people down at Oxford would be willing to begin trading with us which was what we planned all along, we wander around the country picking up items to trade for when the idiots are all dead, that was always the plan." He continued.

"By the sound of it, they're getting it together down there so what I'm thinking is that we take these three back and hand the deceitful little goon over to them for trying to kill the other two, we do that as a good will gesture." He added.

"Untie the two girls tomorrow morning so that they don't run tonight, we'll walk them all back and give him up so they get to deal with their own however they see fit." He suggested. Both daughters reluctantly nodded.

That evening, Robert lit a small fire at the centre of the room and now fully aware of what he wanted to achieve, he glanced across at Vikki.

"Have you met any of the survivors from York?" He asked. Vikki shook her head. Robert glanced beside him at Hope.

"Tell them what the lot up at York are all about." He said. Hope also stared directly at Vikki past the flames, she then explained what they learned when they tortured Bobby Michaels prior to his execution, Jason let out a gasp.

"They wanted to take me up to York to give me to a giant by the name of Abraham who thinks he's the new King of England, women are here to serve men and they own everything, everywhere and there are already more than twenty of them up there with the same opinion as the giant." She explained. Vikki, Jackie and Jason continued to listen to her story.

"You, you personally tortured this Bobby to make him talk?" Jason asked with astonishment. Hope stared across at him and slowly nodded and she displayed a wry grin.

"It was up at Huddersfield, we strapped him to a table with barbed razor wire and made him tell us everything and after he did, we chopped his head off and mounted it onto a pole for them to find as a warning, if and when they came to look for him and they probably did." She replied.

"We also chopped off his hands and feet for our dogs, they seem to like the taste of human." She added. That particular statement sent a chill down Vikki's spine, she somehow knew that Hope spoke the truth.

"So this giant lunatic at York is called Abraham?" Jason asked. Hope returned her stare to him, she didn't nod she only stared and as Jason stared back. He saw only malice and venom in her eyes after she recalled the execution of Bobby Michaels.

Monday May 7th

At around six in the morning as the sun began to rise, Jackie slowly opened her blurred eyes to see only Robert seated across the darkened room where he stared at her. Vikki still slept beside her.

"It would seem that one of my daughters fell asleep during her watch last night." He said. Jackie suddenly turned to see that Jason was gone.

"They're out with the dogs tracking him down, the dogs will sniff him out if he's still close by and he can't have gone far." He added. Vikki also opened her eyes after the sound of Robert's voice woke her from a very stiff and uncomfortable light sleep.

"So now you've only got two to murder." Jackie quietly croaked. She and Vikki stared across at him. Robert slowly climbed to his feet before he removed his large Machete and walked toward Vikki in particular.

"Sit forward." He calmly instructed. For a few moments, Vikki glared back up at him in an eerie and yet somehow peaceful silence, she slowly lowered her head and waited for the razor sharp blow that would finally end her life, but Robert continued to stare down at her.

"I said sit forward, I want to cut the cable tie you two are no threat to us, when my daughters come back with or without him we're taking you back to Oxford so that you can introduce us." He informed her. Vikki slowly raised her head and stared back up at him with disbelief. Tears began to roll down Jackie's cheeks because unlike Vikki, she was not yet ready to die.

Around two hours later, Arya and Hope returned with the hounds and stepped into the darkened dusty makeshift shelter where they saw that their father had freed Vikki and Jackie from their bonds.

"We found their barrow dumped in the river, he took all of the weapons, food and whatever else they brought with them." Arya announced. Both Vikki and Jackie saw that she stared sheepishly at her father because Jason escaped in the night during her watch. Vikki then glanced across the room at Jackie and she took in a long deep breath before she exhaled it.

"Where do you think he went?" Robert asked. Before his daughter could respond, Vikki interjected because she already knew the answer.

"He's going to York to tell the giant psycho that there are nineteen women, guns and a shopping centre full of supplies at Oxford and he'll show him exactly where it is." She uttered. She returned her anxious stare to Jackie.

"He's got the radio too, we can't let them know." She uttered.

Thursday May 10th

Emma Todd and Amy Vinton both fully armed, stood on the main road beside the car park roof on sentry duty. They stared north at the sight of two very large black dogs that trotted toward them, at first neither said a word as they continued to watch.

"If they're starving, they're going to be vicious." Emma eventually uttered. Amy nodded before she removed the safety from her rifle as Emma removed her radio handset and held it to her mouth.

"Guys, we've got two really, really big dogs walking down the road toward us." She nervously announced. There was a momentary pause before anybody responded.

"I like dogs, do they look friendly?" Paul Richards asked from up at the ruins of Oxford Castle. Emma glanced at Amy before she responded.

"They don't look hungry, but I'm not going to walk up the road and ask if they're nice doggies, am I?" She asked. There was no immediate answer from Paul, she knew that he and the others were laughing, but five figures appeared at the roundabout in the distance. At first neither girl recognised any of them, but this new sight caused Emma to return the handset to her mouth.

"Five people have just appeared at the roundabout near you and they're coming this way too." She very anxiously uttered. She also removed the safety on her rifle that was now ready to fire.

"Crap, here we go then." Amy quietly uttered, as both of their hearts pounded. She squinted past the dogs toward the five vague silhouettes in the distance.

"That looks like Vikki and Jackie and they're not carrying guns, but the other three are!" She exclaimed. The two young women began to very tentatively walk north toward the five, the hounds stopped and stared at them.

Cain and Abel stood and watched Amy and Emma as they cautiously passed them on the road and made their way to where their two accompanied friends headed toward them. They finally stopped just past the hounds where Amy nervously raised her rifle and pointed it, she could now see that Vikki and Jackie had definitely been disarmed. Just like she had been taught, she trained her sights on one and it was Robert Early in particular, although she still didn't know if she could actually pull the trigger. Hope Early glared at her from around twenty feet away.

"If you don't lower that rifle away from my dad, I'll cut you clean in half!" She vowed with a sneer. Arya Early suddenly raised and pointed her high powered crossbow directly at Emma who promptly aimed her rifle back. Vikki Annis stepped forward and between them, but adrenalin on both sides was incredibly high.

"Shoot that bitch in the face." Emma quietly uttered to Amy, with regard to Hope Early.

"Girls it's ok, everything's ok they just brought us home!" Vikki insisted. She slowly approached Amy and Emma as the flatbed truck turned onto the road at the north and eventually pulled up directly behind the situation. Robert

Early slowly raised his hands and turned to see Paul, Zack, David, Harrison, Phil and Tess all standing with their rifles pointed at the family.

"You're not as stupid as you look, mate." Paul uttered, as he slowly neared Robert with the rifle still pointed at the largest part of him, his chest. Emma moved to the right of Arya and Amy to the left of Hope in a highly intense stand-off situation, Robert beamed a grin.

'I really like this lot!' He thought to himself. Hope slowly turned her head and stared straight into Amy's eyes with the same venom that she showed Vikki when the axe was pressed against her slender neck. Arya continued to stare with the same malice at Emma.

"Are you going to pull that trigger or shall I scalp you first?" Hope calmly asked Amy, before Robert stepped between them.

"Where's Jason?" David then asked. Jackie turned to face him.

"He was about the shoot us when these guys appeared and stopped him, he's gone to York because there's massive trouble building up there and we need to speak to you all about it." She informed him. David stared back at her with confusion before he shook his head.

"Jason called in on the radio yesterday to tell us that everything was fine and you lot had no signal for a couple of days, he said that you were all making your way back here." He assured her. He watched Vikki then stand beside Amy. She very slowly reached forward and lowered the barrel of the rifle that was trained at Hope's face and she gradually pointed it toward the ground.

"We're both ok, don't shoot her you might piss her off." She very quietly whispered, out of Hope's earshot.

At the town of Peterborough some forty miles from Northampton, Jason Moran sat in the corner of a filthy and mostly destroyed factory building. He ate rations from a can and quietly chuckled to himself as he recalled that Vikki and Jackie pulled the barrow with his rucksack inside it.

His rucksack carried the shotgun that should have been used to kill them both although they were obviously unaware. He still found amusement in the irony that they willingly carried the weapon that was intended to end both of their pointless lives, it was unfortunate that he never had the chance to send that message to Amelia West and Alison Dixon.

Yesterday, he considered that if they somehow managed to survive Robert Early and his psychotic daughters which was very doubtful, they wouldn't yet be back at Oxford and so he called in using the radio handset and reported to Martin Sharpe that for the past couple of days they had no signal. The main group of now twenty eight were still blissfully unaware of what had really happened.

On this day, the radio was switched on beside all three rifles and his sawn down shotgun that were all placed loaded and at the ready on the dust covered floor in front of him, as were all three rucksacks that were filled with food and a few medical supplies. He continued to recall what had happened.

Two days ago at around four in the morning, Jason sat inside the filthy room back at Northampton beside Vikki. In the silence and darkness he pretended to be sleeping and discretely watched Arya nod off back to sleep at the beginning of her four hour watch. Taped inside the back of his trouser belt was a small sharp penknife for such an emergency.

As soon as Arya was again out cold, he very quietly removed the penknife and managed to cut the black plastic cable tie to free his hands. He would never dream of helping Vikki or Jackie because in his mind they should already be dead. He would now leave them for the three savages to deal with.

Thankfully, the barrow outside with the three rucksacks, rifles and his shotgun was for some reason left far enough from the building. There were high winds that masked the sounds as he very gently pulled it back toward the riverbank to where they initially met the three maniacs.

His shotgun was pointed toward the doorway for the entire time, just in case Arya suddenly woke and discovered him missing. For a few very brief moments, he considered returning to the darkened room with one or maybe two of the rifles to slaughter every single one of them which he believed he could probably do, but of course the two hounds had to be taken into account and his next thought caused his heart to pound heavily against his chest. If he shot the dogs first, one or all three of the insane family might have time to get to him, if he shot them first the dogs would undoubtedly attack, so he chose to leave in the darkness now that he was free.

After he removed everything from inside the barrow, he pushed it down the slope and watched it splash into the overflowed River Nene before he initially headed north, but because they had those two large dogs that watched him leave, he then headed east and crossed the freezing river and made his way south to lay low for the rest of the day. He would once again head north after they lost his scent.

What Jason didn't know, was that Arya lay with her eyes closed when he quietly left and as he departed the building, she displayed a wry grin because she and Hope with the two dogs now had something to hunt for sport and fun. The daughters stared at each other in the darkness, they did nothing to stop him but they watched the doorway for every single moment and if he returned like they suspected he might, they were both ready to end his stinking existence. Of course, Jason didn't do that and he survived for yet another day.

His new plan was a simple but effective one, he would only travel at night to avoid being spotted in the open by the plane, he would also zigzag across the country from city to town and continue north toward York to meet this Abraham, who in fact sounded like his type of leader of chosen men, Jason knew that he would definitely qualify as one of those.

He was however blissfully unaware of Abraham's size restrictions regarding chosen men, at five feet nine, he fell short of the mark by some three inches and men before him had already been slaughtered for less. The city of York was however still one hundred and twenty miles away and that was the direct route, but he would not take it. He knew that the much longer journey would take many more weeks, but it would be worth it just to give up those wastes of oxygen down at Oxford.

He also now knew the names and could identify the three psychopaths that executed one of Abraham's men and apparently mounted his head onto a pike for him to find as a warning. While he ate, Jason stared outside of the building with wonder at a huge, heavily damaged face of what was once the top of the iconic clock tower known back then as Big Ben.

Nine months ago during the great storm, a section of the giant tower was somehow hurtled around eighty miles north from Westminster before it finally impacted the ground at Peterborough. The radio handset suddenly 'crackled' into life and distracted his wonderous thoughts before he heard *her* voice.

"Jason, I know you can hear me you bastard and I want you to remember that there aren't many people left, I will find you and when I do I'm going to kill you this time." Amelia West vowed. Jason displayed a grin although his heart pounded. The truth was that he feared her and the shame that she was capable of providing him. She was a mere woman who could easily beat him and deep down he knew it.

"We know what you're doing and where you're going, my only hope is that they don't kill you before I get to you." Amelia continued. Jason stared down at the handset and for a brief moment he considered answering her, but he knew that his voice would tremble just like hers did but for a different reason, hers came from pure anger.

"If and when they come, you'll be the one that everybody here looks for, you'll be in everybody's sights and they might make it to us, but I promise you won't live to see it." She assured him. He quietly chuckled although his heart was now ready to explode.

"You were going to kill my friends and you even took the coward's way out of that, you had a weapon hidden from them because that's the kind of coward you are, you were too afraid to do it like the man we all know you're not." She goaded. There was a pause before Amelia spoke to him for the very last time.

"Did you know that you're not actually big and tall enough, Jason?" She cryptically asked him, to no response.

"I'm going to find him and I'm leaving right now, I'm not appealing to any sense of morality he doesn't have any." She uttered inside Martin Sharpe's radio room, as she climbed to her feet. Also standing inside the room were Reg, Paul, Robert Early, Alison and young Martin who all watched her head for the opened doorway.

"You can't go after him!" Alison called out. Amelia stopped and turned to face her.

"You really think I'm going to let him get away with what he tried to do to Vikki and Jackie?" She angrily asked. Alison rigorously shook her head.

"No, I know you better than that, but two things come to mind right now and the first is that if this is really happening and he's going to York we need you here, we're going to need everybody here for whatever's going to come down that main road and that brings me to my second point." She replied.

"If that's where he's really going, while you're halfway up the country in a couple of months looking for him, Jason will also coming down that main road back to here if they don't kill him for us, so be the smart one and just sit tight and wait for him to come to you." She added. Both Reg and Robert Early nodded in agreement with Alison's common sense and reasoning.

"We need to focus everything on Umar's wall and get ready for this." Reg added. Again Robert Early nodded.

"We'll stick around and help out with whatever you need if that's what you guys would like, I built our fallout bunker I can lay bricks and my girls helped me build it, they're both strong and you can put us all onto your guard duty rotation too." He suggested.

He said, she said

Sunday May 13th

"I think we should fill the plane and fly over York, just to see just how many are up there with this man Abraham." Steve Madison suggested. Reg stared back at him for a few moments before he nodded with reluctant agreement as they sat opposite each other at a table inside the canteen with David, Paul, Alison, Amelia and Robert Early seated around them, who all nodded, Steve then glanced around the table.

"I'm going to help out with manual labour for the walls, so who wants to go up with Hannah?" He asked. It was Amelia who immediately insisted, in the hope that she might see Jason somewhere along the way to make sure that he was definitely headed to York and if there was a possibility to land in a field somewhere near him, she would plead with Hannah to do so.

Arya and Hope Early stood on the large roundabout at the northern end of the main road, they faced north with the two hounds beside them as instructed by their father. They were to stand watch there because he assured them that the great battle that they were made for was coming to Oxford. Of course they had already met with two from York although only one made it back there. They were watched from a distance by two other women.

"Why are they just standing there like that?" Emma Todd asked. She stood fully armed as did Vikki Annis beside her on the same road although much farther south and closer to the car park roof. They stared at the sight of the two heavily armed girls from Wolverhampton with their faithful hounds beside them.

"They do whatever their dad tells them no matter what it is, but they're both incredibly dangerous not to mention absolutely nuts, these are the kind of people that are going to be left to wander around, only the lucky weak, the lucky strong and the lunatics like those two up there." Vikki replied. She nodded in the direction of Arya and Hope.

"They met five of the men from York and that one with light brown hair tricked one of them off his motorbike by pretended to be a crying young girl, as soon as he got near her she chopped his leg off with that bloody great big axe and then the dark haired one chopped his head off with their dad's sword after she shot him in the face with her crossbow." She continued to explain.

Of course, that wasn't exactly what happened at Huddersfield and when Emma later told the story to Amy, it would change a little more and the survivors at Oxford would continue to circulate and interpret the story in their own way with new additions in accordance to human nature. The daughters of Robert Early as a result were slowly becoming almost mythical legends.

"Jackie told Amy and Amy told me that when you two first met them she had never been so terrified in her entire life, even the storm wasn't half as scary as meeting those three for the first time." Emma quietly uttered, again Vikki nodded.

"We all survived the storm, but you don't get to survive those two girls if their dad decides to let it happen." She replied.

"There was a human foot in one of their bags, I saw that with my own eyes." Vikki assured her. Emma cringed at the mere thought of such a grotesque sight.

"Those girls standing up there wanted to kill us just for fun and they would have, it was only their dad that stopped them." Vikki added. Emma again stared at her.

"So, isn't it a good thing that they're on our side now?" She asked. Vikki stared straight back at her.

"I'll let you know, that's if we manage to live through them being on our side." She replied.

Robert Early, Umar Okur and Jake Jarrett measured out and marked the ground at what would later become the two mile long north wall just a few feet from Deborah Lloyd's giant allotment, to keep it inside the new boundary. They also thanks to advice from Robert, marked out the east and west walls to also begin construction there. The wall itself would now be a little more than three miles to the north from the car park roof, this meant that the east and west walls would now both span some five miles in length.

Paul Richards sat on the driver seat inside the cab of the truck that headed toward the roundabout with David Wells at the passenger side. On the flatbed sat Zack Zimmerman, Harrison Bax, Phil Smith and Alan Robbins. They were all now permanently armed and ready for whatever might or might not come to Oxford at any moment as they worked. At the roundabout, the truck slowed to a stop where Hope Early stared up at Paul on the right side, Arya stared up at David on the left and with both windows fully lowered, David tossed a bottle of fizzy pop down to Arya and Paul did the same for Hope and both girls caught them.

"You've been out here for six hours now, do you want somebody to come up and relieve you yet?" David asked. Arya continued to stare up at him and she eventually shook her head.

"We'll cover this day and night between us, you just concentrate on what you're doing, this is where they'll come so this is where we'll wait for them." She replied. David slowly shook his head as he let out a sigh.

"Believe it or not, we managed fine before you came here." He pointed out. His statement caused Arya to laugh with obvious sarcasm.

"No you didn't, we could've walked in here whenever we wanted, you only had guards down at the car park and by the time anybody got to help them it'd be too late for the rest of you, you're an idiot if you thought you were safe in your little bubble down here." She explained.

"Try to remember that nobody is coming to save you from the bad guys, there are no nice policemen anymore, this is where you wait and hold them off, far enough away for others to get ready for it." She replied.

As they continued toward Oxford Castle, Paul and David glanced at each other. On the flatbed at the rear of the truck, Zack, Harrison, Phil and Alan stared at Arya and Hope who both stared back with malice, as if they were the true enemy.

At just after three that afternoon, Jason Moran sat inside the remains of a destroyed building at Melton Mowbray, a little more than halfway to Nottingham from Peterborough. He opened his eyes when he heard a sound approaching from the skies and of course it came from the south.

He again closed his eyes and laughed to himself because those idiots down at Oxford were so predictable, he knew for a fact that seated inside the plane searching for him would be Steve and Reg, as he lay there he fantasised shooting them down.

'Just imagine the grief I could cause down there if I managed to take Reg out.' He considered. Jason however knew that if he couldn't hit the fast moving plane he would give away his hidden location. His plan was always to reach York and leave them all wondering if that was where he had travelled to until it was too late for them. Abraham and his men would suddenly arrive on their doorstep with Jason standing beside him.

If he knew who actually sat inside the plane, the temptation to try to down it may have proven to be too great.

On the right hand seat inside of the plane, Amelia sat and wore the blue headset with attached microphone. She sat beside Hannah who stared down at the ground on her left at an altitude of four hundred feet.

"Do you know where we are?" She asked. Hannah turned her head and briefly stared back before she nodded.

"That's Peterborough down on your side, York is about thirty minutes away." She replied. Amelia stared down at the absolutely destroyed town of Peterborough.

"We haven't seen a single soul alive since we've been up here, it's much worse than I ever imagined especially when you see all of the bodies like this." She uttered through the microphone. Hannah again nodded with acknowledgement.

"I think we may have flown over living people, if we had shortly after it all happened they'd be down there waving their arms and screaming at us, but I think everybody still alive is quickly learning the new rules." She began to reply.

"The new rules are that there aren't any rules it's everybody for themselves, you take whatever you want from whoever you want and nobody will come to do anything about it, so now they're all hiding." She finished.

Around twenty minutes later, the plane approached the city of York from the west at an altitude of just three hundred feet and what they saw made both women gasp. York was a busy hive of activity, particularly around the destroyed Cathedral building that was completely covered with scaffolding.

"Robert was right, look at all of these people, I think they're rebuilding the place!" Hannah blurted, as they flew directly overhead. They both stared down at what looked to be around fifty people, not the twenty that was previously believed.

"If he's also right about this Abraham we're in big trouble, especially if Jason really is heading here." Amelia replied. They stared across the cockpit at each other when something fizzed past the front of the plane and almost hit the propeller, it caused them to immediately turn their startled stares to the front, they then heard a muffled 'crack' that definitely came from the ground.

"What the hell was that?" Amelia asked. Another whizzed past her widow on the right and yet another, this time past Hannah on the left and so she suddenly banked the plane hard left.

"Shit, they're bloody shooting at us!" Hannah squealed in a state of panic, as she opened up the throttle.

"Then get us out of here, now!" Amelia yelled. They promptly headed north and climbed away from the continuing gunfire.

Around twenty minutes later as the plane headed south, Hannah called in on the radio and asked young Martin Sharpe back at Oxford to find Reg and anybody else in authority and bring them to the radio room, she over-emphasised that it was an emergency. Amelia stared across at her while both hearts continued to pound.

"If that lot get to Oxford we're in serious trouble." She uttered. Hannah only stared back at her with terror-filled widened eyes. She had flown solo literally hundreds of times, but never before had anybody ever attempted to shoot down any plane that she flew.

That evening as daylight began to fade, Robert Early approached the large roundabout and headed toward his daughters. Behind him walked Charlotte Strickland with Phil Smith, both fully armed.

"You're being relieved by these two, go back to the canteen and eat you're both on the new guard rotation from tomorrow, two hours on and four hours off." Robert announced to his daughters, both stared at him with disbelief.

"We can cover this between us, dad it's coming this way and we can't trust these idiots!" Hope assured him with frustration in her tone. Robert nodded with acknowledgement.

"I know it is and I know you can, but so can these two fine young people and the two after them, so go back to the canteen and get some rest, that day isn't today." He replied. Just then, the plane approached the main road from the north and flew over their heads as it approached the landing area beside the fuel station.

"Let's go and find out what's really going on up at York!" Robert yelled over the sound of the engine as the plane touched down. Hope then stared directly at Charlotte.

"I'm going to tell you this once, mess up while you're on my post and I'll come looking for you, if you're not already dead by the time I find you!" She snarled. Charlotte stared back at her and trembled as she glanced at the huge axe at her back. Hope then turned her angry stare toward Phil, but it promptly disappeared. To him she displayed a half smile, to a stifled giggle from her sister. Her father also saw it and he also turned his stare to Phil, although there was no half smile from Robert, only the stare.

Tuesday May 15th

Amelia West stood on the fourth floor corridor where she read a brand new form of communication that was crudely taped onto the wall. It was the now twenty four hour, seven day guard duty rotation written by David Wells. As she read it, Hope and Arya approached and she was aware due to the sounds and smells of the two dogs that always accompanied them.

"Are you the one that teaches Karate around here?" Arya enquired. Amelia turned to face them both.

"Our dad said that two of you here do it and he said you're pretty good." Hope interjected. Amelia turned her stare to her and asked why they wanted to know.

"We're apparently not allowed to beat the crap out of anybody here, so we were wondering if you and the other one would like to get a little rough with us, like a play fight." Arya suggested. Amelia stared back at her and then again at Hope.

"You want to fight with me?" She asked with surprise, she watched both rigorously nod. Hope then turned just in time to watch Phil Smith step through the door and into the canteen. Her sister watched her display another smile that was directed toward him, again Arya giggled at that situation. Hope then turned her stare up toward the guard duty rotation, she saw her own name written beside Arya's for a five o'clock in the evening start at the northern end of the main road.

She removed a pen from her sister's brown leather jacket pocket and scribbled out Amy Vinton's name beside Phil's at three o'clock and replaced it with her own. She then scribbled Amy's name beside her sister's to another giggle from Arya, while Amelia also watched.

"You can't just change things around here whenever you like." She insisted. For the very first time, Hope actually smiled back at her.

"If you believe you can't change things, don't change it back because as you just pointed out, you're not allowed to do that." She replied. She then turned and headed toward the canteen where she would soon sit directly opposite Amy, Emma and Phil. She would continuously stare straight at him with Abel the hound beside her. Arya returned her own stare to Amelia.

"Our dad always told us that when this time arrived, we could take whatever we want." She explained and for the first time she also smiled.

Because Amelia was at least another combatant unlike almost everybody else at Oxford, Arya would never show it, but there was genuine respect. Prior to the storm, Arya and Hope also studied various forms of martial art and she knew that a Fifth Dan was heavy duty. Amelia for the first time, displayed a smile of her own.

"About this little play fight, I think it might be a good idea to get some real hand to hand practice in before that lot from York come here." She said with that same smile. Arya beamed a grin and nodded with agreement, so Amelia leaned a little closer to her.

"I'll try to be gentle with you." She whispered, to another beaming grin from Arya.

"Then you're an idiot, I won't do the same I want to see just how good you really are." She whispered in response.

That afternoon, Robert Early walked back toward the Ellington centre from the north with David Wells and Paul Richards. David suddenly stopped and displayed a look of confusion as he stared.

"That's odd, I wrote the guard rotation and I know for a fact that I put your daughters together on it." He assured Robert. They all stared south and saw Hope on duty with the hound Abel, beside her stood Phil Smith. Robert took in a deep breath that he exhaled with a sigh.

"Please accept my apologies, I'll sort this out and whatever you do never have daughters, both times I prayed to the heavens for sons." He quietly uttered. All three men headed toward Hope and Phil, where Robert took a hold of Hope's upper arm and he pulled her to one side as David and Paul walked to where Phil uncomfortably stood.

"You two are looking cosy here, son." Paul said with a chuckle, Phil stared back at him.

"She's completely nuts, she changed the rotation!" He whispered in response. They all turned to watch Robert confront his youngest daughter.

"What's going on here?" He very quietly asked, as Hope stared up into his eyes.

"You always said that when this place was turned to dust we can take whatever we want, I want that." She replied. She pointed in the direction of the very nervous looking Phil. For a few moments, Robert stared across at Phil which didn't help with his already uncomfortable state of mind, before he returned that same angry stare to his daughter.

"You know damned well I meant a weapon or jewellery, not a man!" He snapped, but Hope continued to smile up at her father.

"How the hell do you ever envisage this working out, have you even given that terrified young man a say in any of this?" He just as quietly asked. This time, Hope quietly giggled.

"I haven't had time to give him his say, you're interrupting us, dad!" She replied. As Robert shook his head, Hope continued to giggle.

"Look, you said that we came here to form a friendship with them so that we can trade later, so where better than to find a future mate than here?" She asked.

"We'll be coming here regularly and he'll always be here waiting for me, it makes perfect sense not to mention that I'm doing what you wanted and making friends for once." She continued. Robert stared at her with utter disbelief before he took in another long deep breath and exhaled it.

"We'll continue this conversation later, when we're alone!" He vowed. Hope continued to smile at him as she rigorously nodded.

"I look forward to that, it'll be fun to discuss my future sex life with my dad!" She called out with another giggle, as she watched her now cringing father walk away with Paul and David. She then returned her stare to Phil.

"So, where were we before we were so rudely interrupted?" She asked with a grin. Phil also stared back at her with widened eyes of utter disbelief, but Hope was quite used to that look from men that she met and liked the look of, even prior to the great storm.

At just after five on that same evening, Amy Vinton stood just as nervously at the roundabout. Around ten feet away stood Arya with her dog Cain seated beside her. Amy glanced across at her and then down at the hound from hell.

"How old are your dogs?" She asked. Arya slowly turned and stared back and to Amy's surprise, the older psychotic daughter walked toward her.

"Why, do you want to stroke him?" She asked. Amy again stared down at the large black dog and then back up into Arya's eyes.

"Does he bite?" She asked. Arya displayed a wry smile before she nodded to confirm that yes, he did indeed bite.

"Only when he's told to, but he apparently has something like nine hundred pounds per square inch on his back jaw, so whatever he does bite tends to come off in his mouth." She eventually replied. She then turned to Cain and called him over to where Amy stood and trembled a little, she watched the hound approach before she returned her stare to Arya.

"He probably won't do a thing to you, he's been fed already." She said with another wry grin. Amy stared back down at the huge dog.

"Stroke him." Arya insisted. Her tone sent a shiver down Amy's spine because it was more of an instruction that a suggestion. She nervously reached forward with her trembling hand around an inch from the top of Cain's head, the hound glanced up at it before he seemed to sense the terror and he sniffed it.

"He's wondering if you smell like the other's he's already tasted." Arya chuckled, as Cain's wet nose then very gently touched Amy's palm before he returned to his uninterested, seated posture.

"There you go, he didn't bite your hand off he must like you, or you smell really bad." Arya said. Amy stared at her and after a few moments she spoke again.

"It didn't just happen in August, how the hell did you end up like this?" She asked. Arya turned to her before she smiled.

"Do you mean, how did I become one of the biggest arseholes you've ever met?" She asked in response. Amy continued to stare at her but she didn't answer that particular question. Arya stared down at the ground and chuckled before she finally replied.

"Since we were little girls, our dad assured us that this time was coming and he first taught us how to live through and then after it, but more importantly he taught us about what people would be like after the dust settles." She began. She again glanced at Amy before she stared back down at the ground.

"The silly old fart always believed it would be nuclear war though, not this." She added with a chuckle, she again glanced across at Amy.

"How did you survive?" She asked. Amy stared straight ahead and considered the question at hand.

"It was pure luck really, some of us here worked on the nightshift at a supermarket over that way." She replied. Arya watched her nod to the east.

"Your friend Jason was the manager there, he sent the women home during the storm and the men to hide underground with him until it was all over, the five of us managed to make it to an underground car park." She added, as she vividly recalled that night. Arya nodded with acknowledgement.

"Aren't you one of the three that walked all the way to London and back in the snow?" She asked. Amy glanced back at her and nodded, she saw that Arya again smiled.

"So you're a tough chick then." She commented. Amy for the first time chuckled before she rigorously shook her head.

"I'm not tough, I got thrown into this like everybody else and I'm still terrified all of the time." She replied and there was a pause of a few moments.

"I really do hope Amelia gets her hands on that bastard Jason though, I'd love to kick him in the face before she kills him." She quietly uttered. Arya again giggled.

"Then we'll have to make sure you get to do that one day, you've already earned it." She replied.

At just before midnight, Hope Early sat inside what was once Jason Moran's spacious third floor private living quarters where she brushed out her long straight wet brown hair after a hot shower. Her dark brown leather jacket and pants were slung over the back of a small wooden chair along with her black pullover and t-shirt. Her rifle, heavy axe and many other weapons lay on the carpeted floor beside it, her own hound Abel lay in a nearby corner.

Abel would however be woken when the door very quietly opened before Phil Smith stepped into the room and just as slowly and quietly closed it behind him. Hope turned on her seat, dressed in only her black cotton underwear to see him very nervously standing there, she displayed a warm smile.

"Take your clothes off and get into bed, this is our room now." She cooed.

Monday May 21ˢᵗ

At around five in the morning, Jason Moran reached the town of Scunthorpe, just fifty miles south of York. He was now anxious, no longer of what lay behind, but the possibilities of what could await him at York.

He knew from idle gossip provided by Robert Early and his daughters after they boasted of torturing Bobby Michaels, that this Abraham was all about power and at six feet seven inches, he could take pretty much whatever he wanted whenever he wanted it. Jason was also aware that those words were spoken to intimidate Jackie, Vikki and himself at the time.

He also knew from that darkened dusty room at Northampton prior to his escape, that Abraham's chosen men were all were burley, well fed men. Jason envisaged a ravaging, lawless Viking hoard. He recalled that Bobby Michaels told Arya and Hope that if a man wasn't powerful when he arrived at York, Abraham would execute him on the spot for all to witness, or make him fight a chosen man in some kind of arena to prove himself worthy of becoming one himself and if the new prospect lost that fight, only execution awaited him.

Jason did however have valuable information to offer, which was of nineteen women down at Oxford, many weapons, still an entire third floor that was filled with supplies and a completely filled warehouse. He also knew the names of the three that tortured and executed one of Abraham's chosen men and to prove that he knew, he always recalled the name of Bobby Michaels.

In two days from now, as he thought out his approach to York and more importantly how to approach and manipulate this Abraham when he arrived there, Jason would head to the city of Leeds which was in fact a similar distance to York from where he currently sat. At Leeds he would continue to plan and then approach York from the south-east, but only when he was good and ready to do so.

Friday May 25th

Jason finally left the city of Leeds at around eleven in the morning and began the final walk. This time he headed north-east for just twenty four miles to the outskirts of York. He still had to reach the Cathedral without being killed by one, or several of Abraham's chosen men before he could even reach the big man himself.

He trudged through corpse-ridden fields with the main road to York always on his right side until he reached what remained of Tadcaster, some fourteen miles from Leeds. There, he would stop to eat and maybe spend the night before he continued for the last ten miles. He knew that making it to Abraham was going to be no easy task, Jason was no very large, no obvious chosen man and was already beginning to lose his nerve.

Two hundred miles to the south at Oxford, Sue Cole stood on guard duty at the northern roundabout with Maria Nightingale. Her stepmother Jackie stood at the southern end of the main road with Tess Morking. The second pair stared to their left and watched Umar, Jake and Robert erect scaffolding in the distance.

At the far corner in front of the rice pit, the southern wall now stood at around ten feet tall and ten courses of brick in width after they solved the problem of a lack of mortar. Some five miles to the north at the early stages of the northern wall, Paul, David, Amy, Arya, Hope, Zack and Harrison, finished digging out the identical two mile trench to lay dark grey foundation stones before construction would begin there. When the large stones were laid, the same would begin at the east and west walls. They all knew that time was now of the essence because men from York could be here any day, if Jason had in fact travelled to there.

Four miles further north, Vikki, Phil, Alan, Emma, Wendy and Charlotte carried broken bricks and rubble to the centre of the road, where it was dropped or tossed to create a *'broken brick mountain'* as Reg described. He used the description to emphasise the size required in order to completely block the road so that whatever vehicles approached, would travel no further south. The same concept was planned for every road that led into Oxford from any and every possible direction.

"If they want to come here, they'll have to do it on foot and become much easier targets, they won't be able to drive here on any road." Zack announced a few days ago, to a rigorous nod of approval from Robert Early.

'What a clever idea!' He thought to himself. He glanced across the canteen toward his daughters, they both stared back as everybody listened to the plans for defence of the Ellington centre. He nodded with a smile, meeting the men from York on foot was something that would very much suit the family, if and when that moment arrived.

On this day inside the canteen, Reg, Alison, Amelia, young Martin and the two nurses Katie and Lisa all stood inside the canteen around two joined tables where the large map was again laid out on top, Joanna stood behind and watched with baby Emily.

"We're going to create a bottleneck from the roundabout to here." Reg explained, as he pointed down to the northern end of the main road on the map. He went on to explain that because there was no hope of finishing the high walls before the men from York arrived, alternative defences were the only available option.

Reg planned to construct large, three inch thick solid steel *'shields on wheels'* as he called them, with rectangular firing slots. The shields could be manoeuvred to face a threat from any direction, although if the half brick mountain road blocks did their job, the only approach to the Ellington centre would be on the main road from the north or south, or through the surrounding fields although that effort would come with extremely dire consequences.

"The only way they can get to here will be down this main road, Zack and Robert are going to bury land mines in all of the surrounding fields today." He announced. He tapped his forefinger down onto the roundabout on the map, he then turned to Katie and Lisa.

"You'll need to have an aid station ready for if and when somebody from here gets hurt." He informed them both. The two nurses glanced at each other as the reality started to sink in, as did Amelia and Alison. They all then turned to stare at Joanna with the baby, but she simply smiled back at them all.

"We'll help, it's going to be all hands on deck." She informed them, as she gently rocked baby Emily on her hip.

Saturday May 26th

At Tadcaster, Jason Moran woke with a start to the sound of distant echoed hammering that came from York Cathedral, some ten miles or so to the north-east. He glanced down at his wristwatch to see that it was almost seven thirty in the morning, today was the day that he had planned for since he first learned of what was happening at York. Instead of relishing this moment, he now feared meeting Abraham because of what could occur as a result.

Jason simply wasn't a large man and those stories told to him by the Early daughters had taken their toll, Amelia's comment on the radio regarding him not being big and tall enough also played on his mind, but he knew that he had to do it. Amelia West and Alison Dixon needed to learn lessons in respect and manners toward men like himself and as he fully awoke, Jason had an epiphany. He suddenly knew some of how to construct this meeting with the giant in order to use his hoard so that he could teach those lessons.

He read the handwritten signs at Leeds and at Tadcaster that Hope Early blabbed about after Bobby Michaels revealed everything. Jason had since seen those signs with his own eyes, signs that invited survivors to York Cathedral. He then began the walk back to what was left of Leeds to think again, but this time with a still formulating brand new plan.

'So, exactly how do I get this Abraham's attention without getting killed before I even meet him?' He asked himself. He continued to think through his new plan of action, those handwritten invitations back at Leeds were in fact the key

to his success in realising this meeting of two great visionary minds.

Later that same evening at the city of Leeds, twenty eight year old Gary Smyth slowly drove over dust covered bones, rubble and anything else in his path on the inner ring road. He suddenly slammed his foot down onto the brake, his car skidded to a halt as he stared at one of Abraham's handwritten invitations. Something was attached to it, something that definitely wasn't there before now flapped in the breeze.

Jason sat huddled inside what remained of a factory building at the opposite side of the ring road, he watched Smyth remove the single sheet of paper from the handwritten sign and read the new one. Smyth then turned and glanced around, he knew that he was being watched from somewhere by a hidden outsider.

He was a very well-built man of around six feet two or three inches and these days like many other chosen men, he sported a Mohican style haircut. He continued to stare around the immediate obliterated vicinity and searched. Jason continued to watch as his heart pounded heavily against his chest.

"Why don't you just come out and speak to me?" Smyth yelled at the top of his echoed voice, but Jason was a survivor and he definitely wasn't about to do that or even respond to the question.

'Just take that note back to Abraham like you're supposed to.' He thought to himself, as he watched in hiding. He didn't dare say it out loud because the huge man would

know exactly where he hid, instead he watched Smyth eventually return to his battered blue car. He stopped and stared around again before he climbed back into the driver seat and restarted the engine. Jason breathed a sigh of relief as he watched Smyth drive away and head back to York.

'Shit, he was a big guy!' He told himself, while his heart continued to pound.

Sunday May 27th

Abraham Bridger climbed from his powerful motorcycle and casually walked the short distance into Leeds on the York Road. When he reached the inner ring road, he stopped and held out his arms and even from a distance, it was immediately clear that he was considerably larger than Gary Smyth.

"I'm here unarmed, just as you asked!" He called out using his deep, booming voice that echoed through the destroyed remains of Leeds city centre. With absolutely terrified widened eyes, Jason stared at the six feet seven inch man mountain from behind a crack in the wall. Abraham really did resemble a Viking, a Barbarian with his long hair and long bushy beard and of course yesterday, the large man with the blue car sported a just as terrifying appearance with his Mohican.

Once again, Jason's heart pounded as he watched Abraham search for him amongst the rubble and ruins. He genuinely wanted to step out from the building to show his presence, but absolute fear gripped him and prevented that from happening. He now fully understood that he was in way, way over his head, but the obsession with teaching Amelia West and Alison Dixon the lesson that they both deserved was somehow greater and he had already come this far to lose his nerve at the last hurdle.

"You know the names of the three that executed Bobby Michaels and I want them, I want to hang the bastards from their scrawny necks outside York Minster, he was a chosen man and I'm more than willing to pay you for those names!" He continued. Again there was no response from the absolutely terrified Jason.

"I also want you to tell me about Oxford, I read your note and you have a few debts to pay down there and I get that, so come out and we'll talk about that too, we could take that place down there and you could run it for me!" Abraham again called out with a half-smile, although his patience was already wearing thin.

"Let's do this together, just like you suggested!" He yelled. Just then, he turned his head to the right and saw Jason slowly appear at the opened doorway of an obliterated factory building. Abraham saw even from fifty feet away that Jason visibly trembled as he very nervously approached with his sawn down shotgun pointed directly at the giant, who displayed a wry grin as he watched him very slowly and very nervously approach.

"I told them, that's exactly where I wouldn't have waited." He very quietly uttered, as the terrified, much smaller man gradually closed in. There was then a very heavy thud that turned Jason's world to darkness, before he slumped down onto the ground.

"He was in the SAS my arse, the little idiot didn't even know we were behind him." One of Abraham's chosen men chuckled. He had just rifle butted Jason at the back of his head and knocked him clean unconscious and he continued to laugh, as did the two very large men beside him, Abraham nodded.

"Drag his sorry carcass back to York so we can question the little bastard when he wakes up." He instructed.

Around five hours later, Jason slowly opened his eyes with a dried bloody wound at the back of his head, it came with an absolutely thumping headache. He lay on the hard stone floor of a partially rebuilt huge reception room inside York Cathedral, his blurred eyes glanced around the massive, still heavily damaged once ornate grey and white room.

"We call this room the Arena, it's where any new man that isn't strong and at least six feet tall proves himself by fighting one of my chosen men, maybe you've heard of this place too." Abraham called from the opposite end of the vast room.

"If you can't fight, the already proven chosen man will kill you for extra food and a woman for the night, we have fourteen women here for chosen men to use." He added. Jason slowly sat upright while his head continued to pound, he soon realised that he was completely alone inside the room with Abraham.

"I…I can fight, but I came here because I've got information for you." He quietly croaked in response. When he stared back at Abraham, he saw that the giant sat on a huge solid oak throne-like chair, he nodded in response to Jason's comment.

"In your note, you also told me you were in the SAS, but my men crept up on you too easily so I know that statement was a crock, the man that popped you at the back of the head really was in the army and you didn't even know he was there, so why would I believe anything you tell me now?" He asked. He saw that Jason again began to tremble as stark reality once again dawned.

"His name was Bobby Michaels, the guy they executed was Bobby Michaels and I know the names of the three that did it, Bobby Michaels rode down to Huddersfield from here with another man on motorbikes, they told me the story and what they did to him." He very nervously replied, as he slowly climbed up onto unsteady legs.

"What are their names and where are they now?" Abraham enquired in a calm tone of voice. Jason continued to stare back at him for a few moments.

"The father's name is Robert Early, his two daughters are Arya and Hope, they also have two Doberman dogs." He replied. Again Abraham nodded, he knew that Jason this time spoke the truth, Robert Pritchard told him of large hounds that chased him at Huddersfield.

"I...I don't know where they are now, but I met them at Northampton." Jason added with a nervous stammer. Once again Abraham calmly nodded.

"Now, what's so special about Oxford?" He asked. Jason again glanced up from the recently laid, uneven grey stone floor.

"There are about thirty people living down there in an underground shopping centre with tonnes of supplies, food, medicine and anything else you might want and nineteen of them are just women." He very nervously explained.

"But they're heavily armed and the shopping centre isn't on any map because it was due to open just after the storm, only I know exactly where it is and you'll never find it without me." He replied. Abraham again chuckled.

"Then it looks like you get to live clever little man, for now anyway." He replied. His cold blue eyes watched Jason almost sigh with relief.

"I'll be sending a scouting party of five men down to Oxford and they'll leave tomorrow, you'll go with them to show them where this place is and you'll also come back here with them, if you try to run they'll be instructed to cut your head off and bring it back to me as a trophy." He announced. Jason continued to anxiously stare at the giant.

"There is one more thing, a request." He quietly replied. Abraham continued to stare back at him.

"There are two in particular down there that I owe big time, if it's possible I'd like to be the one that deals when them after we take the place." He quietly uttered, with almost a plea in his tone. His request caused Abraham to again chuckle.

"Let me guess, I bet they're two of the women not the men, fake little SAS man?" He asked with a sneer. There was no response from Jason, Abraham's assumption was correct, the reference made by Jason was to Amelia West and Alison Dixon and it would have to happen *after* Abraham and his men had finished with them.

Monday May 28th

At around nine in the morning, Jason stood outside at the front of York Cathedral beside the giant Abraham as many, many more than the previously suggested twenty large men worked on reconstruction of the vast building. He watched with amazement as two huge men lifted a second dark green, forty five gallon drum that was completely filled with diesel onto a small open backed truck. Two more on top of the small flatbed just as effortlessly grabbed and carried it to the front.

"Like we talked about last night, when you get down to Aylesbury, stop the truck and walk into Oxford from the east so they don't hear the engine and when you get there, this one will show you exactly where they are." Abraham instructed Andy Clarke, who nodded as he glanced down at Jason before he returned his stare to the giant.

"What if there's nobody there?" Clarke enquired. Abraham also glanced down beside him at Jason.

"Then you get to kill this little runt for lying to me and don't forget to bring his head back, but I'm sure they're down there, thirty or more of them and you know what to do when you find them, make the offer and give the terms of their unconditional surrender or we go down there and lay siege to the place." He replied.

Thursday May 31st

During the early hours of the morning, the wheels of the small open backed truck slowly crunched and bumped over rotten corpses as it entered the town of Aylesbury from the north, just twenty miles east from the Ellington centre. Twenty five year old Brian Jonas sat at the back directly opposite Jason.

"You'll stay here and guard the truck." He announced. Jason eagerly nodded, regardless of the protection that he returned with, he didn't relish the thought of a direct face to face confrontation until it was safe to do so and that would be after whoever survived at Oxford had been completely subdued.

Brian Jonas stood at around six feet one and he sported that same Mohican hairstyle for the purpose of intimidation. Also seated at the open backed rear was twenty five year old Adrian Hooper who also stood at over six feet tall, as did twenty nine year old Alex Harper. All three were ordinary hard working men prior to the great storm, not the lawless Barbarians that they now were under the guidance of Abraham Bridger.

Driving inside the green cab was the largest man of all Darren Bishop, who stood almost as large as Abraham himself as six feet five inches. After the truck slowed to a stop, Andy Clarke climbed out from the passenger side at a mere but rotund five feet eleven, although he was of course one of the original trio along with Abraham and Clive Henderson.

"We'll get to Oxford to watch and stay there for the night, then we'll pay them a visit at around ten tomorrow morning." Clarke informed the four chosen men who all nodded. He then turned his attention to Jason.

"We don't need you to come we're here to intimidate them, wait here and guard the truck we'll be back tomorrow afternoon and don't build a fire they might see one from here, we don't want them to know we're there until we walk toward them in plain sight." He instructed.

As a local man, Jason obviously knew the area well and he also knew every way to the Ellington centre from Aylesbury. An hour after he gave directions to the five much larger men, they left for Oxford and a short while later, Jason followed although using a much shorter, more direct route to observe whatever was going to happen from a safe distance when they arrived there and more importantly, to witness first-hand what would happen at Ellington tomorrow morning.

Amy Vinton and Wendy Jones stood fully armed on sentry duty behind Reg's latest engineering creation, while Phil Smith and Charlotte Strickland patrolled the southern end of the main road. Amy and Wendy stood behind a recently tried and tested on the rifle range, three inch thick and moveable, large plate steel shield that spanned the entire twenty five feet width of the road. The recently built barrier was also eight feet tall with nine small rectangular shaped firing slots cut into it, five feet from the bottom.

At the southern wall, Umar continued to build as quickly as he could with help from Amelia, Alison, Vikki, David and Maria. It was Maria who stirred boiling rice inside the pit where the east corner now stood at sixteen feet, surrounded by scaffolding with the beginnings of the wooden walkway at the top. Alison and Vikki were being taught by Umar to lay bricks in order to speed up the process of construction, so that he could soon begin at what would become the adjoining five mile long east wall.

Back at the Ellington centre, inside the lower ground floor maintenance area, Reg and Jake busily worked at a second, identical steel barricade on wheels, that would by the end of the day also stand on the main road, this time to face south. All hands would then be used to hurry the construction of the surrounding high walls, although everybody deep down knew that they would never be built in time if Jason had travelled to York.

Five miles from Umar at the opposing north wall, Robert Early laid bricks on top of dark grey foundation stones and was teaching Harrison and Emma. Labouring for them were Jackie, Zack and Sue Cole. There was a sense of anxious urgency around the Ellington centre because everybody knew that if Jason was definitely making his way to York to inform the giant would be King of their existence he would, or should at least be there by now.

The psychotic savage would know exactly where they were and they were by no means ready for him to make an appearance with however many large men could possibly accompany him. Amelia and Hannah saw many, many more than twenty from the air.

Inside the field to the west with eight black and white cows, stood Tess Morking and Deborah Lloyd, they were both also fully armed. That field was still completely exposed, as was the field to the east where Arya and Hope Early patrolled and impatiently waited for battle with Cain and Abel beside them. Just beyond both fields were some eighty buried and armed land mines of various sizes and ferocity.

Steve and Hannah Madison would soon relieve Tess and Deborah, who would both rest for four hours only to relieve the two behind the barricade on the main road. Amy and Wendy would later relieve a pair to the south. When evening came and construction halted, others would join the guard duty rotation, while bricks laid with makeshift mortar slowly hardened and settled.

From inside the obliterated remains of what was the familiar giant superstore where he worked prior to the great storm, Jason Moran stared with utter horror, the two psychotic girls with their father had joined the group at Oxford. He watched the daughters from a safe distance as they menacingly paced back and forth across a field with their giant hounds. He had no idea that between them, just twenty five feet from where he crouched was the first buried land mine, that would at the very least blow both of his legs clean off should he inadvertently step onto it.

"What the hell are they doing here?" He quietly asked himself with frustration. From what he already knew, the insane family were without doubt a game changer.

Jason had no idea of where Andy Clarke and the four large chosen men were hiding and also watching, but he knew that they had to be somewhere around by now, which meant that he in fact hid from both groups after he was specifically instructed not to be there, but his obsession with the demise of Amelia and Alison would never allow that to happen, he had to watch their humiliating subservience with his own eyes.

Friday June 1st

Hidden inside a destroyed building north of where Oxford Castle once stood, Andy Clarke and the four large chosen men sat inside a dust covered darkened room. In preparation, they discussed what they had observed since they arrived during darkness of the night before.

"They're armed yes, but they're mostly women and they don't look like they know what they're doing with those weapons, we could probably take the place right now just the five of us." Adrian Hooper suggested. Andy immediately nodded with agreement.

"The runt was actually right about them, but I've got instructions from Abe if the place looks as it does." He replied. The four men sat and stared as they waited for him to continue.

"The five of us are to walk down that main road and give them an ultimatum, we'll tell them who we are, where we're from and that there are a hundred more up at York and if they want to live, they have to accept that they now live under our rules." He explained.

"We'll tell them that we're going to drive the truck here and they'll fill it with supplies from that warehouse and they're to hand over five of the women to take back to York with us, then they get to live past today." He added.

Twenty minutes later, the five men left their shelter to make their way south to the Ellington centre.

"Intimidate the crap out of them, stand over them and make them all terrified of the sight of us." Clarke reminded his huge, very heavily armed and savage looking men.

By pure chance, Paul Richards, David Wells, Phil Smith and Sue Cole stood behind the high and wide steel barricade at the northern end of the main road during a rotation changeover. They watched through the small rectangular firing slots, five very large men casually stroll toward them.

"My God they're all massive, look at the size of them!" Sue very nervously blurted, as David spoke on the radio handset to warn everybody else of the situation. Four of the men stopped around twenty feet from the barricade and only Andy Clarke continued, he also eventually stopped at around five feet from the shield where he stared at it.

"Get your leaders out here, we know you've got people in charge!" He insisted with an arrogance in his loud tone. He stared unafraid at four rifles that all pointed directly at him through the narrow firing slots of a rusty steel shield.

"Who are you and what do you want?" Paul called out. Clarke continued to stare, still seemingly unafraid at the protruding rifle barrels.

"I'm here to make an offer on behalf of the new leader of this country, now get yours out here to speak to me." He again insisted. The four even larger, terrifying looking men stood menacingly and then strolled closer to the barricade, to around five feet behind Clarke.

"Keep your rifles pointed at him and if he lifts that shotgun, don't think just shoot then turn your rifles to the other four, they can't hurt you behind this thing we tested it on the range, but you can hurt them." Paul quietly whispered. He stepped out from behind the barricade and approached Clarke, who watched him with the same arrogance.

"Are you in charge here?" He asked, he watched Paul shake his head.

"You haven't made an appointment and I'm guessing you're from York, so I suggest you boys turn around and walk away while we still let you." He replied. The long black barrel of his older rifle pointed at Clarke's huge round stomach. Paul knew that if he pulled the trigger, the round would pass straight through and completely rip out the large man's back before it also took out one of the men behind him.

"How would you know we're from York?" Clarke enquired, as he and Paul stared into each other's eyes and neither flinched.

Jason Moran hid behind a large tree, he watched Clarke and the other four walk from the roundabout toward the barricade, he then watched Richards and Clarke talk on the road, but of course he couldn't hear the conversation from around a quarter of a mile away.

He glanced to his left and watched Robert, Arya and Hope Early head up the main road toward the two men, from the car park roof and behind them, Amelia and Tess who were also all heavily armed. Jason's heart pounded as he watched from a safe distance.

He then saw that from the car park roof, many more disperse across the field toward the beginnings of the north wall. He recognised Zack Zimmerman, Alan Robbins and Harrison Bax who all lay in the long grass where they aimed their rifles at the four chosen men.

'We're outgunned by a mile, what is that fat idiot playing at?' He anxiously asked himself. He knew that there was nothing that he could do about it, of course this time he was on the opposing side of the Oxford dwellers.

"There's only one scenario where you all get to walk out of here, son." Paul quietly assured Clarke. The obese man watched Robert and his two daughters with Amelia and Tess approach. He returned his stare to Richards with absolutely no idea that three who approached were in fact the executioners of chosen man Bobby Michaels.

"If you're not in charge here get whoever is to me, is it those five?" He asked. Paul slowly turned to see exactly who approached.

'Oh shit!' He thought to himself.

With some confusion, Clarke soon turned to watch Robert, Arya and Hope pass him as they headed toward the four large men behind, but Amelia and Tess stopped and stood in directly front of him.

"What do you want dickhead, where's Jason Moran?" Amelia abruptly asked.

Hope Early stood directly in front of the largest of the four men behind Clarke, she stared up and into the eyes at six feet five inches of Darren Bishop. Her father and sister stood in front of Adrian Hooper and Alex Harper, leaving just Brian Jonas unchallenged, although at least five rifles now pointed at him from across the fields and he knew it.

"We've been sent here to trade with you, but before you make a regular donation you should know that there are more than a hundred of us up at York, all waiting to come and rip this place and everybody in it apart." Clarke sneered. He stared back down at Amelia who calmly nodded.

"There'll be ninety five of you, if you don't tell me where Jason Moran is before you run back there." She assured him. Clarke was no longer Amelia's main concern, from the corner of her eye she could see that Hope Early stared with that same venom up at the largest of all. Huge Bishop stared back down at her with a wry grin, but Hope was now very quietly talking to him, goading him into action, as every person in that stand-off heard Clarke loudly state his terms.

"Your walls aren't built, more than a hundred men all fully loaded can take this place out from all directions in a day, that's if you don't agree to my terms right here right now." He mentally recited Abraham's handwritten note in his trouser pocket.

"You're nothing, we'll burn this place to ash with you all locked inside it." He vowed.

Huge Darren Bishop continued to smile down at the little girl who continued to goad him into some kind of action. Amelia, Paul and her father could see what she was trying to do, although none would remove their stares from whoever stood directly in front of them. Clarke then returned his attention to Paul Richards.

"We've got a truck not far from here, you'll fill with supplies for us to take back to York, we'll also be taking five of your women with us, consider it a tax." He uttered, but before Paul could open his mouth to speak, Amelia did so on his behalf.

"Hope, do it now!" She called out.

Hope's menacing stare up at Bishop suddenly turned to a wry smile to match his, she then nodded with acknowledgement for Amelia to see.

"Am I one of the women that you want to take back to York?" She asked Bishop with obvious sarcasm in her tone. Clarke turned to watch with confusion whatever was about to take place.

"I only ask because the last time I met one of your friends Bobby Michaels up at Huddersfield, he wanted to take me there and I had to chop his head off to show him that I didn't want to go." She quietly informed him. From behind her, Andy Clarke's face reddened with pure rage. Bishop now stared down at her with the same anger after her revelation.

"So, are you going to try to take me, you big fat, slow dumb dickhead?" She asked. Paul Richards slowly raised his rifle and pointed it directly at the back of Clarke's head. He nodded to Amelia to move her away from his line of fire.

Bishop could see that Hope had a huge axe somehow strapped to her back along with a rifle, but she had no weapon close to hand and because other rifles pointed directly at the four men, his new plan was to grab her, to use as his personal human shield. There was a highly intense moment of terror for all concerned, they had very suddenly reached that point, Darren Bishop would be the first to make a move.

He suddenly lunged at Hope and grabbed her before he effortlessly pulled her toward him, he turned her around to face Amelia before he then lifted her completely from the floor to hold her in front of him. If anybody fired a shot, they would now hit her. Hope stared directly at her father and displayed a smile.

"What an idiot." She giggled.

Without uttering a word, Robert lunged the razor sharp tip of his broadsword up and forward, just past his daughter's face and straight through the neck of Bishop. It came out at the right side causing hot blood to splatter onto the face of Brian Jonas.

Before he could react in any way, the sword was just as promptly pulled out from Bishop's neck and Robert ferociously swung it as hard and as fast as he could. Brian Jonas suddenly lost his head as a result. The bodies of both chosen men slumped down almost together onto the ground, with Hope Early sprawled, still grinning on top of them with a nick on her left cheek, a gift from her father.

Adrian Hooper and Alex Harper, who both stood to the right of where Darren Bishop had just lost his life, now stared at Arya with absolute terror in their eyes. Her high powered crossbow was already now pointed directly at Hooper's face from very close range.

"Take a moment to remember boys that you were nothing but ordinary men before the storm, we've never been ordinary and with that in mind twitch, fart or smile I dare you." She almost eloquently reminded him.

Hooper slowly opened his mouth to nervously speak as beads of sweat trickled down his scarlet face, to Arya that constituted a twitch. She pulled the trigger to immediately send the bolt straight through his face and out from the back of his head. Hooper was the third of five to slump to the ground with a heavy thud and so far, with no Oxford casualties. Hope climbed back to her feet after falling with Bishop, she dusted off her brown leather clothing before she reached behind and removed her large and heavy axe, she stood in front of Alex Harper and stared up into his absolutely terrified widened eyes.

"That means my sister's winning, if you're sensible and don't open your mouth like that idiot just did you get to walk away, somebody has to carry fat boy behind me back to wherever you left your truck." She quietly uttered. She then smiled up at him as her sister chuckled beside her with another bolt already loaded onto her crossbow, aimed at Alex Harper's face.

"Are you going to open your mouth and make me chop your head off?" Hope then enquired. Harper didn't move a single muscle to assure her that he wouldn't. Andy Clarke angrily turned to find himself faced with the long barrel of Paul's rifle pointed directly at his face and he also stopped dead in his tracks.

"You point that thing at me and kill me if you like, but he'll still come here with all of them and he'll rip you lot to shreds." He vowed, to a nod from Paul.

"Don't worry about this thing pointing at you, worry about her." He replied. From the corner of his eye and unbeknown to Clarke, Paul watched Hope walk to behind where Clarke stood. She pulled back her heavy razor sharp, double sided axe and swung it as hard as she possibly could.

Her axe immediately severed both of Clarke's large feet from the ankles with that single blow although his boots remained where they were. Everybody heard the crunch of bone before he fell to the floor, screaming in absolute agony as blood spurted from both now fully opened wounds.

Twenty minutes or so later, all concerned from Oxford stood on the main road and watched Alex Harper struggle to carry Andy Clarke north toward the roundabout. Hope stood beside Amelia where she removed with her fingers, shreds of flesh and bone from the razor sharp blade of her axe before she returned it to her back. She picked up from the ground, two black leather boots with feet still inside them before she stared at Amelia and displayed a smile.

"Are you coming out to play with us next time, little Miss Karate expert?" She sarcastically asked. She then barged past Amelia and made her way back toward the Ellington centre. Amelia turned to watch her walk away, but she then turned back to watch Robert approach as he stared toward the field on his left side.

"Now that we know they're definitely coming here, let's get some more mines buried in the fields all around the car park!" He called out to Zack. The former soldier nodded and when Robert turned again, he also stopped where Amelia stood.

"Ignore my youngest, she gets a bit excitable after a fight." He quietly uttered. Amelia only stared back at his blood soaked face, but she had nothing to say to him she watched him then smile.

"Try to remember, it was you that told her to start that, your instruction was red rag to a bull for my daughters." He reminded her.

Nobody from either side knew that as soon as the incredible violence began, Jason Moran sprinted past Headington and made his way back to Aylesbury and the truck. He didn't once look back after he witnessed from a distance, Robert Early violently thrust the tip of his sword through Darren Bishop's neck and out through the other side and in the same motion, cleanly cut off the head of Brian Jonas. That was the moment when Jason hastily retreated to live through yet another day.

Around four hours later, when he finally reached the truck at Aylesbury, he immediately started the engine and sped north, bumping over rotten bones as he headed back to York without waiting for Alex Harper and Andy Clarke. He presumed that they perished with the other three, thanks to that damned psychotic family.

At a later date, the corpse of Andy Clarke would be discovered with the telling identification of no feet, not far from the underground car park at Kidlington where Amelia survived what everybody still believed was a single vast storm named Ella. Clarke perished due to the vast loss of blood.

If Alex Harper then travelled back to the truck at Aylesbury, Jason had already left and whatever happened to Harper is still unknown. He never returned to York and was never seen or heard of again, but he somehow survived the storm during the August of the previous year and become one of the very few to survive the Early family.

Jason raced back, but not to York. He once again travelled to Leeds as fast as he could, but would much later inform Abraham of what happened to his chosen men, particularly Andy Clarke who was one of the original three, in the hope that the real battle for Oxford would now begin.

After three days and two nights of driving, Jason holed up alone for a further four days inside an obliterated building at the city of Leeds before he returned to York. At Leeds, he would deeply cut his own face, chest and stomach several times using his faithful penknife and other sharp objects, to make it appear that he was involved in a great battle where only he somehow survived, after they were suddenly ambushed. He was certain that nobody else would return to York to say anything to the contrary and Abraham would clearly see that yes, he really could fight.

The four days at Leeds were used to allow his new, self-inflicted wounds to heal a little and to make the great battle seem more recent than it really was. He would appear to Abraham like a surviving, ready to fight hero whereas Jonas, Harper and Bishop in his version of events, fled like cowards as soon as the fighting started, but were cut down as they ran. In his revised version, unfortunately Clarke and Hooper also died during the battle. As for Jason, he chose to voluntarily return to York alone just like a chosen man and as he suspected, the giant would become more than outraged.

As for Jason Moran, he would once again somehow manage to live through yet another day.

Your world history lessons will continue …

Printed in Great Britain
by Amazon

47258631R00205